Dorie's brother needed that money, so she'd have to convince this ex-cop....

Bret rubbed his hand over his neck and said, "You have to admit that I'm not responsible for my father's mistakes."

"What about the Donovan family honor? Doesn't that mean anything to you?"

A grin tugged at his mouth. "I think our family honor, if we ever had any, went up in smoke at the craps table in Mountain City. Let me sleep on this. I'm going to try to work something out that's fair to everyone."

"So I'm supposed to just go away and come back tomorrow?"

"You don't have to leave. If you attempt the drive down the mountain in the dark, you could end up wrapped around an oak tree."

"Okay, I'll stay. But I'm sleeping with one hand wrapped around my can of Mace."

Bret placed his hand over his heart. "Ouch." And then he smiled, and she felt that sense of comfort again. And she didn't like it all that much. A girl gets to feeling too comfortable with a man, and that's when her life starts unraveling.

Dear Reader,

Have you ever happened upon a special place, one you knew would stay in your memory forever? I had just such an experience at the Walasi-Yi Outfitters in the north Georgia Blue Ridge Mountains. A rustic building of wood and stone, the campers' store and refuge was old, solid and welcoming. Its enduring architecture made the structure an integral part of the mountain environment.

I saw many hikers with rugged shoes, hats to shade their faces from the sun, and large backpacks. I also saw dogs with their own packs, slung like saddlebags over their backs.

The store had everything a backpacker could need. Freeze-dried foods, lightweight cooking utensils, sleeping bags, bug spray. Most hikers came for an hour or so and then continued on their way, refreshed and restocked for the rest of the journey.

I longed to place a story in this setting, and Blue Ridge Hideaway provided the perfect opportunity. I hope you will enjoy Bret and Dorie's journey, and maybe even trek through the beautiful Blue Ridge Mountains someday. If you see the Walasi-Yi, stop and visit.

I love to hear from readers. You can contact me at cynthoma@aol.com or visit my website, www.cynthiathomason.com

Cynthia

HARLEQUIN HEARTWARMING

Cynthia Thomason

Blue Ridge Hideaway

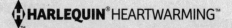

Recycling programs
for this product may
not exist in your area.

ISBN-13: 978-0-373-36646-0

BLUE RIDGE HIDEAWAY

Printed in U.S.A.

H HARLEQUIN®
™ www.Harlequin.com

CYNTHIA THOMASON

Cynthia inherited her love of writing from her ancestors. Her father and grandmother both loved to write, and she aspired to continue the legacy. Cynthia studied English and journalism in college, and after a career as a high school English teacher, she began writing novels. She discovered ideas for stories while searching through antiques stores and flea markets and as an auctioneer and estate buyer. Cynthia says every cast-off item from someone's life can ignite the idea for a plot. She writes about small towns, big hearts and happy endings that are earned and not taken for granted. And as far as the legacy is concerned, just ask her son, the magazine journalist, if he believes.

This book is dedicated to my beloved husband,
Buddy, who walked many trails with me.
I will remember every one.

CHAPTER ONE

"THIS IS IT!"

Dorie slammed on her brakes, bringing her work-weary Ford Ranger to a shuddering halt in the weeds bordering the two-lane North Carolina Route 23. "The place actually exists!"

A shaft of sunlight had managed to spear through the gloom of gray clouds, illuminating an arrow and the words *The Crooked Spruce* crudely painted on a roadside plaque. Another few minutes and dusk would have settled, making it likely Dorie would have missed the sign altogether.

She turned her wheel sharply to the right, grinding her front tires on the road's gravel approach. "You'd better be here, Clancy! I didn't drive all this way to find out I've been on a wild-goose chase."

The sign nailed to a wooden post could have been constructed twenty years ago or only yesterday. The road looked as if it hadn't been regularly navigated since…well, in a long time.

Dorie tossed aside the penciled map the clerk at the convenience store had scribbled for her twenty minutes and twelve miles ago. He hadn't been much help, telling her he had seen the name Crooked Spruce on a small sign on a rural highway.

"No kidding, it's a small sign," she mumbled, starting the ascent up the mountain. When she'd asked the clerk if he'd ever been curious enough to investigate the place, he'd scratched his chin and told her to come back and tell him when she found out what it was.

Armed with this scant information, Dorie drove under the canopy of tall trees whose bare limbs waited for the first leafy buds of spring. She shivered in the skeletal shadows of branches dripping with the icy remnants of a late-afternoon shower. She'd left the balminess of a sixty-three degree day in Winston Beach, North Carolina, at noon—more than six hours ago. Here in the mountainous region of the same state, she'd had to stop and put on her parka to ward off a twenty degree dip in temperature.

Her pickup's engine labored on the steep climb up the mountainside. And with each rounding of narrow curves, Dorie's heart beat faster. For the half mile she'd driven so far, she'd noticed rugged pathways cut into the forest, some still patchy with snow. Perhaps cabins existed in the woods, but she hadn't seen any sign of human life. No wonder. Who would be out on this blustery March day?

After a few minutes, another signpost loomed ahead of her. This one, obviously new and professionally constructed, arched across a substantial wooden entryway and identified her destination with two bent, short-needled trees burnt into either side of the words *The Crooked Spruce Outpost*.

"Clancy Donovan, it's just like you to hide away in some backwoods place where the only living creatures who see you have four legs." She aimed her truck into a clearing. "But you can't hide from me now, and you'd better still have my money."

About a hundred yards ahead, Dorie discovered a peaked-roof, two-story log building about the dimensions of a double-wide trailer. And this remote pocket of civilization included a population of at least one.

Dorie narrowed her eyes at the man perched near the top of an eight-foot ladder. Could that be Clancy? A quick appraisal of the man's wide shoulders under his plaid wool mackinaw and his crop of thick coppery hair sticking out from a baseball cap convinced her that he wasn't. What little hair hippie-throwback Clancy had was gray and usually tied in a leather strap at his nape.

She searched in her purse until she wrapped her hand around the container of mace she'd bought for this trip. Not that she believed she'd need it. She could handle Clancy. But the guy on the ladder was another story. Besides, a woman traveling alone should always be prepared for emergencies.

Dorie shifted the Ranger into Park a couple dozen feet from the structure. The man must have been oblivious to the not-so-stealthy approach of her eight-year-old truck since he didn't interrupt his work to check out her arrival. Flecks of brown paint fluttered to the ground as he scraped a putty knife under the eaves of the building's large screened porch.

She turned off the engine, and the truck made its customary hundred-thousand-mile wheeze, a cross between a cough and a hiccup, and Dorie held her breath. No way the man could ignore that sound.

He turned suddenly, dropped the putty knife to the tray attached to the ladder and pulled foam-covered earbuds from his ears. He peered into the window of her truck. Dorie's gaze connected with his dark eyes, the color indistinct in the shadow of the building's overhang. Could be deep brown or charcoal. She wondered why it mattered. He wasn't Clancy. From the relaxed way he balanced his substantial height on the ladder, he had to be at least thirty years younger than the stoop-shouldered man she'd come to find. Gripping the mace, she exited the car and stood by the driver's door.

"Hey, there," the man said, his voice exhibiting neither malice nor welcome. "We're not open yet. Not for another month."

"Fine with me," Dorie said. "I'm not here to take advantage of your services…." She glanced into the porch and noticed assorted outdoor furniture stacked up, apparently not in use at this time. "Whatever those services may be," she added.

The earbuds dangling over his shoulders, he stepped down from the ladder and flicked a button on an MP3 player attached to the top flap of his jacket pocket. "Okay, then what can I help you with? You take a wrong turn?"

The sad irony of his question almost made her laugh out loud, though this guy couldn't know the downward spiral the past six months of her life had taken.

"I'm looking for someone," she said. "A man."

His mouth quirked up in a little grin. "Like I said, we don't open for more than four weeks. You might have more luck finding one then."

She released a breath of frustration. "You don't understand. I was told a particular man might be here. I've driven a long way to find him. His last name is Donovan."

He walked toward her. A slight limp in his right leg contrasted with the fluid movement of the rest of his body. He held out his hand. "Well, then, you're in luck, after all. I'm Donovan."

She stared at his hand as she backed away from him. "No, you're not Donovan."

He dropped his hand to his side and pierced her with a sharp gaze, with eyes that she now realized were dark brown, like the color of a pinecone. His look was half puzzlement, half irritation. "I'm sorry, but you're not likely to win this argument," he said. "I do know my own name."

She wasn't handling this well. She was nervous, tired and, of all the outcomes she'd gone over in her mind during the drive from the Outer Banks, the possibility of finding two men with the same name in the same place wasn't one of them. "Sorry," she said. "I'm looking for Clancy Donovan. Do you know him?"

"Clancy, eh? You're close. I'm Bret Donovan."

He was about to speak again as a shout came from the side of the building. "I heard a car. Who…?"

Holding a scrub brush, Clancy Donovan stopped dead, dropped a bucket of murky water next to his rubber boots and gaped at Dorie. After a few seconds during which he obviously pondered the ramifications of her appearance, he said, "Oh, shoot. Dorie. How did you find…?"

She advanced on him. "You sorry son…"

"Watch your language," Clancy said. "We've got a child living here."

She pressed her lips together and did a quick survey of the property. She didn't see a kid, but decided to try and rein in her temper, anyway.

Bret quickly blocked her path. "Luke isn't due back until tomorrow. You know that," he said to Clancy. Then, turning to Dorie he said, "Looks like you've found what you came for."

She tried to sidestep him. He put his palms up and stepped with her, a frustrating no-win dance she didn't appreciate. "You're not going to keep me away from him," she said.

While staring into Dorie's eyes, Bret spoke to Clancy. "I take it you know this woman, Pop?"

Pop? Clancy has a son? He'd never mentioned having any family. She'd thought he was a lonely old man, a *conniving* lonely old man who drew unsuspecting victims into his seedy con games. At any rate, she'd never have picked this Bret fellow to be Clancy's offspring. He was at least five inches taller than his father, and despite the catch in his walk, definitely an impressive guy. And, since everyone knew blood was thicker than water, possibly a dangerous one.

She flexed her grip around the mace and positioned the index finger of her right hand on the spray trigger in case this encounter turned into a two-against-one situation.

"He knows me all right," she said. "Tell him, Clancy. Tell him just how *well* you know me."

Bret's face tightened into a frown of disapproval and Dorie realized how he might have interpreted her words. "Not like that!" she said. "How could you think…?"

He removed a stained Florida Marlins ball cap, pushed strands of hair off his forehead and resettled the hat low on his brow. "Let's all calm down a minute." He held his calloused, long-fingered hand out toward Dorie a second time. "Look, Miss…"

"My name's Howe," she said, keeping her hand on the trigger. "Dorinda Howe. Dorie."

He lowered his hand again. "Dorie, I'd feel a whole lot better if you'd put away that can of pepper spray."

She'd thought she'd concealed the canister from view. "How did you know…?"

"It's an old habit from a previous profession. Back in those days, I never approached anyone without looking at what might be in their hands. That applies especially to unannounced visitors who seem to have a serious ax to grind about something." He cocked his head to the side and managed a small grin. "But here's a tip. If you want to be really sneaky with that thing, you should choose a color other than hot pink."

Very funny. She didn't bother explaining to him that she came from a worse-for-wear seaside village with a rowdy population and a high crime rate—a far cry from the typical Outer Banks tourist spot. Canisters of mace went fast, black being the popular seller. Maybe it was just as well he knew about her weapon. Neither of these men would try anything, knowing she could temporarily send them into fits of coughing with a couple of well-aimed bursts.

"I think I'll hold on to it, junior," she said. "If it's all the same to you."

He scowled but didn't press her to give up her protection. "Fine, but at least put it in your pocket. I don't want it going off accidentally."

There was something rational and calming about the level tone of his voice, and Dorie decided to trust him that far. Besides, a damp, bitter wind had suddenly swept down from the mountaintop, and she needed both hands to zip up her parka.

Bret turned to his father. "Pop, I think you'd better tell me what's going on."

She crossed her arms over her chest, and glared at Clancy. "Go ahead, tell him, *Pop*. And while you're filling your son in with all the details about our recent history, I'm going to be right here listening to every word just so you don't forget to mention the exact amount of money you owe me."

BRET HAD A bad feeling about this. In the forty-eight hours since his father had arrived without notice, nothing suspicious or sinister or even questionable had happened. Bret had allowed himself to ease into a sort of complacent acceptance of Clancy's appearance even though gut instinct told him to keep his guard up—what he usually did when his dad was in his life. And now this—a woman about as mad as a hen in a hatbox threatening the peace and tranquility he'd come to the mountains to find. Past experience had taught him that this woman's desperate situation, whatever the details, was probably Clancy's fault.

He did a quick appraisal of Dorinda Howe. She had guts even if she didn't have the stature to back them up. At a little over five feet tall, with slim legs encased in a pair of straight jeans and most of the rest of her concealed under a hood and a light parka, she didn't look capable of tangling with a dragonfly. But looks could be deceiving. And she did come packing mace.

He glanced up at the craggy summit of Hickory Mountain. The sun had slipped toward the valley behind them. In another ten minutes nighttime would descend on the mountainside, and this little patch of land would be about as dark as any place on earth. Bret ought to be putting his tools away and securing the property from bears and raccoons while he still had some daylight. But the normally relaxed ending of his day was obviously not going to happen.

Dorie rubbed one hand up and down her arm while keeping a tense fist near the pocket where she'd put the canister.

"You're freezing," Bret said. "And it's only going to get colder. We're supposed to dip into the upper twenties tonight."

"Doesn't this mountain know it's the end of March?"

He smiled.

"Whatever. I don't plan to be here to watch the thermometer drop," she said through chattering teeth. She glared at Clancy. "My business shouldn't take long."

Bret swept his arm toward the building. "Let's go inside. I turned the furnace off this morning since I knew I'd be outside most of the day, but I can at least start a fire while we wait for the heat to kick on again."

She studied his face a moment before eyeing the lodge with definite longing, but she didn't take a step. "I don't know…"

"Look, you'll be fine. Nobody's going to hurt you." He jabbed a thumb in the direction of her pocket. "If anything, we're scared of you."

She remained still, apparently considering his promise.

"We'll just get out of the wind while we talk this over. Besides, I don't know about you, but I could use a cup of coffee."

She looked one more time at both men before nodding. "Yeah, coffee sounds good. And there's another thing…"

"Oh?"

She pointed to the lodge he'd been working on all day. "I'm hoping you have modern facilities in there."

Understanding her concern, he said, "All the comforts of home. Plumbing included."

She stepped back, clearing a path for Clancy. "You go first. I don't want you behind me."

He frowned but moved ahead of her. "And I don't want that can of pepper spray to come out of your pocket," he said. He stopped at the door Bret held open and looked over his shoulder. "Don't try using that stuff on me. My son here used to be a cop."

As Dorie followed him inside she spared a quick glance at Bret. "A cop, eh? And while you were protecting and serving your community, how many times did you arrest your own father?"

Bret let the door shut behind him. "Never had to." His lips curled up in a grin. "We always lived in different cities." He started to recite directions to the bathroom, but stopped when his cell phone rang. "I've got to take this. It's my son, and I don't always get clear cell service on this mountain."

"Sure, go ahead."

Anxious as always to hear Luke's voice, Bret waved Dorie to the hallway bathroom. "Hey, buddy, how's everything going?"

In a hyper, enthusiastic voice, Luke regaled his father with the latest escapades he'd enjoyed with his cousins.

"Can't wait for you to get home tomorrow," Bret said. He hoped his son felt even a small percentage of the longing he himself was experiencing at seeing the boy again. They had been apart almost a week now, and to Bret, that was far too long.

"Me, too, Dad," Luke said. "But I was wondering why Aunt Julie has to bring me home tomorrow. Why not Sunday? School doesn't start until the next day."

Bret hid his disappointment behind parental prerogative, stopping just short of saying, "Because I said so."

"We talked about this already, Luke. Saturday is the day Aunt Julie can come up here, and Saturday is the day you're coming home. Okay?"

"Sure. I'll see you tomorrow."

Bret disconnected and stacked logs in the fireplace. He struck a match and blew on the kindling, creating a nice start to a fire. Aware that his father was fiddling with the coffeemaker, he waited to see if Clancy would offer an explanation for Dorie's accusation. But the only sounds in the room were the crackle of the flames and the hiss of the brewing machine.

Crouched in front of the hearth, Bret turned to his father and said, "I'd really appreciate it if, before she comes out of the bathroom, you'd tell me what you did to that woman."

Clancy stared at him before taking a seat on a bench at one of the recently assembled wood picnic tables in the center of the all-purpose room. "Why are you assuming I did something to her?" he asked, doing his best to affect a tone of wounded feelings. "Maybe she did something to me. Maybe she showed up here on some crazy vigilante mission, and I'm caught in her crosshairs. Maybe…"

Bret stood, placed his hands on his hips, and fixed his gaze on the entrance to the hallway. "And maybe you owe her money like she said."

Clancy threw his hands up. "I helped her,

that's what I did! She came into my place looking for a job, and I did her a good turn."

Dorie stormed into the room, her jacket draped over one arm. "That's how you're telling this story? A person could end up homeless because of your *good turns,* Clancy. In fact, I practically have!"

She marched to the table. Wavy strands of wheat-colored hair fell to her shoulders. She raked her fingers through wispy bangs nearly covering eyes that snapped with blue fury and shoved her other palm under Clancy's nose. "Give me my money. And don't tell me you don't have any of it left!"

He made a show of twisting around to reach into his back jeans pocket. When he pulled out his wallet, he withdrew some bills and crammed them into her hand.

Dorie stared at the pile. "That's it? There can't be fifty dollars here."

"Fifty-two," he said. "Take it or leave it."

Dorie stuffed them in her pocket. She looked up at Bret who'd been watching the show with a pretty good idea of how it would end up. His expectations were right on. His father had been up to his old tricks. He'd obviously conned this woman somehow, and he'd run away to the mountains to lay low.

"Arrest your father, Mr. Police Officer," Dorie said. "He's a liar and a thief."

"That may be so," Bret said. "But I'm an *ex*-cop, remember? I can't officially arrest anybody."

"Well, you've got a problem then, junior. I'm not leaving here without my five grand."

Bret looked at his dad. "Five grand, Pop?"

Clancy shrugged. "Can't remember. Might have been."

"So what are you two going to do about it?" Dorie asked.

Bret blew out a long breath. He was going to have to tell this woman that he wasn't responsible for his father's debts. And when he did, was he going to have to wrestle that can of mace out of her grip?

"Right now I'm going to put more wood on the fire," he said, buying some time. The room was growing colder by the minute, but the chill he felt now had little to do with the plunging temperature outside.

CHAPTER TWO

WITH THE FIRE roaring nearby, a whisper of heat coming from the floor vents and her hands wrapped around a steaming cup of coffee which Bret had refilled twice, Dorie felt a subtle hint of encouragement seep into her bones. Tension eased from her shoulders. She let out a long breath and took an even longer one deep into her lungs.

As her body let go of some of the day's anxiety, she made a thoughtful appraisal of Bret Donovan that went beyond his obvious good looks. He had been attentive and responsive to her story. Perhaps, she almost allowed herself to believe, even a bit sympathetic. Could she conclude now that he was nothing like his father and would do the honorable thing and make amends for what Clancy had done to her?

A few minutes ago she'd paused in relating the events which had led her to Clancy more than three months ago. She waited for Bret to respond to what he'd learned so far.

He set his coffee mug on the table. "So this company you sold the rights to, this Family Picnic Company, was your principal livelihood?" he said.

"That's right. And along with my partner, we made a decent living."

"So, if you don't mind my asking, why did you sell your half to your partner?"

"I had to. I needed money."

She didn't elaborate about the small cottage her mother had left her when she ran off. He didn't need to know that. The simple two-bedroom house wasn't worth much, but Dorie was determined not to sell it. So she told him how she and her friend had started the Family Picnic Company to cater to people who wanted to host outdoor events, barbecues and such. She would hitch a wagon that carried ribs and all the makings of her secret sauce and baked beans behind her Ranger. Her partner would tow the funnel-cake-and-candy-apple cart, and they would set up anywhere folks wanted to treat friends and family to an outdoor party. Once word got around, she was busy almost every weekend.

Other than admitting she needed money, she hadn't given Bret specific details explaining why she'd been forced to sell her only means of support. When she'd gone to work for Clancy a few months ago, she hadn't even told him that crucial bit of information, and he hadn't asked. Now, even if she told them, she doubted the heartless father and his ex-cop son would understand her need to pay the fees of the high-priced attorney she'd hired to defend her brother. Especially since her brother had been accused, wrongfully she believed, of participating in a shooting. The money she'd gotten from the sale of her share of the picnic company had gone to the firm of Hawkes, Schreiber and Bolger, and more was owed now.

Maybe Bret wouldn't ask her why she needed the money. The honorable thing would be to just give her the five thousand dollars and send her down the mountain. Maybe he even had the cash squirreled away at The Crooked Spruce. The outpost was so remote, there would be little danger of theft. And a lot of people didn't trust the bank anymore. If Bret didn't have the cash, she'd take a check. Once she was gone, he could get

Clancy to pay the money back any way he could.

"You must have needed money pretty badly to take that step," Bret said.

"I did," she said. "I sold my share of the business because I owed money and was obligated to pay it." She speared Clancy with a telling look. "That's what honest people do when they have a debt."

He stared at the ceiling.

"Now I need what you owe me, Clancy." *Especially since I've found out that my financial responsibility to Jack's defense is just beginning.*

Bret sat across the picnic table from her. He put his elbows on the top and leaned forward. Those soft nut-brown eyes, which had captured her imagination an hour ago, now seemed capable of reading her thoughts. She looked down, avoiding his gaze. She'd never been in trouble with the law, but still, after what Jack had been through, she didn't think she'd ever be comfortable under a cop's intense scrutiny.

"So how does all this lead up to you getting a job working with my father?" he asked.

She focused on Clancy. His hands were

clasped on the tabletop. His attention could have been fixed on the tiny hairs on the backs of his fingers. Since he wasn't looking at her, maybe he was finally embarrassed about how he'd misled her. Or maybe he was trying to figure out another plan to get away with cheating her.

"You know your father owned the Crab Trap, a bar on Winston Beach?" she said to Bret.

He admitted that he was aware of his father's business venture. "I never saw the place for myself," he said. "For the short time my dad owned it, I was—" he stopped, glanced at his father "—I was indisposed for a while and couldn't visit him."

The vagueness of his answer registered as a tingle of alarm down Dorie's spine. Maybe the ex-cop had some secrets of his own. "I had been in there a time or two after Clancy bought it," she said. "The Crab Trap catered to a local crowd, people who had been around Winston Beach for a long time."

"So not your typical tourist types?"

She shook her head. "Definitely not. The Trap was filled with old-timers, bikers and roughnecks, mostly."

Bret smiled. "And one Dorinda Howe."

"I wasn't a regular. But the day after I sold my business, I drove by the place and saw a help-wanted sign in the window. Being unemployed at the time, I went in and applied for the waitress job."

Clancy finally raised his head to stare at his son. "Which I gave her because of the generous nature of my character."

Bret frowned. "Right. Go on, Dorie."

"Oh, that much is the truth, minus the generous nature part. He gave me the job."

"I sure did," Clancy said. "I figured she could make the Trap the place to go for barbeque in the area, plus clean up the image a bit. A win-win for both of us."

Dorie frowned. "But what Clancy isn't telling you is that he had the Crab Trap up for sale at the time, which totally affected my job security. But that was okay. He had a right to sell it. Only thing is, he didn't own the building. He was only leasing it, so he didn't have much real property to sell. He was trying to find a buyer for his license, the equipment, which basically included the beer taps, furniture, grills and deep fryers." She leveled an icy stare at Clancy. "And, what he calls the goodwill he'd established by running the place."

Clancy put one finger in the air. "That's right. Goodwill. It's not easy to put a price on that."

"But you did," Dorie said. "You put a price of twenty thousand on it."

Bret's eyes widened. "Jeez, Pop, I only lent you three thousand to start up that business last year. Did you get twenty grand for it?"

"Of course not. That was just my asking price." Clancy's eyebrows came together in an insolent gesture. "I ended up getting only fifteen thousand."

Dorie could sense the wheels turning in Bret's head. After pausing a moment, he said, "And out of that fifteen thousand, you owed me three and Dorie five?" At least Bret was remembering his math correctly.

"And I earned every cent of it," she said. "Your father never would have sold the Crab Trap if I hadn't come in there and made a deal with him to turn it into a presentable establishment that would appeal to buyers."

"What exactly did you do?" Bret asked.

"A whole lot more than any other so-called waitress would have done. I used my special recipes to bring in crowds. I changed the advertising so he'd attract a better clientele, revised the menu to include healthier food and kids' meals. Handed out coupons all over the area so we'd attract the few tourists who actually stopped on Winston Beach."

She looked at Clancy and was gratified to see that he was listening and didn't appear ready to argue. "Basically I was his nutritionist, marketer and public relations department. In addition to all that, I scrubbed years' worth of old grease off the walls," she added.

"You did all that for a waitress's salary?" Bret said.

"No. I'm not that gullible. What I asked in return was a regular job as the waitress with salary and tips, and a percentage of the selling price up to five thousand dollars. Clancy and I agreed that he would keep anything over five grand. At that time, five thousand was what I needed."

"Okay. Sounds fair enough," Bret said. "Did you get this agreement in writing?"

She fished in the pocket of the jacket beside her on the bench and produced a wrinkled envelope. After removing a one-page document which she smoothed over the surface of the table, she said, "Check it out for yourself." She pointed to the financial terms and then to her signature and Clancy's at the bottom. "We both signed it."

Bret studied the paper and then looked at his father. "That's your handwriting, Pop," he said. "This isn't the fanciest contract in the world, but I think it would hold up in court."

Clancy crossed his arms over his chest and scowled. "Whose side are you on?"

"I'm on the side of what's right. Did Dorie fulfill her part of this contract like she says?"

Clancy stubbornly stared into space for several uncomfortable seconds before finally, almost negligibly, nodding his head. It wasn't a definitive admission, but he wasn't denying Dorie's story.

"Her contribution helped you sell the place?"

"I suppose."

"You *know* darned well it did," she said.

Bret shrugged. "Then you owe her, Pop. And you owe me three grand. That was the deal we made when I lent you the money." He waited for his father's reaction, and when the old guy didn't so much as blink, he said, "And funny thing, Pop, when you arrived here, I asked you about the Crab Trap and you told me there had been a kitchen fire and you lost everything."

"I might have said that," Clancy mumbled. "But I was just stalling for time before I paid you back."

Bret looked down as if he was used to this kind of scenario from his father. "You've got the money, right? I mean you obviously didn't have it in your pocket a few minutes ago when Dorie asked for it, but you've got it somewhere, don't you?"

Clancy stared blankly.

Dorie bit her bottom lip and tried not to squirm. What would she do if Clancy didn't have the money? There was no doubt he was a weasel, but even a weasel couldn't lose fifteen thousand dollars in a little over a week. Could he?

"Pop?"

Bret's gaze zeroed in on his father's eyes under the ledge of Clancy's bushy white brows. Clancy shifted away from his son's stare.

"The money's in your room, isn't it?" Bret said. "Or safely in a bank somewhere?"

Tense seconds ticked by until Clancy fisted

his hands and made a sound between a moan and a snarl. "Not exactly."

"What does that mean?"

"I had it for a while."

Skepticism etched itself in creases around Bret's eyes. "How long is a while? And what happened to it?"

"I didn't come straight here after leaving Winston Beach," he said.

"Where did you go?" Bret's voice reflected uncertainty, as if he expected the ceiling to suddenly cave in on them. As if he'd experienced other symbolic ceilings caving in during his lifetime. "Pop?"

"I was trying to turn that money into a whole lot more," Clancy said. "I was hoping to give you that three grand with interest."

"Where did you go?" Bret asked again. This time the words seemed ground out of some dark place inside his memory.

"I drove up to Mountain City, West Virginia, for a few days."

"Mountain City?" Bret closed his eyes and took a deep breath. "Why did you go there?"

Dorie leaned forward, trying to read both men's faces. "I know exactly why he went there, Bret, and so do you."

Bret hammered his fist on the table. "Good grief, Pop. You lost that money gambling!"

"I figured I could turn that fifteen grand into five times that much. I've always been lucky...."

"You've never been lucky with dice!"

"That's not true. Why, lots of times I've..."

"How much?" Bret asked. "How much have you got left?"

Clancy turned his palms up on the table as if he somehow expected riches to fall into them. "I have...well, I *had* fifty-two bucks."

Dorie stood, marched around the table and loomed over him. But at only five feet three inches, her looming capabilities were limited. Still, she was gratified when he cringed.

"Fifty-two dollars?" she said, pulling the bills he'd given her earlier from her pocket. "*This* fifty-two dollars? This is all that's left of fifteen thousand?"

He stared at the table. "'Fraid so. I had living expenses for that week, too. Hotels and meals..."

Her entire body tensed before a trembling began in her legs and worked its way through her. She closed her eyes, fighting the desire to strike out physically at the man whose face swam before her, but what good would that do? She'd only end up in the same sort of place she'd visited two days ago when she met with her brother in a dank, gray-walled prison room.

She pictured Jack's face now and drew strength from the past. Since their father, a shiftless man with no ambition, had left them after Jack was born, Dorie had always been the rational child, the dependable one. Their mother stuck around until Dorie was legally an adult, and then she saw her chance and left. After that, Jack had counted on Dorie. And he needed her now more than ever.

In the visitor's room at the Broad Creek Correctional Facility, Jack had sat across from her, his hands folded, his gaze imploring her. "What do you mean he's gone?" he'd asked when she'd given him the bad news about their funds being missing.

"He just up and left after he signed the papers on the Crab Trap."

"But that's your money. You earned it!"

"I know, Jack, and I've spent the last five days trying to find out where he might have gone."

His fingers tightened until his knuckles turned white. "And did you? Find out, I mean."

"I think so. I hope so." She'd explained about locating one of the regulars from the Crab Trap who'd spent long hours talking to Clancy about whatever old guys reminisced over. He'd been reluctant to tell her what she wanted to know, but finally relented when she made him see that Clancy had treated her unfairly.

He'd told her that Clancy had talked about going to the mountains to find someone he knew. He remembered Clancy mentioning a place called The Crooked Spruce in the Blue Ridge chain. So Dorie had searched for The Crooked Spruce on Google, and come up with one reference only. Somebody had applied for a vendor's license for a new business in western North Carolina.

After visiting with Jack and reassuring him that she would do whatever she could to get his defense rolling again, she'd packed a bag and headed for the mountains hoping to surprise Clancy at his hideout.

Now, even though she'd found him, she'd hit an even more impenetrable stone wall. She opened her eyes to erase the image of

Jack's face—desperate, sad, knowing she was his only hope. It wasn't fair. Just because Jack had gotten into a few scrapes, the police seemed to believe he was guilty of shooting and killing a convenience store clerk in Winston Beach. But he'd been almost as much of a victim as the clerk had. Dorie knew that. She believed his story. He was only sixteen years old, her baby brother. She'd taken care of him all his life. She wouldn't stop now.

She let out the breath she'd been holding and fixed Clancy with her iciest stare. "You're going to get the money," she said. "You're going to pay me what you owe me. I need that money."

The only sound that registered in her brain was her own heartbeat, pumping blood furiously through her veins. She'd never known she could feel such animosity toward another human being.

Clancy didn't blink, but she knew he was aware just how fragile her emotions were at this moment, just how close to the edge of rational behavior she felt and how precarious his situation was. He swallowed and ran a finger inside the ribbed neckline of his T-shirt. "It may take a while…" he said.

"I don't have a while. And I'm not kidding. I'm not leaving here without five grand."

Clancy darted a look at his son who'd remained silent. And then the old guy sort of smiled, attempting some of that charm he'd used to sucker her into revitalizing his restaurant. "Bret?" Despite his silly grin, his voice quivered on the brink of panic. "Don't let her near the fireplace poker."

Bret stretched out his leg, rubbed a hand over his thigh and winced. "I don't know as I could stop her, Pop."

"I'm not going to kill you," she said. "How would I get my money that way? I'm just going to haunt you and threaten you and make your life miserable until I get every last cent."

Clancy turned his hands up on the table. "I don't know how…"

Bret rose slowly, as if even that simple movement pained him. He took a few steps toward a doorway that led from the room. "Pop, can I see you in the kitchen?"

"Sure thing." Clancy stood and strode after his son, moving so fast that Dorie could only conclude that he was grateful to be anywhere but in the same room as her.

"Don't even think about going out a back door," she called after him. "You won't get very far in the dark on this mountain. And I can run faster than you."

Bret stood in the entry, his hand on the door. "Don't worry. I'll bring him back."

She believed him. In fact, she was dangerously close to putting too much faith in this younger Donovan. He had that kind of face a person could trust, though she saw now that it wasn't a perfect face. His complexion was ruddy from mountain winds. His eyes were crinkled at the corners from the accumulation of his life experiences, many of which Dorie suspected had been hard, especially knowing his father. Strangely, these imperfections only gave a sense of solid strength to him she could identify with.

She could imagine him assuming a commanding stance whether he was talking with his father or a suspect. Yes, with his legs braced, his shoulders back and his penetrating gaze on a person's face, he could convince anyone to do the right thing. At least Dorie hoped so.

"We'll be back," Bret said. He watched his

father slink into the kitchen. "And then I may just turn him over to you and a couple of hungry black bears."

CHAPTER THREE

ALONE IN THE ROOM, Dorie wondered what she was going to do if she couldn't squeeze five thousand dollars out of these two men. Bret must have some money, especially if he owned this entire piece of property. She allowed herself to hope that he would bail his father out of this jam.

She stifled a yawn and shook her head to clear her mind. Her brain was fuzzy from lack of sleep. She hadn't eaten anything since this morning except for a candy bar she'd bought at the convenience store. Her bones ached from sitting behind the wheel for hours. Her emotions were frayed beyond what should have been normal even considering the abundance of stress in her life lately.

Before leaving Winston Beach seven hours ago, she'd spent most of the morning at the attorney's office, trying to convince him to keep working on Jack's case. Counting on finding Clancy, she'd promised the lawyer more money soon and had finally extracted a promise from him that he would pass along the paperwork he'd accumulated to a new associate in the firm who would "revisit" the facts of the case and see what he could do. Dorie hadn't met the associate, a man named Eric Henderson, but she had to accept Mr. Schreiber's recommendation that this new attorney was clever and hardworking. Not to mention expensive. Waiting to hear from him only added more anxiety to an already-troubling day.

She got up from the picnic table and rolled her shoulders to relieve tension that had left a dull ache in her neck. She walked around the room and tried to concentrate on details of the basically Spartan environment. Besides the pair of picnic tables, which took up much of the center of the space, there was one long, dark pine buffet table along the wall that flanked the kitchen door. The fireplace, almost large enough for two men to squat inside, filled much of the opposite wall. A comfortable pine-framed sofa and pair of chairs faced the fireplace, and a flat-screen television was mounted above it.

One of the longer walls consisted mostly of windows which looked out on the screened porch. The opposite wall was lined with pine shelving. The scent of freshly milled wood was still strong in the room, suggesting the shelves were new. There was a state-of-the-art computer on a corner table.

The ambiance of the room was masculine but peaceful, an homage to simplicity and nature. She breathed deeply, attempting to infuse her body with the tranquility of her surroundings even though there was nothing tranquil about her life now. And, as it turned out, nothing simple about what she'd come here to accomplish.

She returned her focus to the door, walked closer and tried to hear what the men were saying. Clancy's low, guttural mumbling was easy to identify. Dorie couldn't tell what he was saying, but his muffled words seemed argumentative.

The steady timbre of Bret's voice was just as distinctive as his father's but for a different reason. She wasn't able to make out the specifics, but Bret seemed to be countering his father's grumbling with rationality.

She exhaled slowly and leaned against the

door frame. She wanted to believe that Bret would devise a plan to pay her back, but her instincts warned her to remain wary. Even so, hope began a slow, steady battle with her skepticism.

Her thoughts backtracked to when they had all entered the lodge. Bret had removed his mackinaw, hung it on a rack by the door, along with the Marlins baseball cap he'd been wearing. Maybe his cap was from Florida, but he seemed much more at home in this rugged, harsh climate.

Dorie twisted so her shoulder was against the door, her ear close to one of the dark-stained panels. The conversation inside seemed to have reached a lull, prompting her to put even more faith in Clancy's son. If he was reasonable, she could be, as well. She wouldn't fall into the trap of judging all police officers by the few who'd treated Jack with such overt prejudice. That would be no more justified than watching cops judge her brother by the standards of all troubled teens.

Yes, Bret would make this right. He would understand that his father had cheated her and, recognizing that their family honor was at stake, very well might assume responsibility for paying her the money his father owed. In a few minutes, with five thousand dollars in her pocket, Dorie could be on her way back to Winston Beach.

BRET PACED. It's what he'd done back when he was on the Dade County homicide division and all the clues had been there, in front of his eyes, and he hadn't been able to put them together. It's what he did now when he was worried about his son, Luke, and wondered if the decision he'd made for both of them was the right one. It's what he did when he thought of Miranda and how he could have saved her if only...

Clancy sat at the kitchen table, his hands folded, his gaze fixed on his son. They'd discussed and argued the details of the debt, and Clancy had admitted his guilt.

"Look, Bret, I know how you must be feeling. I screwed up again. I get that. When I'm able to put a few bucks in my pocket, the old demon comes back, and I just have to risk it on the bigger payoff."

"How many times are we going to have this conversation, Pop?"

"This time is different, son. This time I really disappointed you. I'll make it right. I'll stay here and work on this project of yours until I pay you back the whole five grand."

"Pay me back? Now I'm supposed to hire you on top of everything else?"

"You told me you were going to hire somebody. Why not me? I can work hard."

Bret stopped walking, turned and faced his father. Yes, he had admitted that he'd need to hire a helper to get the camp up and running in time. And his dad did have skills. "You bet you will," he said. "I own you until this place is open and then some."

"Fair enough."

Bret stared at the door. "But what about that woman out there? What do we do about her tonight?"

Clancy had the decency to look at least a bit guilty. He avoided Bret's stare. "Maybe she'll accept payments. I'll send her a little every month until we're square."

"You think that's going to make her happy? Because I don't. She wants the whole thing. I can't see her leaving this mountain without the five grand."

Clancy seemed to shrink in his chair. "She

does seem determined. Tell me, son, do you have five thousand dollars?"

Bret had known this question was coming. Still every muscle in his body tensed. His reserves were running low. He'd spent most of his savings and the majority of his disability checks to get The Crooked Spruce ready. The last thing he wanted to do was pay his dad's debt. Yes, he had five thousand, but he wasn't ready to admit that to his father.

"Oh, sure, Pop." He pulled out a drawer. "It's right here in the kitchen junk drawer!"

"I didn't mean here at the outpost. I meant anywhere."

"Do you know what she needs the money for?" Bret asked.

"Haven't a clue. She said she owes somebody. All I can say is that I don't believe she's in trouble with bad people or anything. She was a good worker. Came in every day. Never caused any problems."

The law enforcement wheels in Bret's head continued to piece together the story of Dorie Howe. "Doesn't mean she's not into something illegal or dangerous, Pop. In my business—my former business—you learn that even the most innocent-looking people can be hiding something." And with that can of mace and a hundred pounds of grit packed into her little body, Dorie Howe could be hiding plenty.

At the image of her pretty face scowling up at him, he couldn't resist a secret smile. He shook his head. *Good grief, Donovan, you've been away from women too long!*

"Why don't you check her out?" Clancy said. "Call one of your contacts from the force."

Bret had been thinking the same thing. Dorie had proved her case, and Pop definitely owed her, but she was so desperate to get the money that Bret's cop instincts had gone on instant alert. Did he have the right to check her out? You bet he did. She was on his mountain, mixed up in his family. He not only had the right. He had an obligation. Especially with Luke due back in the morning.

Luke. Thinking of his son brought to mind a whole different set of responsibilities. He honestly hoped the kid had had fun with his aunt and cousins the past week. He'd certainly been anxious to go, though Bret had been reluctant to agree to the time away. True, this mountain location wasn't everything a ten-year-old could hope for. But Bret still believed he'd made the right decision to get them out of Miami, away from the bad memories.

And he'd done all he could to make the move seem like an adventure. In just a few months he'd taught his son survival skills, introduced him to tools and construction, taken him to town a couple times a week to rent video games, see movies, eat pizza. He'd thought he had all the bases covered, and yet the boy still seemed unhappy much of the time. And too excited about going to Atlanta with his aunt Julie.

He refocused on his father and the current problem. "What do you know about Dorie, Pop? Family, friends, that sort of thing."

"Not much. I didn't ask her a lot of personal questions when she applied for the job. She was like a saving grace when she walked in the Crab Trap that day, willing to work to put a little spit and polish on the place. A few people she knew stopped in from time to time, and they talked. I don't know what about, but they seemed to like her. Left her good tips, I remember. I knew about that picnic company and how it was her living. But

I just figured that made her more valuable to me. She knew something about food and service."

Bret took a sip of his coffee. "I'm going to call Rob at the department," he said. "Let's see what we can find out about Miss Dorie Howe." He paused before adding, "She is a 'miss,' right, Pop? No husband or mobster boyfriend to show up here one day?"

"Not married," Clancy confirmed. "And if she has a boyfriend I never met him. She's a cute little thing, though, so…"

Bret had already determined that for himself but wasn't about to let Dorie Howe's cuteness deter him from what he thought was right. "Never mind, Pop," he said. "As long as some husband isn't going to follow her up here and put another plug in me."

"Heaven forbid," Clancy said. "Can't go through that again."

Bret took his cell phone from his back pocket. "Reception is always better at night," he said. "Less interference from the towers. I'm going to give Rob a call now. Should have info by the morning."

"What about this evening? What are you gonna do about Dorie?"

"I'm not her keeper, Pop. But I certainly don't want her driving that beat-up truck of hers down the mountain in the dark. And it's freezing out there. The only place she can stay is that fleabag motel by the convenience store." He tapped the phone against his thigh. "I'll tell her she can stay here tonight."

"Okay, you do that. And I'll make sure my door's locked."

DORIE JUMPED WHEN the knob turned, and she quickly put a few feet between herself and the door. The men came out of the kitchen. Bret looked at her, but his face was unreadable. In fact, father and son could have been a pair of granite bookends for all the clues she could derive from their expressions. But that didn't mean she wasn't going to get good news. She stood straight, hooked her thumbs into the pockets of her jeans and said, "Well?"

His gaze never wavering, Bret rubbed his hand over the nape of his neck and said, "I need to sleep on this, Dorie. There are extenuating circumstances I need to consider."

"What extenuating circumstances?"

"Well, for one, you can't possibly think I have five thousand in cash in this building."

That would be nice, but also unlikely.

"But I might have a plan."

A plan? The only plan she was interested in was one that put five thousand dollars in the palm of her hand. She narrowed her eyes. "What are you suggesting?"

"I'm going to try to work something out that is fair to everyone."

"Everyone?" She glared at Clancy. "I couldn't care less about being fair to your father. He cheated me. He obviously doesn't understand the meaning of the word *fair*."

"I know it seems that way," Bret said. "But you have to admit that I'm not responsible for his mistakes."

Yes, she supposed she did have to admit that. But doing so wouldn't get her the money, so she said, "What about the Donovan family honor? Doesn't that mean anything to you?"

A grin tugged at his mouth. "I think our family honor, if we ever had any, went up in smoke at the craps table in Mountain City."

"So I'm supposed to go away and let you two 'sleep on this'? I guarantee you I won't be having such a good night's sleep while you're deciding my future."

"About that…" Bret said. "There are no

places I'd recommend for you to stay in this area. So I'm suggesting you don't have to leave here."

"Yeah, right. Like I'm going to stay with you two."

"That's exactly what I'm hoping you decide."

She put her hand up to stop all discussion of bunking anywhere within a mile of Clancy Donovan. By morning, he'd have devised a plan to steal back the fifty bucks he'd given her. "Thanks, but no—"

"You can't attempt the drive down the mountain in the dark, Dorie," Bret said.

"That's why they invented headlights."

"Still, one wrong turn and you could end up in a gully or wrapped around an oak tree. In these temperatures, there will be icy patches, and I'm guessing you don't have all-weather tires. You're used to driving near the beach. This mountain is a whole different story."

She pondered her options. She didn't want to accept what these guys believed might pass for hospitality. The last thing she wanted was any reason to be grateful to them. One night under their roof didn't compensate for the money Clancy owed her.

Apparently assuming her silence meant she was considering his advice, Bret continued. "You can stay here or your closest choice is the Sleep Haven Motel next to the convenience store. Did you get a good look at that place?"

She had, and she'd been glad she planned to get her money and leave for Winston Beach without a layover. The only kind of "haven" the motel appeared to offer was for roaches.

Her attention switched from son to father. Bret seemed to be sincere. And he'd more or less promised her an answer, or a *plan* by the morning. Clancy hadn't looked at her since he'd come back into the room. His eyes remained fixed on a knot in the wood plank flooring.

She huffed in frustration. "Okay, I'll stay. But I'm sleeping with one hand wrapped around my can of mace."

Bret placed his hand over his heart. "Ouch." And then he smiled, and she felt that sense of comfort again. And she didn't like it all that much. A girl gets to feeling too comfortable with a man, and that's when her life starts unraveling.

"We're perfect gentlemen, aren't we, Pop?" Bret said.

Finally Clancy looked up and met her gaze. "You might be, son, but I don't think Dorie will believe it of me."

"Anyway, I'm glad that's settled," Bret said, glancing over his shoulder at the kitchen door. "When I was talking to Pop just now, I opened a couple of cans of stew and set a pot on the stove to heat. It might be ready by now. I don't know about you, but I'm starving."

Her mouth watered just thinking about it. "I could eat, I guess."

"Fine. I think a meal will do us all some good. Have a seat and I'll bring out the grub."

She almost laughed out loud. "Grub? What is this place, junior? A Boy Scout camp?"

He gave her a serious stare. "Funny thing. That's exactly what it used to be. But not anymore. Now it's for grown-up Boy Scouts. Ones with money who are looking for a whole new level of merit badges."

He went into the kitchen and Dorie wondered what he meant. What kind of a place had she wandered into?

CHAPTER FOUR

DORIE USED A thick slice of bread to soak up the last of the gravy in the bottom of her bowl. "This came out of a can?" she said when she realized Bret was staring at her, an amused expression on his face. Let him laugh if he wanted to. It wasn't a crime to be hungry.

"Sure did. Got it at the big box store in Asheville the last time I went for supplies.

"Well, it's good."

The wine was good, too. Dorie had been surprised when Bret had brought out the bottle and two glasses. She'd smiled at the images of moose on the tumblers—the glasses were definitely more suited to iced tea or, as in Clancy's case, a frothy serving of Guinness.

Bret held the bottle over Dorie's glass, but she covered the opening with her hand. "No more for me. I need a clear head to deal with the Donovan men."

He added an inch or two to his own glass. "Oh, come on. You don't think we're all that scary, do you?"

"No, I guess not." *But this place is.* She stared out the window to the exterior of the porch where a single exposed lightbulb attracted hardy insects not burrowed in somewhere against the cold. Beyond the porch, the woods were black. "Does it always get so dark up here?" she asked.

"On this side of the mountain, yes. On the other side, the direction the sun sets, it stays lighter a bit longer. But this is the country. We don't exactly have streetlights on every corner. We don't even have corners."

She definitely wasn't used to outdoor living of this magnitude. Living so close to the beach when she was growing up, Dorie had gone to the ocean nearly every day, but then her mother had run off, and at eighteen, Dorie had suddenly been in charge. Her beach visits had become less frequent. The brief note her mom had left saying she was sorry, and they'd be better off without her hadn't excused her abandonment in Dorie's mind.

But the small wood-framed cottage her mother had purchased for the family worked just fine for Dorie and Jack and, amazingly, had been paid off a couple of years before Linda Howe's departure. Dorie had had to borrow against the house on a couple of occasions, and she'd only been late on her loan payments a few times. Though built in the fifties, the bungalow was Dorie's pride. The house wouldn't last forever in the punishing sea air, but she kept the appliances up and regularly painted and repaired what needed attention. And she enjoyed the lights that illuminated her street every night.

She casually stretched to cover any sign that the darkness bothered her. Then she picked up her bowl and glass and headed toward the kitchen.

Bret rose and took the dishes from her. "I'll take care of this." Glancing at Clancy, he said, "On second thought, Pop, the least you can do is clean up."

"I suppose I could." Clancy stacked the dishes and went into the kitchen.

Dorie put on her jacket. She didn't look forward to going outside in the cold but she needed a bag from her truck. Luckily she'd packed a change of clothes and a few grooming products just in case.

Bret gave her a quizzical look. "Where are you going? I thought we'd decided you'd stay here. I really don't think you should drive on that road tonight."

She almost smiled. "Worried about me, junior?"

"I'd worry about anyone foolish enough to attempt that narrow path in conditions like these."

"Well, don't be. I'm not going anywhere. Despite your announcement of a possible plan, we didn't actually come up with a solution that works for me." She fumbled with her zipper. "But a girl can only carry so much in her pocket. Mine was used for mace, so I have to get my toothbrush out of my truck."

"Want me to go with you?"

"You're offering to escort me a few feet out your door? I don't think so, junior. I'm not afraid of a few fireflies." Lies, all lies. In Dorie's mind there could be plenty of larger creatures out there that would scare the daylights out of her.

"Leave the door open and yell out if you need me." He covered her hand with his and helped yank the stubborn zipper to her neck. When the pulse in her wrist quickened, she pulled her hand free.

"I'm glad you're staying," he said.

"Yeah, well, I'm hoping you're my fairy godfather and you're going to slip five thousand dollars under my pillow tonight."

"I don't exactly keep five grand in small bills around this place," he said.

"And I don't believe in fairy tales."

She went out the door and, without looking in any direction other than her truck, she dashed off the porch and flung open the passenger door. With one quick swipe, she had her pack under her arm and was running back.

Bret had settled at the picnic table again and was rubbing his thigh much as he'd done before. She set her pack on the table and sat across from him.

"What's wrong with your leg?" she asked, surprised that she might actually care.

"Job-related injury. I'm still in recovery mode."

"Related to your painting-and-scraping job or your cop job?"

"The latter."

"So were you a cop here in North Carolina?" She thought that because of Jack's involvement in a shooting, that might be an important detail to know. Maybe this ex-cop was one of the good ones, and she could actually tell him why she needed the money and how Jack had been treated so unfairly by the police in Winston Beach. On the other hand, maybe he was part of some brotherhood of North Carolina cops and wouldn't feel a bit of sympathy for Jack. Because the local police believed Jack was guilty, Bret automatically would, as well.

"Miami," he said without adding details.

"And so you gave up the excitement of police work in a city like Miami, Florida, to commune with nature?"

"I moved here because I wasn't crazy about working a desk job," he said. "Among other reasons."

Earlier, she'd come up with a few explanations for his hermitlike existence—an unfavorable internal affairs incident at his old job, a love gone sour or being stalked by a vengeful parolee he'd put away. Now, hearing this scant bit of information, she figured he was in the mountains because he'd suffered an injury and could no longer serve as an active-duty police officer. That had to be tough.

"So what is your purpose here?" she asked. "Besides peeling off old paint?"

"That's just part of what I've done to this place," he said. "And what I still need to do. The Crooked Spruce is more or less the realization of a dream of mine. I don't know if you looked around when you first drove up, but the property extends for a couple of acres. There are a few rudimentary cabins out back of this one. An old bathhouse and a shed. The buildings are pretty weathered but still stable enough."

Once she'd arrived on Crooked Spruce property, she hadn't seen anything but the main building and Bret Donovan up on the ladder. Still, after Bret's description, she didn't think she'd missed much. "So this really was an old Boy-Scout camp?" she said.

He nodded. "It was closed down almost thirty years ago when attendance fell off. The state of North Carolina took over the deed and held on to the acreage. Why, I don't know. They didn't do much to beautify the place. But I guess even the minimal upkeep needed to stop the structures from falling down wasn't justified, so some bureaucrat up in Raleigh convinced the state to put the place up for sale about a year ago."

"And you bought it?"

"I did."

"Cops make pretty good money in Miami, I guess."

"We make a little higher than the national average, but I had only saved enough for a down payment on the property." He leveled his index finger against his brow. "I'm up to here in mortgage debt. And I've just about maxed out my credit cards."

She was sorry to hear that, for Jack's sake, but couldn't help pointing out the obvious. "But you had enough to loan Clancy three grand when he needed it."

"Yeah. I wish I still had it. I didn't realize how much fixing this place up would set me back. If I had that three grand now I'd hire plumbers and carpenters, and other experts who wouldn't have to dance around the code-enforcement guys." He shook his head. "Never mind. I'm learning a lot thanks to the library of do-it-yourself books I've collected in the past few months. And they know me pretty well at the Home Depot."

"I guess you're not planning on bringing back the Boy Scouts."

"Not hardly. The Boy Scouts haven't been interested in this property in years. No reason to think they would be now."

Dorie looked around the lodge room. "This must have been the main structure."

"Yep. The kitchen was here when I bought the place. I put in the fireplace and shelves and bought the furniture."

"It's kind of a shame, you know," Dorie said. "I would think all this woodsy-ness and outdoor living would still attract young people. But I read somewhere that there aren't as many Boy Scouts as there used to be."

"I read that, too."

"Too bad," she said. "In my opinion, that leaves a void that should be filled somehow. Kids need guidance, even if it's not from a parent." She paused. "Especially if they don't have parents." She thought of Jack and how staying in a place like this might have helped him on his road to adulthood. Under the mentorship of a good adult he might have learned responsibility and finished high school. He might have been saved.

"Maybe so, but it won't be filled by me. I'm catering to an entirely different clientele. Grown-ups with money, I hope."

She stared out the window where the bugs had increased in number and were circling the lightbulb in a frenetic search for warmth. Right. Rich people with designer insect repellent were going to flock to this backwoods location. "You know, junior, this isn't exactly the Ritz-Carlton."

He frowned. "Would you quit calling me junior? I told you my name's Bret."

"Okay, Bret."

"And this wasn't meant to be the Ritz-Carlton. It's an outpost."

"Which is what exactly?"

He explained the dual purpose of his camp. An outpost was a sort of refuge for folks on the trail, a spot where they could shower and sleep one night in a bed. But The Crooked Spruce would also serve as an outfitter's store, a place where hikers could purchase gear they had forgotten or suddenly decided they needed.

"So what's your plan for attracting the jet-set crowd?" she asked.

"I'm planning to cash in on one of the latest fads of corporate ladder climbers."

She snickered. "What fad is that? CEOs like freeze-dried food and sleeping bags now?"

He shrugged. "As a matter of fact, they do. Believe it or not, Dorie, guys like to prove their mettle on the open trail under seemingly harsh conditions."

"Seemingly harsh?"

"Oh, sure. The weather, the setting, the wildlife. All that can be harsh, but comfort is only a matter of the gear you invest in."

"And where do you find these adventurous CEOs?"

He proceeded to tell her how he hoped to market his new enterprise by saturating the internet with advertising about his Blue Ridge Mountain outback experience. He'd started to put together a list of sites frequented by over-stressed executives and people looking for a different vacation experience, one that got them about as far away from city life as possible.

"This part of the Blue Ridge, what's called

the old Timber Gap Trail, is just far enough from the well-traveled Appalachian Trail to be tempting to men wanting to hone their survival skills," he explained. "On this mountain you won't find campers every few hundred yards, so the guys who'll come here are on their own until they hit The Crooked Spruce."

"And you think that's what the modern executive is after?" She gave him a skeptical look. "What makes you think the Caribbean or Europe isn't their destination of choice?"

His eyes burned with a secret enthusiasm she had yet to fathom. "Look at all the reality shows on TV now," he said. "Bosses disguising themselves as workers, millionaires going into ghettos, normal suburbanites taking on survival experiences. I'm telling you, the modern man secretly yearns to explore his wild side."

His excitement might have been infectious, but no way did Dorie believe folks used to comfort and convenience would enjoy trekking across a mountain that barely allowed her pickup to climb it. Still, she had seen some of those television shows and the guys who attempted a less civilized life didn't want to come across as weak.

"Maybe those execs you hope to attract will get a kick out of a night or two under the stars," she said. "But I'm thinking that when their tootsies start to chafe in the cold and they find something curled up next to them in a sleeping bag, they'll hightail it back to Asheville."

"That's where the outfitter plan comes in," Bret said. He pointed to the shelves lining one wall. "I'm going to fill those shelves with everything the guys might have neglected to buy in the first place, or replacements for anything that proved disappointing." He enumerated on the fingers of his left hand. "All kinds of camping gear, warm clothing, meal packs, tools…"

"Snake antivenom."

He ignored the comment. "Sleeping bags…"

"Three-hundred-dollar sleeping bags, I'll bet," she said.

"Right. And once the cabins are fixed up, I'll have the facilities for warm beds and hot meals." He leaned forward, his gaze intent on her face. "It's my firm conviction, and my *hope,* that once the city boys get partway down the trail, they'll spend whatever they have to in order to make it all the way to trail's end and not come off looking like they don't have what it takes."

"So the success of your little venture depends on the macho stubbornness of your customers combined with an inbred inability to adapt to this environment." She raised her eyebrows and added, "And the extravagant use of their credit cards."

He gave her an admiring stare, apparently impressed that she'd zeroed in on the brilliance of his plan right away. In a way, the idea was brilliant if one didn't consider that Bret Donovan had inherited the same scheming genes that dominated his father's actions. But at least junior's plan was legal, and he was only bilking those who could afford it.

"You think it will work?" he asked.

He wanted her opinion? Well, okay. She had one. "Maybe. There could be enough Paul Bunyan wannabes out there who might find your wilderness experience satisfying." He started to respond, but she held up her hand. "But, honestly? I just don't see the point."

"What do you mean?"

She considered not telling him. She didn't want to make an enemy of Bret Donovan. She needed him to make good on his father's debt, but he had asked.

"Nothing," she said. "I was just thinking that this place probably was a pretty good Boy Scout camp."

"I imagine so," he said. "And I don't disagree with you that places like The Crooked Spruce could help shape young lives. I've seen enough troubled kids in my former profession who might have benefited from the responsibility and work ethic that a youth camp could provide, but I've moved on from that life and its problems. And I wasn't responsible for the Boy Scouts leaving. So if they don't want to come here anymore, why shouldn't I take advantage of what they left behind?

"Bottom line," he said. "The Crooked Spruce is mine now. I need to make a living, and this is what I want to do. This may have been a decent Boy Scout camp, but it's going to be an even better outfitters."

"Yes, it will. Still it's kind of a shame…."

"Dorie, I can't fix people. Lately I've barely been able to fix myself."

She shrugged. "Fine. Good luck. Now where do you suggest I bunk tonight?"

"Pop and I sleep on the second floor. But you'll be staying in the spare room down here." He pointed toward the hallway where she'd gone to use the bathroom. "It's the last door down on the right. Technically it's a storeroom right now, but there's a bed in there. Not fancy, but it's clean. You can use the bathroom down here and avoid bumping into Pop and me."

"All right."

He walked slowly to the kitchen, favoring his right leg. Obviously the inactivity of the past few minutes had affected him. Before going in, he stopped and turned back to her. "I hope we can work this out," he said. "What happened to you isn't right."

"We agree on that." She waited for him to elaborate. When he didn't, she said, "So you never told me what's wrong with your leg."

He paused as if debating whether or not to tell her. Finally he sighed and said, "A few months ago, when I was still a cop, I got shot in a botched liquor-store robbery."

She couldn't control her reaction. A startled cry came from her throat.

"I know," he said. "Sounds like a cliché, doesn't it? Liquor-store robbery in the middle of the night. But it happened. And I got a bullet in my thigh for my troubles."

Her mind flashed back to the details of Jack's case. A convenience store robbery. Three teenagers. One gun. A downed store clerk. She flinched.

"Hey, it's okay," he said, misinterpreting her reaction. "I'm getting better every day. You know the worst part? The shooter only got a light sentence. He'll be out in three years if he doesn't screw up."

He stared around the room, a faraway look in his eyes. "So, yeah, The Crooked Spruce used to be a Boy Scout camp, but here's some irony for you that came out in the trial. The guy who popped me was once an eagle scout. Had more medals than a five-star general. Guess you never can tell about people."

She didn't know how to respond. It was a crazy bit of irony.

He could have gone into the kitchen, but instead he held up one finger. "One more thing."

"Yeah?"

"You got anything against kids?"

"Of course not. Why?"

"My ten-year-old son's due back tomorrow. He's been staying with my sister over spring break from school. He's a good boy. Quiet. Won't bother you too much."

"I don't have a problem with that...if I'm still around when he gets here."

"Okay, then. We'll talk more in the morning."

Dorie looked at the door after Bret had closed it. Questions flooded her mind. How did a ten-year-old like living on this mountain? Where was the boy's mother? What kind of a father was Bret? She came to the same conclusion she often did about children who lived with only one parent. They were luckier than those who had none at all.

CHAPTER FIVE

"SORRY TO CALL so early, Bret, but last night you made this sound like a priority so I got on it first thing."

"I appreciate it, Rob." Rubbing the sleep from his eyes, Bret prayed his cell phone wouldn't conk out before he got the info he needed. He grabbed the tablet he kept on his nightstand and prepared to take notes. "I knew you'd have the resources at Dade County P.D."

"You want to tell me why you wanted me to look up this woman? She do something to you?"

"No. Actually it's the other way around. What I mean is, I'm trying to clear up a problem she had with my father."

"So I don't need to suggest a warrant for one Dorinda Howe?"

"Not necessary. I can handle everything from here." *And besides,* he thought, thinking of the spare bedroom downstairs, *I know right where she is. Or where she's supposed to be.*

"Okay. I've got some facts about your Miss Howe. In the past year she's gotten a speeding ticket and some parking fines. She's also had some credit problems dating back a few years. Been late on payments and once was turned over to collection. As far as criminal activity, though, she's not even a blip on our system."

"That's good. But it sounds like she's got a problem handling money, like maybe she could be in some kind of trouble."

"I suppose. Still, I don't show anything specific here. But I don't want to think of you tangling with her younger brother. That kid has a rap sheet that's been building for a while."

"She has a brother? So he could be a problem."

"Not right now," Rob said. "He's locked up tight as a tick in Broad Creek, so you can put him out of your mind."

"What did the kid do?"

"Let's see here. Jack Howe—let me scroll down. Joyriding in someone else's car, vandalism in a public park, some petty robbery, stuff like that."

"And for these crimes he's in Broad Creek?" Bret asked, knowing the maximum security prison was for serious offenders.

"Hang on. I'm not at the bottom of his stats yet," Rob said. "The most recent stuff is at the end. By the way, how's the leg?"

Bret automatically placed his hand on his thigh, an involuntary reaction. He tried not to favor his right leg first thing in the morning. Pain after a night of immobility was common, and he just had to walk it off. "Getting better," he said. "Giving the injury a good workout by climbing ladders and replacing shingles."

"Someday I'm going to come up there and visit your slice of paradise, Bret. Sounds like just the R and R I need."

"Hope you do that, Rob. I had cops in mind when I bought the property. Cops and overtaxed corporate execs. No better place to release tension than this old lumber trail."

"Sounds good. Tell your boy I said hi. How's he doing?"

Bret knew his friend was truly interested, but he didn't want to delve into the honest answer to that question. Luke was due back in a couple of hours, and Bret was anxious about how his son would react to being on the mountain again, especially after a week with his cousins, cable TV, nonstop video games and Happy Meals.

Luke didn't openly complain about the life he now shared with his dad on the mountain, but he often hinted that he wished things were different. Bret knew the kid had issues, both with the death of his mom and the recent move.

"He's doing fine," Bret said, wishing, hoping, it was so.

"Whoa!" Rob said. "Here's something of interest."

"About Jack Howe?"

"Yeah. He's in Broad Creek on suspicion of robbing a convenience store. Says here somebody got plugged."

"What?"

"I gotta go, Bret. The precinct captain is calling me. I'll make a copy of everything the brother is in jail for and call you back."

Bret wanted more details but he knew he couldn't keep his friend from his duties. He simply said, "I owe you, Rob. Thanks again."

He disconnected, slid his cell phone into his pocket and headed for the stairs. His heart pounded when he hit the last step, and he speculated about the exertion of the past few seconds. Why was his pulse racing? Was he concerned about the level of crime Jack had committed? He had to face Dorie this morning. And he wouldn't jump to any conclusions until he had all the facts.

SHE STOOD AT the counter, her back to him. She apparently didn't hear him come in. Dressed in a yellow sweater, faded blue jeans and yellow sneakers, she brightened up his drab old kitchen like a sunflower that had just taken root in his pine flooring.

"Good morning," he said.

She turned. Loose hair brushed her shoulders. Strands caught the dawning sun coming in the window and reminded him of dew on petals. Bret couldn't take his eyes off her. Jeez, where was all this poetic nonsense coming from this morning? Sunflowers, dewy petals. Mountain life was turning him into Longfellow.

She dropped coffee grounds into a mug.

"I found some instant. Hope it's okay if I make a cup."

"Of course. You don't have to ask. I'll brew a real pot if you want me to."

"Not for me. I use instant at home. Can I get one for you?"

"Thanks." He pulled out a chair and sat. "How'd you sleep?"

She turned back to her task, and he watched the subtle movement of her shoulders as she poured water from the kettle. "Fine. Better than I thought I would." Carrying his mug to the table she said, "I had everything I needed and more. Forty-eight rolls of toilet paper, thirty-six paper towels, Kleenex, a case of bug spray…" She stopped and smiled.

"I told you that room was used for storage."

"Yeah, you did."

"Did the sounds of our mountain creatures bother you?"

"I found them rather soothing in a way." Then, as if worried she appeared too complimentary about the accommodations, she backtracked. "Of course, I'm anxious to get

back on the road. I'm not much of a country girl."

"Sure. I understand." He added sugar from
the bowl on the table and stirred. He noticed
she left her coffee black.

She took a sip. "So…where are we this
morning on this plan of yours? You think it
through?"

Right to the point. "I did. Can I ask you
something?"

"I guess. As long as I don't have to answer.
You're not asking as a cop, are you?"

"No. As a friend."

She gave him an odd look he couldn't in-
terpret for sure, but he figured it meant she
didn't think of him that way.

"Are you in some kind of trouble, Dorie?
Maybe financial trouble?"

She eyed him over the rim of her mug.
"Now that sounds like a cop question to me."

He chuckled. "Old habits. But I am curious. I have the money to pay you. Despite
being in debt over this place, I have kept an
emergency cash reserve. The money's in the
bank in town. But this being a Saturday, the
bank will be closed. In Mountain Springs,

our banks keep true bankers' hours. I won't be able to get the money until Monday."

"Is your check good?"

"Right now it is. But my funds are extremely limited. And as I pointed out yesterday, I'm not responsible for my father's debts."

She frowned. "I'm not arguing that point. But we're not going through all this again, are we?"

"I'm just saying, maybe it's the cop in me, after all, but I don't especially want to hand over five grand to you if I don't have a good idea where it's going. I could be contributing to something illegal or at least dishonest."

"The only dishonest thing about that money is the way your father stole it from me."

"I get that, and I'm not arguing with you, either. But I could use some information, Dorie. Can you tell me what you need the money for?"

She scowled at him. He wasn't surprised. Tact wasn't his strong suit. "I don't have to tell you that," she said.

"No, technically you don't," he agreed.

"But you said you owed it to someone, and, since it's my money…"

She started to interrupt and he put his hand up. "I know. It's your money."

"That's right."

"Okay, but it's my money that will leave my bank account, and I'd kind of like to know the particulars." *Like is some loan shark after you to pay him back?* Bret had had experience with scum like that, and he actually considered that he might be able to help Dorie out of a jam.

"I guess you would like to know," she said. "But I'm not going to tell you or your father anything about that money. It's mine. I want it back. End of story."

He took a sip of coffee. This wasn't going as he'd planned. "Not exactly. At least it's not the end of the story if you want the money to come from me."

The scowl stayed in place. Both hands tightened around the mug until he thought she might crack the crockery. Finally she said, "So that's your big plan? You're hold-ing the money hostage until I tell you where it's going, who I owe?"

"I don't look at it that way. It's a lot of

money. At least it's a lot to me right now, the situation I'm in. But I know Pop cheated you, so I'm willing to pay it."

She smirked. "Great."

"But I'm not going to hand it over just like that. Here's the deal. Tell me where this money has to go and I'll send it directly to the person who's waiting for it. That way your debt is paid and we eliminate the middle man."

"Meaning me? I'm the middle man?"

"Well, you are."

"That's preposterous. I'm the one who is owed the money. What I do with it isn't your business."

"Maybe not, but I'm not giving it to you without knowing where it will end up. The person you owe the money to is the true destination, and I don't know anything about him or her."

"You don't need to! And you don't pay a debt by attaching all sorts of conditions on it!"

"You're wrong, Dorie. Again, it's not my debt, so I think I have every right to place a condition on paying it." He wasn't going to relent. "Don't forget, I know my father. This money could have started a dirty trail of deceit that's going to end up with whomever you have to pay it to. I'm not about to finance anything illegal. You could be mixed up in something…"

"I'm not! As for your father, that's anybody's guess."

"Exactly my point. I'm offering you a fair deal, Dorie. Tell me where to send the money, and I'll put a check in the mail on Monday." He waited for her reaction. All he got was a glare that tightened his gut.

He was absolutely certain that he was doing the right thing. Sure, she had a point about her privacy, but he didn't know where that money was going. Maybe her con brother was into something in jail. Maybe Dorie was afraid of someone and paying protection money. That possibility worried him more than he wanted to acknowledge. Also, maybe she wasn't as squeaky clean as her record of parking fines and financial problems indicated.

The stalemate went on for a full minute while he grew more uncomfortable. She tapped her fingertip on the coffee mug, further grating on his nerves. He was being hard on her, but she'd showed up on his doorstep yesterday a perfect stranger asking for five thousand dollars. And she'd been mixed up with his father! That fact alone was enough to make him suspicious.

"This is a way out of the problem, Dorie," he said at last. "Look at this from my point of view for a moment."

"As if we haven't been," she said.

He pressed on. "I'm an ex-cop. I'm on disability from the Miami Police Department. If I end up involved in something illegal, I could lose my monthly payments."

He didn't know if that was true or not, but he figured she'd believe it.

He looked around his kitchen. "I'm deep into this place. It's a hardship for me to give you this money now, when I'm so close to opening. And remember, I hardly know you. Once I'm satisfied about where the money is going, I'll settle your debt and take it out of Pop's hide, but I'm not giving you the money directly."

"This is ridiculous…"

"It's the deal." He shrugged with pretended indifference. "Take it or wait for Pop to settle up with you."

She drummed her fingers on the table, took a deep breath. He knew she'd agree. She had to.

"Okay, but it will have to be a cashier's check. This guy won't take a personal check from someone he doesn't know."

"No problem, but again, it will have to be Monday. The bank's…"

"Yeah, I know."

"You can stay here until then."

"Goody."

He smiled. "Like you said, plenty of paper towels and bug spray."

She stood. "I'll go to my room and get the name of the person you should send the check to."

His instincts went on overdrive. "You don't know the name?"

"It's a group of people. I'm not sure of the spelling of the main guy. Then if it's okay, I'll use your computer to find his address."

Despite the vagueness of her answer, he nodded. She started for the exit, but he stopped her at the kitchen door. "By the way, Dorie…"

She turned, stared at him. "What?"

He got up and walked to the sink to rinse

out his cup. "Were you ever going to tell me your brother's in jail?"

DORIE'S KNEES LOCKED, preventing her from scurrying into the hall as if she hadn't heard his question. She felt ambushed and grasped the door frame for support. "What did you just ask me?" She almost didn't get the words out before her lungs emptied of air.

"Your brother." His voice was calm, as if he'd planned this confrontation to watch her squirm. "I understand he's in jail."

"How did…" She stopped herself and re-phrased. "Why would you think that?"

He leaned against the counter. "Is that why you need the money, to help him?"

Oh, no, he wasn't going to get her to admit to something by tricking her into a confession. She might have told him about Jack on her own, but now she realized he was still cop enough to pull a couple of tricks out of his sleeve.

"I don't have to tell you why I need the money," she said again. "It's bad enough that you conned me into giving you the name of the person I owe."

"And once you do, you think I won't be able to track down who that is?"

His expression was a little too smug. He was too certain of himself. And she suddenly figured out what was going on. Anger built inside her until she felt it thrumming in her temples. "You've checked me out! You and your cop buddies! How dare you? You're acting like I'm the one who committed a crime here."

"Of course I checked you out. I don't know you. I'm sending someone five grand on your say-so. Only an idiot wouldn't investigate your background."

"Or a self-righteous cop who doesn't want to admit his father is a crook."

"I admitted to my dad's faults. I know him better than anyone else does except for maybe my mother. You didn't show up here with a revelation my family and I haven't heard a hundred times before."

She took several steps back into the kitchen. She thought he might inch his way down the counter. Most men backed up from her when she was as hot-tempered as she was right now. But not Bret. He just calmly scooped more grounds into his coffee mug and put the kettle back on a burner. She wished she had that can of mace right now. She'd spray him just for the heck of it.

He set the cup on the counter. "You want to sit back down and tell me what's really going on?"

"So you can judge me? Make conclusions about something you know nothing about? I'll pass."

He smiled. Smiled! "Believe it or not, I thought maybe I could help you. I have known quite a few people who have gone to jail."

"I'm sure you have. Criminal activity is in your gene pool."

"Unfortunately that's true. But so is a commitment to the law. So if you want to tell me what you need the money for…"

"Are you going to back out and not give it to me?"

"Why would you think that?"

"I figured maybe you'd change your mind now that you know about my brother. It seems like cops judge all kids by the actions of a few, assume someone is guilty just because of his associations."

"I'd prefer to believe I'm not like that."

She crossed her arms over her chest. "Right. So here you are, an ex-cop who got shot by a guy robbing a liquor store, and you're going to tell me you don't have a preconceived opinion about my brother because he's accused of killing a convenience store clerk? I don't be…"

She stopped talking as if a bucket of cold water had been tossed over her head. The room had gone deathly silent. Bret's face blanched and his eyes widened.

"Say that again." The words seemed to come from the dark place of his own misery.

She drew in a sharp gasp. "Oh, my gosh, you didn't know that part."

CHAPTER SIX

"MURDER? I KNEW someone was shot, but this... Your brother killed someone?" He closed his eyes for a few seconds and drew in a long breath. When he looked at her again, he seemed almost calm. She wondered what kind of mental discipline he'd mastered to pull that off. She was clenching her hands to keep them from shaking.

"I didn't mean to tell you that," she said. "At least not in that way."

"Obviously. But now you have, and you should sit down."

"I don't want to sit." The words were a feeble attempt at displaying confidence she didn't feel. She couldn't very well refuse his request. She'd opened her big mouth and let spill the secret she'd wanted to reveal only on her own terms. She went to the table and pulled out a chair. "I suppose I could use another cup of coffee."

"Forget the coffee for now. We have some important matters to discuss."

"By *discuss* do you mean under conditions of intense interrogation and mental torture?"

He pointed to the chair. "Please, sit."

She did.

He sat across from her. He checked his watch. She recalled that his son was due back soon. Maybe he would ask her to be gone by the time the boy was supposed to be home.

"Let's start with the easy questions," he said. "How old is your brother?"

"He's sixteen."

"Let me guess. He's a good kid, just had some bad breaks, tough life, no one to love him…" He stared at her. "Have I got that about right?"

She met his gaze and didn't blink. "Yes, minus the sarcasm. Although he's always had me to love him."

"Why don't you tell me his story—the one from the night he shot a store clerk."

"Jack didn't shoot anybody."

"Fine. Tell about the night a store clerk got shot and Jack just happened to be there."

She tamped down her anger and proceeded to relate the details of the store robbery, all the while keeping a close watch for changes in Bret's expression, signs that he was believing her. The facts were simple, and she told them in fewer than five minutes. He remained stone-faced, like any cop she'd ever met. They were all experts at making the interrogation victim squirm.

"So, Jack thought he and his buddies were just going in the store to buy beer with a false ID?" Bret said when she'd finished.

"Yes, that was the plan. Nothing criminal was planned as far as Jack knew."

"Buying beer with false identification is illegal. I'm sure Jack knew that."

She didn't respond. He was just baiting her now.

"And according to my source, Jack had been guilty of several crimes in the past."

Not being able to deny that, she remained silent.

Bret continued. "Things got out of hand, as you say, and one of the boys, the hot-headed one, as you describe him, shot the store clerk."

"That's right. The clerk became confrontational, pulled a baseball bat from behind the counter and threatened them. Vince, that's the boy's name, took a gun from his belt at his back where he'd hidden it and shot him." She considered what else she might say and opted for the truth. "I've never cared for Vince. Anytime Jack has gotten in trouble, Vince has always been the ringleader. He probably mouthed off to the clerk when the man didn't automatically ring up their beer."

"The gun was behind Vince's back?"

"That's right."

"It was concealed from the clerk."

That sounded like an incriminating statement, and Dorie evaded the answer. "I can't say for sure."

"But you can say for sure that Jack was an innocent bystander? He didn't know Vince had a weapon?"

"That's right. As for Jack being innocent, he wasn't innocent in providing a false ID. Just the shooting."

"But you said he drove the getaway car?"

"Vince threatened him. Anyway, the car was Jack's, and yes, he drove it."

"Did Vince corroborate this story?"

For the first time, Dorie looked down. This was the part of the story that could lead to

Jack's conviction for a crime he didn't commit. "No."

"How about the other boy?"

"No."

"That must have been a tough break for Jack."

This was ridiculous. Bret didn't believe her, and Dorie saw no point in continuing his line of questioning. "Look," she said, "it's obvious you don't buy this story…."

"I haven't said that."

"No, but I can tell. And it's okay. This isn't your problem. Jack is my problem."

"True, but our problems have become intertwined. You can't deny that you've become a problem in my life."

"Your problem is with your father, not me."

"Look, Dorie—" his voice mellowed "—I can't explain this, but when you drove halfway up a mountain to a place you didn't know in that old truck with nothing but a can of mace to fend off who-knows-what, you became of concern of mine."

That stopped her. She wasn't just a problem? He was concerned? Yeah, about giving up five grand.

"Just send the money, Bret. I wish I could

get out of here today. I would if there was a decent place to stay around here."

"Nobody's asking you to do that."

"Okay, but I promise, I'll be gone by Monday afternoon as soon as I'm convinced that money is on its way. And besides hounding Clancy to pay you back, you can forget me and go on with your nice little life of peeling paint and gouging executives."

"Now that's harsh, but the circumstances at this point involve a murder charge. You certainly can't blame me for wondering about the money." His gaze was intense. "Who gets this five thousand? A guard at Broad Creek? Vince? Is this money being used to extort a confession or an alibi?"

She stood so she could face his stupid allegations on her own two feet. "A lawyer gets it, okay?" she practically shouted. Bret had gone from concerned citizen to cop again. The man was a chameleon. But now that the story was out, her reservation about revealing everything related to Jack's case no longer seemed important. "It's for Jack's defense."

At least he had the decency to remain quiet for a few seconds which was a good thing because Dorie was caught between rage and tears. She'd had enough. The five thousand was honestly owed to her. She wasn't asking for more than she was due. And she was done jumping through hoops to get it.

"Oh. A lawyer. Okay, that certainly is another possibility."

She was mollified to an extent, but still angry. "That's right it is. As far as I'm concerned, it's the only way out for a sixteen-year-old kid whose guilt was prejudged by—" *No, Dorie, don't blame the cops. You've come this far.* She swallowed and ended with, "For a kid who is currently residing with hardened criminals."

He nodded once. "Go get the address."

"Fine."

"And Dorie, I really am sorry I came down so hard on you."

"You did, you know?"

"When you said Jack was being held on murder charges I forgot for a minute that I'm just a civilian these days."

"Look, Bret, I'm not doing anything wrong. I have a brother in trouble. I need a lawyer to help him. And I need money that is owed me to pay that lawyer. You can stop imagining undercurrents of criminal activity."

"Fair enough."

She was in the hallway when he called her name. She came back to the kitchen. "What now?"

"While you get the address I'll start fixing some eggs. You like eggs, don't you?"

"Of course."

"How do you like them?"

"Scrambled. With cheese."

"I can do cheese."

In the hall on the way to her room, she ran into Clancy. "I suppose you have something to say, too," she snapped at him.

"I was going to say good morning, but now I think I'll mind my own business." He scooted by her and went to start the coffee-maker while mumbling, "Did I miss something?"

"No," Bret said.

Clancy muttered about the early hour and then added a comment in the same complaining tone. Dorie figured he was talking about her. Well, so what? She'd said a few choice things about him in the past week.

She returned with the address of Jack's

lawyer, quickly ate cheesy eggs with ketchup and even admitted to the chef they were pretty good. Actually they were the best she'd ever had. After promising to do clean-up duty, she went out the back entrance of the lodge to make a phone call. She climbed about a hundred yards up the slope of the mountain before she got a clear signal on her cell.

"Hello. Broad Creek Correctional."

Dorie recognized the gravelly voice of Brad Cantor, the prison employee who answered the phone and usually greeted her when she came in the visitors' entrance of the facility. He was a nice guy, but he always made certain she walked through the screening machine and regularly checked her purse for contraband. Still, she liked him well enough. He reminded her of a country grandfather. He always asked how she was and listened to her answer.

"Hi, Brad. It's Dorie Howe. I was hoping I could talk to Jack."

"His block just finished breakfast, Dorie. He should be back in his cell by now. Hold on and I'll try to put you through to the phone there." There was a pause before he said, "How you doing, by the way?"

"Well enough. Thanks for asking." She made a point of being polite to all the staff at Broad Creek. She only hoped Jack was doing the same.

Brad put her on hold. She was used to the wait. Inmates couldn't have cell phones. Nor were they allowed to have internet privileges unless they were doing research or school work. Dorie had never been denied phone access to her brother, but she hated that the District Attorney had decided to try him as an adult and therefore assigned him to Broad Creek. Connecting to him generally took several minutes.

"Dorie, is that you?"

"It's me, Jack." She pictured him leaning against the cement block wall that held the old-fashioned black phones, the kind that used to be in booths by every gas station. "How's it going, kiddo?"

"I heard from that lawyer who looked at my case when we fired the public defender."

That was good news. At least Grant Schreiber had kept his word to contact Jack. "He told me he's appointing an associate to review everything, a guy named Eric Henderson."

"That's probably the guy he said was coming out to see me in a few days. Have we got any money to pay him?"

"We will have," she said. "The law firm should still have about five hundred left from the sale of my business. Even without the five thousand, that should be enough for the associate to drive out to Broad Creek and interview you."

"Okay."

"Just be honest with him about everything, Jack. Tell the truth. You don't have anything to hide."

"I know that, but what if he won't take my case? What if he says we don't have a chance?"

Dorie could sense his frustration. "Don't borrow trouble, Jack. We're paying this guy to find a way to acquit you."

"Yeah, you're right. So, did you find Clancy?"

"I did."

"And he gave you the money he owes you?"

She thought of Clancy sitting in the kitchen

right now, waiting for his coffee to brew. Had she not shown up yesterday, he would have started his day believing he didn't have a worry in the world. Now at least he knew he couldn't hide from his responsibility.

"Not exactly," she said. "I've got some bad news. Clancy spent the money."

"All of it?"

Dorie told him about Clancy's wayward trek to the casino.

"That stupid jerk! I told you not to trust him."

She did a mental ten count. "Jack, be fair. It seems you and I both have issues trusting the wrong people."

"Yeah, I guess we do. I wouldn't be in here if I hadn't trusted Vince and Tony. Now what are we supposed to do?" Jack asked her. "You said we'd have the money to pay the lawyer."

"We will," she said. "Clancy has a son here, and he seems reasonable. He and I have worked out a plan to get my five thousand back. The whole amount should be sent to Grant Schreiber on Monday. He will have it Wednesday at the latest."

Jack blew out a long breath. "Okay. Because what Clancy did is a crime. *He* should be stuck in this place. Not me. He stole from you, Dorie."

"Yes, he did. And, Jack, I'm going to stay here in the mountains for a few days, just to confirm the transfer of the money. But if you see the new lawyer before I get back, tell him to proceed."

"I will, but, Dorie, I need you here. You're the only person who comes to see me. Your visits are all that keep me going."

Dorie couldn't ignore the desperation in Jack's voice. And she understood. He was just a kid, stuck in a man's world, and with the worst possible sort of men. "I'll be back as soon as I can. But right now getting the money is top priority."

Another long silence until Dorie broke it. "Jack, tell me you'll stay strong. This will all be over soon. I won't stop until your name is cleared and you're free. I promise you that."

"I know that. And I'm sorry for wimping out on you. I'm sorry for everything. I know you're doing all you can."

"Just hang tough, kiddo."

"Sure, I will. And I'm fine. Don't worry about me."

Like that was possible.

"It's not so bad," he added. "I'm adjusting."

She knew he was teetering on the edge and exaggerating his state of mind for her sake, and she was grateful for his effort. She hated being this far away from him. For the past eight years, since their mother left, it had been just the two of them, surviving by depending on each other. She wouldn't let him down. "That's the brother I know and love," she said.

"You're at that place you told me about, right?" he asked. "That Crooked Spruce place?"

Relieved that the conversation had gone in a less painful direction, she gave him details about the outpost. "It's still really cold here," she said. "And the cell service is iffy, especially for my carrier." She rubbed her arms through her sweater. "In fact, I had to climb halfway up Hickory Mountain to get a cell phone signal to call you. I'm freezing my butt off."

She looked down at the cabin. Through the porch screen she saw Bret dressed only in a flannel shirt and jeans. He struggled with a large carton, cutting the packing straps and tearing at the taped seams. Dorie wondered what was in the box. But mostly she marveled at how natural he looked, immune to the cold that caused her beach bones to ache.

"Call me when you can," Jack said. "I won't try to reach you unless I have to."

"You got it. We'll stay in touch. And Jack?"

"Yeah?"

"I love you, baby brother. We'll get through this."

"I know, Dorie. Someday, when I'm out of here, I'll pay you back…"

"Hey, let's worry about that later. One day at time, okay?"

She disconnected and headed back down the mountain pathway. Hearing her approach, Bret turned and raised his arm in a casual wave. Her heart gave an odd little kick in her chest and an unaccustomed warmth spread through her chilled body. She tried to shrug it off. She climbed the steps and went onto the porch. "What are you doing, there, junior…I mean Bret? Unpacking a gold-plated heater to sell the execs?"

He ripped open the lid. "Funny. Actually this is a porch swing my sister sent me as a sort of lodge-warming gift. Since she's due here any minute, I figured I ought to put the thing together."

"Need any help?" The offer slipped out of her mouth with relative ease. As long as she was stuck here for the next couple of days, and since the important details had been more or less worked out, she supposed she could pitch in around the place.

He stared at her a moment and then jerked his thumb toward a toolbox on the floor. "How are you with a screwdriver?"

"Flat head or Phillips?"

"Flat."

She dug through the jumble of tools and found the right one. "Stand back and watch."

CHAPTER SEVEN

EASY TO ASSEMBLE with two people on the job, the porch swing was a thing of beauty and expert craftsmanship. Imported from Scandinavia, it was made of teakwood, polished to a fine satin sheen. The swing could easily accommodate three people, but with an assortment of plush cushions and a woolen throw, Dorie could picture someone stretching out for a gently swaying nap.

Bret attached the bronze-colored chains to large metal hooks in the ceiling which he'd oiled so the swing didn't make a sound when he set it rocking. He stood back and looked at the results of their labor. "What do you think?"

"It's gorgeous," Dorie said. "Maybe you could add a couple of pillows at the arms to make it even more inviting...."

"This is a man's retreat, Dorie. We don't need fluffy pillows." He scratched his chin.

"For that matter, as nice as this thing is, we don't really need a swing."

"Are you saying women aren't allowed here?"

"Not at all. I'm just saying that I doubt many will come."

"You might be surprised. Women are executives, too, you know. And many of them are wilderness campers. If they come, now they have a swing…if they can keep the men off it."

He chuckled. "We'll see. I'll keep track of my guests and email you the gender ratios."

The thought of giving Bret her email address, remaining in touch even to a small extent, brought a tiny flutter to her stomach. Of course, they wouldn't stay in touch. He wouldn't send her any numbers. He'd just be happy to know he was a vision in her rearview.

He pointed to the arched driveway entrance to his camp. "Just in time. My sister will be pleased to see the swing all assembled."

A minivan pulled up to the lodge. Three boys got out and ran up to the porch. One of them, a slender kid with hair slightly darker than Bret's light brown, headed directly for Bret. He reminded Dorie of her brother at that age. Hair in his eyes, suntanned and healthy, baggy pants, a hoodie and Converse sneakers.

"Dad!"

Bret wrapped his arms around the kid. "Welcome back, Luke. Did you have a good time?"

"Best ever. It was great."

"Best ever, eh?"

Did Dorie imagine the veil of disappointment in Bret's eyes?

Bret held the boy at arm's length and ruffled his hair. "You avoided all barbershops, I see."

"No time," Luke said.

A woman, tall, plumper than her brother, with highlighted dark hair, came up onto the porch. "I suggested haircuts for all of them," she said. "But I was vetoed."

Bret gave the other two boys quick hugs before opening his arms to his sister. "Thanks for this, Julie," he said. "I'm sure you had your hands full this week."

"Nothing to thank me for, Brat. You know I love McDonald's and Dave & Buster's."

Not wanting to intrude on a private family moment, Dorie remained in the shadows behind the swing. She wondered why Julie had mispronounced her brother's name. Mistake?

Luke caught Dorie's gaze and lightly tapped his father's arm. "Dad?"

Bret looked down.

"Somebody's here. Is she a hiker?"

"Oh, sorry." He motioned Dorie over. "This lady stopped by yesterday to check the place out."

Julie's eyes widened and she looked Dorie over with interest. Dorie felt a flush creep up her neck. She hoped Julie wasn't adding her own interpretation to Bret's innocent explanation.

Bret made introductions, and even though she knew the names wouldn't matter soon, Dorie committed them to memory. Julie was Bret's older sister. Her sons, Mark and Randy, his nephews. And Luke, his pride and joy.

"Why don't you boys go inside and find Grandpa?" Bret said.

"Grandpa's here?" Luke shouted and all the boys stampeded inside.

"Oh, boy, Grandpa," Julie said, giving Bret a familiar sort of look. "Talk about having your hands full." She focused on Dorie when the boys had gone in the lodge. "So what do you think of the place?"

"It's interesting," Dorie said. "Quite a concept."

"Yeah, you've done a good job with the place, Brat," Julie said to her brother. "I'm proud of you. You going to be ready by May first?"

Bret shrugged. "As we say up here, 'If the creek don't rise.'"

"Ho, ho, ho!" Clancy's booming voice preceded him out the porch door. "My baby girl is here!"

Julie put a smile on her face. "I saw the old Honda," she whispered to Bret. "I knew before your announcement that you'd had an invasion of the dad variety." She hugged Clancy. "Pop, what's new?"

"Same ol', same ol'." He quickly glanced at Dorie and looked away. "You know me."

"I do." Taking Clancy's arm, Julie ushered him inside the lodge. "Let's check up on those boys before they destroy everything Brat's done so far."

When just the two of them were left on the porch, Bret said, "That's my family. Now you know all of them, minus my mom. And, of course, Julie's husband, who's always at home making money to support my sister's extravagant habits." He looked at the swing. "Like buying expensive presents."

"I saw her looking at it," Dorie said. "I'm glad we got it assembled in time."

"Try it out," he said. "You can be the test subject."

She'd been dying to do just that so she took advantage of the offer. She sat on the far right side, leaving plenty of room. Amazingly Bret sat, as well, hugging the other side.

"It's all right," he said.

"It's wonderful." She set the swing moving with her toe. "By the way, why does your sister call you Brat?"

"You don't think it's appropriate?"

"Well…"

"Actually, it started the Christmas morning Jules was thirteen and I was ten. I got a spy set, and for the next three years my sister's life was a misery of espionage. Since then, the name just stuck."

The sun had made its way over the mountaintop and it warmed the porch through the tin roof. Dorie felt lazy and comfortable.

The swing was as smooth as a metronome. The breeze held just a nip of coolness. The company…best not to think about that. She stood. "I'd better get inside and do the breakfast dishes before your sister thinks you left that mess."

"And I guess I'll give Pop time with Julie while I peel more paint." He rose and walked toward the door. "Call if you need anything."

She went inside, cleaned the kitchen and had just sat down with a second cup of coffee when Julie came in with a cooler and set it on the counter. Dorie held up her mug. "I'm buying."

"Sounds good."

While Dorie served the coffee, Julie unpacked the Styrofoam box and piled food next to the sink.

"What's all that?" Dorie asked.

"Lunch. I figured I'd probably have four hungry men to feed. Now I have five, counting Pop. I never know if Bret's going to have anything in his fridge. And I couldn't chance putting my two eating machines back in the van on empty stomachs."

"Looks like you've got enough for an army," Dorie said.

"I do. Three kinds of deli meat, potato salad, chips and fruit. Obviously I'm hoping you'll volunteer to eat some of it."

"That's nice of you, but I have things to do…."

Julie waved a package wrapped in butcher paper under Dorie's nose. "Roasted seasoned chicken breast. You can't tell me you're that busy."

Dorie laughed. "I'm not. But I get to help."

"You're on." Julie went to the cupboard and removed plates and glasses. Dorie retrieved condiments from the refrigerator.

They worked side by side sharing inconsequential bits and pieces of their lives while watching the three boys through the kitchen window. After a few minutes, Julie said, "So how long have you known my brother?"

Dorie paused. An honest answer would only result in more questions. But she liked Julie and she decided to take a chance that a simple but truthful statement would satisfy her. "I don't know him well," she said. "Like he said, I just got here yesterday."

Julie meticulously sliced a tomato. "To check the place out, right?"

Dorie layered slices of roast beef on a platter. "Not exactly."

"You're not interested in The Crooked Spruce as a vacation destination, then?"

Dorie shook her head.

"I didn't think so." She put the tomato slices on a plate next to lettuce leaves. "I know it's none of my business, but I guess the big sister in me takes over at times, and I get curious."

"I understand," Dorie said. "I'm a big sister myself."

"So, had you met my brother somewhere before coming here?"

"No. I didn't know he would be here. I didn't even know he existed."

Julie set her knife on a plate and looked at Dorie. "Now this is getting really interesting. Then why did you come up this mountain? Hardly anyone knows this place is here. I can't imagine that a young woman like you would be interested in The Crooked Spruce." She smiled. "No gender bias intended."

"None taken."

When Dorie didn't immediately provide more information, Julie chewed on her bottom lip. "Oh, no," she said after a few seconds.

"Oh, no, what?"

"You didn't come here for Bret. You came for Clancy!"

"Well…"

"What did he do now?"

Dorie didn't want to explain her situation again so she just said, "He's your father, Julie. I don't really need to bore you with details."

"Oh, yeah, he's my father, all right, so nothing you could tell me would surprise me. But it's your call whether to fill me in with his latest escapade." She washed a second tomato under the faucet. "But I'll just guess that it has something to do with money. And I'll also guess that you don't owe *him* any."

Dorie smiled. "I don't want to tattle. Especially now that I'm seeing some positive characteristics in Clancy."

"Yeah? Like what?"

"It's obvious he loves his children."

"Yes, that's true," Julie said. "After Mom divorced him, for reasons that were never really explained to Bret and me, Pop did the best he could. Sometimes he even gave us the majority of his paycheck before he wandered off for a day or two." She smiled. "Bret and I learned money management at an early age. Most of that knowledge stuck with Bret. Not so much with me."

"Did your mother move away?" Dorie asked, thinking of her own situation.

"Not for a while. She stayed close enough to supervise our upbringing. She even made a few halfhearted attempts to redeem Pop. But when Bret and I were teenagers she moved to California. She wanted us to go with her, but by then we liked our schools and our friends. We even liked Pop, with all his faults. So we decided to stick it out."

"That must have been hard," Dorie said.

"It was, but we always stayed in touch. And we visited her. Truthfully I never had any hard feelings toward Mom. Can't say the same for Bret, though. He was the youngest. I think he resented her move."

Dorie unwrapped a package of sliced turkey. "I'd say you both turned out pretty well."

"We've had our issues, but who hasn't. I guess I'm kind of scatterbrained. At least that's what my family believes."

Dorie smiled at her. "Scatterbrained in a

good way, I'd say. I haven't seen that trait in your brother."

"Oh, no. Bret's biggest problem, in my opinion, is that he's like a moral compass, a straight arrow to the point of almost being stuffy. And he's a planner. You know…save a hundred pennies and someday you'll have a dollar."

Dorie layered bread slices on a plate. "Seems like his plan worked well for him in the case of The Crooked Spruce. This could be a good investment."

"It's more than an investment," Julie said. "It's a necessity."

Though she wanted to know what Julie meant, Dorie didn't feel comfortable prying into Bret's private life, so she kept quiet.

"Did he tell you anything about his wife?" Julie asked after a moment.

"No." She didn't know if she should hear such personal details from Julie. "He's been trying to work things out between your dad and me. We haven't talked about personal stuff." *Well, I have because he coerced details out of me, but he hasn't.*

"He's a private person. Always has been,

but he's gotten even more introverted since Miranda was killed."

"His wife was murdered?"

"No, not murdered. She died in a boating accident. She was on a Sea-Doo in Biscayne Bay and collided with an eighteen-foot speed boat. It was horrible. Both Luke and Bret saw the whole thing from shore."

The tragic story along with the scents and sight of all that food spread out in front of her suddenly made Dorie feel nauseous. She backed away from the sink.

"Are you okay?" Julie asked. She pulled a chair from the table for Dorie to use. "I'm sorry. We've lived with this for over a year now, but I forget how it sounds to people who didn't go through it."

"That poor little boy," Dorie said. "And Bret…"

"It was really rough for a while. The paramedics tried to save Miranda, but she died before reaching the hospital. And you know the irony of the whole thing? Bret didn't approve of her getting the wave runner, but she wanted it so badly. So she talked her father into buying it for her. She came from this wealthy Miami family. Her daddy was very indulgent, couldn't refuse her anything."

"And Bret didn't have a say in the purchase?"

Julie smirked. "Oh, he had plenty to say. He and Miranda fought, but when that shiny thing appeared in the driveway, Bret knew he'd lost the argument. For a long time he blamed himself for not sticking to his guns on this one. Now it seems no one can get him to give an inch on any issue. It's like he's become this moral vigilante for the world."

Julie sighed. "I think that's why he moved up here, just to get away from people who screw up, like the guy who shot him, his own father and Miranda's father, who constantly tries to get his hooks into Luke."

"I can imagine that Bret doesn't want Luke too influenced by Miranda's family."

"That's right. In fact, I think sometimes Bret goes too far the other way in ensuring that Luke isn't spoiled." She returned to the sink and continued with lunch preparations. "At first I tried to reason with Bret," she said. "I told him that we live in an imperfect world. If you're not out there dealing with the screwups, they'll eventually find you, anyway."

Just like I found Bret, Dorie thought. *He was content making his plans and fixing up his isolated world, and then I showed up proving again how his father cheated somebody else.* "I can't believe Bret is as normal as he seems to be," she said. "He's had to deal with a lot."

"Yeah, he's keeping it together now. For Luke's sake, especially. Though the kid is lonely, and Bret doesn't seem to know what to do about it. We come up from Atlanta to see them whenever we can."

"I'm sure that helps." Dorie couldn't count the times she'd wished she'd had a supportive family around her.

"They'll be okay, though," Julie said. "They've got each other, and it's a strong bond between them. Bret's a bit overprotective, but I suppose I can't blame him."

Dorie recalled the uncomfortable questions and hidden accusations Bret had made this morning. All at once, his actions didn't seem so outrageous. Of course he would check out a suspicious person who came to his camp. And he would question her motives and background. He had his son to think about. She hoped he trusted her now. She was glad that the facts were out in the open and he knew the truth. She even wondered if he might reveal more of his own past to her.

"Do you want a glass of water?" Julie said, drawing Dorie away from her thoughts.

"No, I'm okay. I was wondering about Bret's mother. Was she any help when Miranda died?"

"Maisie was as much help as she could be from her cabin in Nettles Canyon, California. I know her heart ached for him, and she wanted to comfort him. But she's a spiritual person, and her way of reaching out to Bret was to try to convince him that Miranda is part of the greater spirit world now."

"That made him feel better?"

"You've met Bret. Not so much. But at least Maisie tried. Her yard is filled with wind chimes and bird feeders. She's happy in her canyon and never leaves, didn't even come here for Miranda's funeral. Bret was really bummed about that."

"So how often do you get to see her?"

"More than you'd think. Bret doesn't want to deprive Luke of his grandmother, so he and I take the boys at least once a year. We all sleep in bedrolls on Maisie's living room floor. The boys run like wild wolves around the canyon and Bret and I help Mom prepare the homeopathic oils she sends around the country to people who have everything from bunions to anxiety."

Dorie couldn't prevent a sputter of laughter. "Somehow I can't imagine your brother brewing bunion cures."

Julie smiled. "I know, right? My husband always gets a good laugh out of that. He won't go near the place."

"And I'm sorry Clancy and Maisie didn't make a go of their marriage," Dorie said. "Just from the little you've told me, they both seem a bit unconventional."

Julie sighed. "Every time we visit her, Maisie asks about Pop. I don't think she ever really got over him. She just kind of gave up trying to turn him into someone responsible." She sat down at the table with Dorie. "Now you know nearly all the quirks about us. I probably said too much, but you seem like a nice person, another victim of Pop's who's just trying to get what's due her." Julie laughed. "I guess that's the difference between me and Bret. I tend to trust everybody, even if they're the wrong people, like you did by trusting Pop."

Dorie felt better, stronger for knowing the truth. "I'm glad you told me. I'm only going to be here a couple more days and then these three guys can get back to life as usual."

"Whatever that is." Julie pushed back from the table. "We'd better get this food ready. I've got to be back in Atlanta before dark."

They set platters on the counter, but before calling the men in, Dorie asked, "How do you think Bret will react to hikers coming to The Crooked Spruce? He can't check out each and every guest."

"No, but I think his visitors will just trickle in at first. And he's got a guy lined up from his days at the police academy, an ex-cop like himself who's coming to stay and help with security. That's my little brother. Covering all the bases."

All but one, Dorie thought. *Has he figured out how to deal with his own heartbreak?*

FOR DORIE, WHO couldn't remember a leisurely meal with family in…well…maybe ever, lunch was over much too soon. Besides the food being great, it was a true family gathering that included Dorie almost as a member. No one broached any of the unpleasant topics that had been discussed lately. Bret kept the boys involved in conversations. Clancy teased all his grandsons equally, and they responded as if he were Santa Claus, a superhero and a comedian all in one.

Julie mentioned all the places she'd taken the boys the past week and gently reminded her brother that "civilized society" offered numerous advantages. She admitted, though, that she'd always liked the mountains and asked Dorie if she was from the area. When Dorie said she was from coastal North Carolina, Julie, a true diplomat, said she liked that part of the state, as well.

"Okay, you two," she said to her boys when lunch was over. "We've got to roll. Tell your cousin goodbye and warn him that I'm not going to leave without getting a huge monkey hug from him." She smiled at Bret. "I'll take a hug from you and Pop, too, but you probably won't give me one when I tell you that I'm leaving you with the dishes."

"Clean-up is my job," Dorie said. "It's the least I can do after sharing this feast."

"Okay, then," Julie said. "It was nice meeting you, Dorie. I hope everything works out like you want it to." She passed a quick glance at her father. He looked away.

Bret walked his sister and nephews to the van. Clancy stayed in the kitchen with Dorie and carried plates to the sink. "I appreciate your not telling the boys and Julie about our little problem," he said.

"Our little five-thousand-dollar problem, you mean?" she said.

"Yeah, that one. I've got good kids. Better than I deserve. Neither Bret nor Julie has ever told the boys that I have my faults. I don't think they've figured out yet that I have any."

She filled the sink with water. "I don't see any reason to burden a kid with details he can't do anything about, anyway. Or things that he'll probably discover for himself in time."

"You're right, I suppose. I'm just borrowing time. But thanks, anyway."

"You're welcome, Clancy. You've got a really great family. You're lucky."

"No thanks to their mother and me, I guess."

He picked up a dish towel and began drying the plates she stacked in the drainer.

Bret walked in when the last dish had been put away. "My timing is perfect, I see." He looked at Dorie and his father and apparently sensed renewed tension between them. "What did I miss? Something else going on between you two?"

"Nope," Clancy said. "Dorie just has a way of pointing out the things I'm too dense to see for myself. And on that note, if you don't need me for an hour, I think I'll take a nap." He walked out of the kitchen.

"Thanks for handling kitchen duty," Bret said to Dorie.

"No problem. If I'm going to be here until Monday, I might as well help out."

"Still, under the circumstances…"

"Forget it. Like you said, my problem with Clancy shouldn't be your problem. But you got stuck with it. And me. In fact, if there are any chores that need doing this afternoon, just point me in the right direction."

He looked surprised. What did he think, that she was a freeloader sleeping in one of his beds and eating his food without offering some sort of payback? Dorinda Howe had worked for everything she'd ever owned, and she always paid her fair share, one way or the other.

"What's the matter, Bret?" she said. "You don't think I can handle a few simple jobs around here?"

"No, ma'am. I don't think that at all. I've seen you with a screwdriver. I was just wondering how you are with a paintbrush."

"I'm not exactly an artist, but I think I can stay in the lines. So tell me what needs painting and I'll get started."

"I'll do that."

"One more thing…"

"Yeah?"

"Where's the nearest Walmart?"

"Not far. About two miles to the highway and then it's off the first exit going north. You planning a trip?"

"Thought I'd go tonight. If I'm sticking around until Monday, I need to pick up some things."

"Walmart?"

They both turned as Luke came in the kitchen.

"Can I go with you, Dorie?"

"Sure, if you want to." Remembering her

place, she looked at Bret. "If it's okay with your dad."

"It's okay, isn't it, Dad? I can go with Dorie."

His brows came together in a scowl. "No, Luke. It most certainly isn't okay."

CHAPTER EIGHT

HIS MOUTH OPEN, Luke stared as if Bret had just slapped him. "Why can't I go?" he said.

Bret paused a few seconds to come up with a reasonable explanation, one that wouldn't insult Dorie, and finally resorted to a parental cop-out. "Because I said so."

"That's no answer," Luke said. "I still have money left from what you gave me to spend in Atlanta. I want to go to Walmart and get one of their video games on sale."

"Sorry," Bret said, purposefully avoiding eye contact with Dorie. "And if you have so much money left, you can give it back to me."

"That's not fair!"

Bret took a breath. Why did kids always seem to use that one-liner about fairness? Whenever one kid got to do something another couldn't—not fair. Doing homework before video games—not fair. Being denied permission to go away from the camp with someone the parent hardly knew—not fair.

He sensed Dorie's gaze on him and felt the hairs on his neck prickle. He didn't want to get into this discussion with her, not after they'd all shared such a companionable meal. Thankfully, after a few moments, she said, "I'll just go out to the porch where you left the paint cans. You want me to start painting the trim?"

"That would be good."

Once she'd left the room, Bret told Luke the trip to the store was not up for further discussion.

"I want to know why I can't go."

Bret sighed. Apparently the discussion was going to happen whether he wanted it to or not. His kid had been home less than two hours and they were already getting into an argument.

"I like Dorie," Luke said. "Aunt Julie told me she likes her, too. Don't you like her? Is that why you won't let me go?"

"I like her well enough."

"She's not a safe driver? I'll wear my seat belt."

"I don't know how she drives." Bret sat

down at the table and folded his hands on top. "The fact is, I don't know much about her at all. That's why you can't jump in her truck and take off."

"Then what's she doing here, anyway? You're always talking about strangers and stuff, so I figure she can't be a stranger or you wouldn't let her stay, especially before the camp opens."

"No, she's not really a stranger." How to explain this to a ten-year-old kid? "Grandpa knows her. She's a friend of his, sort of."

"What kind of friend? She's not his girlfriend, is she?"

"Of course not. Why would you get that idea?"

"Because Grandpa doesn't have a lot of friends. That's what you always told me. And Grandma Maisie left him a long time ago, so I figure maybe he likes Dorie."

This conversation was going way off track. "She's just someone he knows, okay? She used to work for him."

"So he trusts her, right?"

"I guess."

"Then I'll go ask Grandpa if I can go to Walmart with Dorie. He'll let me."

Was this his little boy who was suddenly working angles like a streetwise teenager? "No, you won't. I'm your father, and I said you couldn't go. That's the end of it. Besides, you just got back from a week away. Maybe I want to spend time with you."

"Then spend time with me at Walmart and go with us."

"Luke…"

Dorie popped her head in the kitchen. "Sorry, boss, but your paintbrushes are all dried out. I think someone forgot to wash them the last time they were used."

Pop! "Great. I don't have any others. I guess I'll have to buy some new ones."

"I can pick them up for you when I go to the store later," Dorie offered.

Bret couldn't ignore Luke's pointed stare. "That's okay," he said. "How about if we all go together? I'll drive us in my truck."

"Works for me," Dorie said.

"Works for me," Luke said. "As long as I get to spend the rest of my Atlanta money on a new game."

BRET'S SELF-CONFIDENCE plunged even as his admiration for Dorie grew. He'd never before felt so jealous. He'd been envious of guys who'd advanced ahead of him in the police department, but jealous? No, not him. Still he had no other way to explain what he was feeling now.

During the ten-mile trip to Walmart, Dorie and Luke, sitting next to each other in the cab with Bret, had challenged each other to name the products advertised in television jingles. Dorie had proved that she knew more about video games than just the titles. At the burger place next to the superstore, where Bret had offered to buy dinner, she'd showed her knowledge of milk shake flavors and all the varieties of cookies available at the supermarket.

When they got to the store, Bret said he'd stay with Luke, and Dorie should go off and do her own shopping. Before she left them, they passed a shelf of puzzles near the games department, and somehow Dorie talked Bret into buying a three-hundred-piece one of the X-Men, saying it would be a fun family activity.

A jigsaw puzzle? She had to be kidding. Bret had a camp opening in a few weeks. He had cabins to fix, a bathhouse to modernize. He didn't have time to put puzzles together. But, giving in to her gentle prodding, he bought it, anyway.

And then, when they passed the store salon, Dorie talked Luke into getting a haircut, saying that things like that were important for guys in the fifth grade. While waiting for his turn in the chair, Luke spotted a friend from school. He enthusiastically introduced Dorie to the kid while Bret waited on the sidelines, paintbrushes in hand. They'd chatted a few minutes and then Dorie had gone off to buy something else while Bret waited for the haircut to be completed.

In the checkout line, Dorie went first. She was careful to hide a couple of pairs of panties under two T-shirts. But Bret had caught a glimpse of them. He'd forgotten how women's undergarments came in such pretty colors. He also realized he'd forgotten to show Dorie where the washer and dryer were in the shed outside the lodge building. He resolved to remedy that mistake when they got home.

On the way back to camp, the spontaneous good humor between Dorie and Luke continued while Bret was reminded that the only times Luke laughed with him were when they were watching a sitcom together or Bret read a joke from a magazine. The natural, uncanned laughter he was hearing now was refreshing. And disturbing.

Back at The Crooked Spruce, Luke was anxious to start the puzzle, so they sat at the picnic table with a fire crackling nearby and followed Dorie's advice to find corners and straight-edged pieces. Soon Clancy joined them. Dorie was content to find pieces related to the blue sky while the guys picked out pieces of Wolverine's costume and adamantium claws. Somehow she just knew that sticking to the hardest part of the puzzle was the thing an adult should do so the ten-year-old could find the exciting pieces.

Luke went to bed at 10:00 p.m. and Clancy soon followed. After announcing that she would turn in soon, Dorie went onto the porch. Bret refilled two hot-chocolate mugs and followed her out.

"A night cap?" he said, handing her the mug. "It helps you sleep."

"Sure. Thanks."

He stood beside her at the porch railing and looked up at the stars visible through the still leafless trees.

"Nice night," he said, taking a sip of cocoa.

"Yeah, it is. I think it's warmer tonight than last night."

"Could be," he said. "Or maybe you're just getting used to the weather."

She smiled. "I doubt that. I've never been too keen on cold temperatures. I like the beach."

Oddly, that statement disappointed him. "Thanks for all the time you took with Luke tonight. The puzzle turned out to be a good idea. And I'd say Luke seems to be quite taken with you."

"Oh, I don't know about that. I'm something different, that's all it is." She wrapped her hands around the mug and looked at Bret. "He's a great kid, Bret. You must be proud of him."

"I am. But this whole move…and other things…haven't been easy for him. I worry every day about whether I did the right thing bringing him up here."

She passed him a knowing look and he wondered what Julie had told her. Probably everything. That was Julie.

"I wouldn't worry too much," she said. "Kids adjust. I think it's much more important that their stability comes from the people who love them rather than the physical things around them. He'll make friends, bring other boys up here to explore."

"That's the thing," Bret said. "He hasn't suggested bringing anyone here. In fact, when he saw that kid at Walmart tonight, that's the first I knew that he was even making friends."

"Some kids just like to keep to themselves. But that can change. I'll bet when he gets more used to this place and the school, he'll invite other boys." She smiled. "And maybe girls eventually."

Bret laughed softly. "Now you're just scaring me."

"Didn't mean to." She stared at the sky for a moment and then said, "Look at my brother, Jack. He lived in the same place all his life—the little cottage we share on Winston Beach. Despite having the same house to come home to night after night, he managed to get in trouble. I suppose I made mistakes with him, was too lenient…"

"You had parents, didn't you?" Bret said. "You can't blame yourself for the scrapes he got into."

"Where our dad is, I haven't a clue," she said. "But our mom stuck around until the day after my eighteenth birthday."

"What happened then?"

"Out of nowhere, she gave me the deed to the house. Said it was all mine. I should have seen it coming, but I was pretty naive back then. The next morning she left a note saying Jack loved me more than he did her, anyway, so she knew she was leaving him in good hands. She had a boyfriend, so she must have gone off with him. I haven't heard from her since."

Bret couldn't begin to comprehend such behavior from a parent. Even Maisie, who wouldn't win any awards for mothering, had been a thousand times more maternal than whoever gave birth to Jack and Dorie. How could any mother do what Dorie's mother had done? "So that was it? It sounds like she waited until you were officially an adult and then took off."

Dorie shrugged. "I guess that was her plan. Thank goodness she didn't leave earlier. Jack was only eight at the time. The state could have come in and taken him to foster care. As it was, Mom left written instructions for me to be his guardian, not that any official ever checked. I don't know what I would have done if I'd lost him."

Bret was beginning to comprehend the weight of responsibility that drove Dorie to make the decisions she did. An eight-year-old was an awesome burden to drop on the shoulders of a young woman. She'd obviously had to grow up fast.

"So, barely an adult yourself, you took on the job of raising your brother."

"I did the best I knew how," she said. "I'd pretty much raised Jack all along, but taking over the full responsibility? Well, I know I must have been lacking in some areas."

He studied her profile in the moonlight. A firm, stubborn chin, high cheekbones that lifted when she smiled, soft eyes with long lashes. She was a blend of strength and fragility. He suspected she knew how to be tough and when to be soft. Nothing he could say would convey his sympathy, and he figured she didn't want it, anyway. So he said simply, "That must have been tough for you."

She nodded. "There were times… But I'm telling you this to point out that kids have so many influences on their lives, sometimes the way they turn out is just dumb luck. We can only do so much."

He couldn't argue. He'd known the most indulgent parents, ones that probably read every book on the subject of raising competent, self-assured kids, who'd raised hellions. And he'd known parents who'd haphazardly fed and clothed offspring who'd ended up at Harvard.

"And there's another thing. At the time, this move was what *you* needed...." She paused. "At least I imagine it was. Luke can't be happy unless you're settled and content. His emotions feed off yours. You ground him. His security is directly affected by how secure you feel."

The woman had some good instincts. The blame that had sat squarely on Bret's shoulders for months now suddenly seemed lighter, less of a burden. Maybe it was time for him to stop beating himself up for taking Luke away from his Miami home and his maternal grandfather.

"I did need to start over somewhere else," he said.

She nodded as if she understood. "We're all human. We all have needs."

He wondered what her needs were now. Had she ignored them for so long that she couldn't even identify them? Had she sacrificed so much for her brother that she didn't even realize what her own life was missing? He sometimes missed having a partner to share his hopes and dreams with, someone to love. He speculated about whether or not Dorie had a man in her life. If so, Bret hoped he was as understanding with her as she must be with him.

"This hot chocolate was just what I needed to help me sleep," she said, pushing away from the railing. "I think I'll take a shower and go to bed."

She smiled at him again, and he wondered if that special look was fast becoming one of his needs.

"Go ahead and make up a list of jobs for tomorrow," she said. "You get my help for one more day whether you want it or not."

He felt inexplicably saddened by the thought that she'd be heading off his mountain on Monday and back to the life that waited for her in Winston Beach. He didn't like thinking of her in that life again, dealing with lawyers and trials. But their relationship so far was only business and the deal they'd made would be concluded. "I appreciate your help," he said.

After she went inside, he waited a few minutes before going in, then washed out his mug, set it next to hers in the drainer and headed for the stairs by her room. As he passed the bathroom she was using, he smelled something enticing that brought back emotions he'd tried to bury. Apples, maybe. Her shampoo? The scent stirred something deep inside him and he realized that the connection he suddenly longed for might be with the woman whose shampoo would linger with him all night.

CHAPTER NINE

SUNDAY, DORIE'S LAST full day on Hickory Mountain, the dawn was crisp and cool and clean. She kept busy with the few simple jobs Bret asked her to do and then she set about thoroughly cleaning his kitchen. While scouring and organizing his supplies, she discovered most of the ingredients she needed to make a barbecue ham casserole, one of her specialties. If it was true that the way to a man's heart was through his stomach, perhaps she could leave a good impression on Bret's heart with her secret sauce. Not that she'd really thought about being in his heart at all. Not that it mattered.

By noon, Dorie had begun to regret that her time at The Crooked Spruce would be over so soon. She'd always loved being by the ocean, but her short time in the Blue Ridge had shown her the beauty of the mountains. The budding trees were a sign of a vibrant spring just around the corner. The mountain paths were mysterious and inviting. The smell of fresh lumber was natural and sweet. But these elements weren't all that intrigued her on that last day. She enjoyed looking out the kitchen window and watching the men work. Honest labor such as she had always believed in. She loved it when Luke burst through the kitchen door wanting a drink or a snack or simply to ask her what she was doing. His youthful demands and curiosity reminded her of the good times with Jack.

But this brief contentment ended midafternoon when a black-and-white patrol car pulled up in front of the lodge. Dorie immediately retreated from the main room to the kitchen. Anytime she'd encountered the police, the situation had gone badly for her. A speeding ticket, a busted taillight—she'd always heard stories of people talking their way out of these dilemmas, but not her. She'd gotten a ticket from some grim-faced by-the-book cop every time. And her mistrust of the law had only gotten worse when her brother had been falsely accused.

Still, her curiosity was keen, so she stood near a partially open door, hoping to hear what was going on. Bret came around the lodge and met the sheriff on the front porch. After polite but manly greetings, he said, "What brings you up this way, Matt?"

"I'm checking on all local residents," the sheriff said. "At least the ones who aren't still in Florida until the temperature rises."

"Looking for something in particular?" Bret asked. "Or someone?"

Dorie peeked through the opening in the door. The sheriff, a big man about Bret's age, rubbed the back of his neck. "You ever hear of Dabney Shelton?"

Bret answered that he hadn't.

"Their family has been in these mountains since the 1800s. And I can't say that the generations have improved with age."

Bret crossed his arms over his chest. "What do you mean?"

"Dabney is trouble. Always has been. The oldest of two boys, he's nineteen now, just got out of jail for stealing computers from the high school. The ones he didn't sell, he busted up on the highway, leaving parts strewn all over. Just malicious vandalism."

Even from a room away, Dorie could see worry lines form in Bret's forehead. His booted foot tapped a steady beat on his porch floor. "You think Dabney might come around here?"

"I wish I could answer that," the sheriff said. "Would make my life a lot easier. All I know for sure is that yesterday what was left of the ramshackle barn next to his daddy's place burned to the ground. That's what Dabney's known for. He's always been a fire starter, though we haven't been able to prove his guilt."

"He doesn't leave evidence, then?" Bret said.

"Not any we can tie to him for sure. And now that he's out of jail, I've heard he's trying to enlist his younger brother, Leroy, into his activities. They've been seen together a number of times in Mountain Spring."

"Does Leroy have a record?" Bret asked.

"Not yet. He's always been a quiet kid, stuck around home, built up a lot of truancies. But he's not a criminal—at least not so far. But I think he can be influenced by his older brother."

"That would be a shame," Bret said. "About those fires, you know my background. Maybe I could help pin Dabney to the crime before he does more."

"I'll let you know. Right now all I have is a strong hunch," Matt said.

"Is the barn the only fire you've had reported?" Bret asked.

"Wish I could say yes, but we've had a couple other suspicious blazes crop up, as well. Luckily we got them under control quick enough."

Bret looked out of his porch screen, seeming to take in his beautiful arched sign. "I can hardly afford a fire around here," he said. "Not after all the work I've put into this place."

"That's why I'm warning you and anybody else on the mountain," the sheriff said.

"I appreciate the heads-up," Bret said.

"Keep a lookout. I know you have law enforcement experience so I trust you to know what you're doing if you see something or someone suspicious. Dabney is a big man over six feet tall and heavyset. Leroy is smaller and skinny. Looks like he hasn't had a haircut in months. If you see them, don't engage them. Call me, and I'll be out here in a flash."

"I will. But I don't know these guys, and

they don't know me, so I can't imagine they'd have a beef with me."

"You're working hard and turning nothing into something," Matt said. "That's enough to get Dabney's attention."

"I'll be cautious," Bret said. "Thanks for coming out."

The sheriff got in his car and drove off.

BRET WAS AS tense as he could remember being since he'd left the Miami police force. When Matt left, he stormed into the house and called for Luke and Dorie. She came out of the kitchen, Luke trailing behind her.

"What's going on, Dad?" Luke asked.

"Just had a visit from the sheriff," he said. "I want you two to pay close attention. There are a couple of bad fellas on the loose around here, starting fires and causing other general mischief."

"It seemed to me that the sheriff wasn't positive," Dorie said. "Like he's assuming he knows the perpetrators without any eye-witnesses or concrete evidence."

Bret narrowed his eyes. "Were you listening to our conversation?"

She shrugged. "No one warned me that it

was a secret. I figure if a law enforcement officer shows up, it's everybody's business, even if he's jumping to conclusions."

Jumping to conclusions? Was she serious? Bret could only shake his head. "Matt's been the sheriff in Mountain Spring for something like ten years. I think that qualifies him to know just about everybody in this part of the Blue Ridge."

"But there's no evidence. Innocent until proven guilty, isn't that the foundation of our justice system? And yet the sheriff, and you it seems, immediately decide that this man, and possibly his brother, are guilty."

He knew why she was playing devil's advocate, and the last thing he wanted to do was bring up the subject of her brother again and her opinion of his treatment by the authorities. She probably figured the Shelton brothers were being railroaded just like her brother had been.

She stared hard at him. "Can't you admit I at least have a point?"

"All I'm going to say right now is that each of us has to be very careful for the next few days. No wandering off the property. Come to me if you see anyone who doesn't belong here." He tapped the side of his head. "Be smart. Be vigilant."

Dorie started back toward the kitchen. "That won't be hard on me. I'm leaving soon, anyway."

Did she think this was a joke? He watched her enter the kitchen and then said, "Luke?"

"Don't worry, Dad. I'll be careful."

"And tell your grandfather to follow the same advice." Bret scratched his head. "Though the word *careful* doesn't seem to be part of his vocabulary."

THE REST OF the day passed without incident and by Sunday night, conversation turned to the quality of Dorie's barbecue and school starting again the next day. On Monday morning, Dorie sat in Bret's truck in front of Pine Crest Elementary School in Mountain Spring, North Carolina. Next to her, Bret looked over his shoulder to the backseat. "You have everything?" he asked his son. "Backpack, lunch, book you were supposed to read over the vacation?"

"Yep." Luke opened the back passenger door and jumped out. "Am I supposed to take the bus home?" he asked.

"Yes. I'll meet you at the stop."

Dorie opened her window. "Have a good day, Luke."

"I will. And Dorie, don't finish the puzzle before you leave. I want to put in the last piece."

"I won't touch it."

"And when you come back, bring another puzzle, okay? Maybe a Batman one. I like doing them."

"You got it, kiddo." She made a thumbs-up sign, and Luke hustled toward the one-story brick building.

Bret pulled away from the curb and glanced at her. "Did you give Luke the impression you were coming back? Because if you did…"

"No, of course I didn't. Some people just have an easier time saying goodbye if they pretend it isn't forever. Luke and I said our real goodbyes last night."

"I just don't want him counting on something that isn't going to happen."

"Neither do I."

"He really likes you, Dorie."

"And I like him."

"He seems content with you here."

"Works both ways, Bret. I never knew there were so many varieties of trees in these mountains, and Luke knows all of them. I suppose he got that knowledge from you."

"I've tried to make this new location a learning experience for him."

"Good job, then."

They arrived at the Walmart again where Bret's bank had an in-store branch. "Okay. Time to go in and get the cashier's check," Bret said. "You sure you still want to mail it? We could have it wire-transferred."

"I didn't want to fuss with getting Schreiber's account numbers. If we send the check by Express Mail today, he'll get it tomorrow. That'll be fine."

They went into the store, proceeded to the bank office and waited a minute before being called to a teller. Dorie provided the information needed to make out the check. She told the teller to assign it to Hawkes, Schreiber and Bolger, Attorneys-at-Law in Wilmington, North Carolina, and said, "Next stop, the post office."

They drove the short distance and Dorie went in to mail the check. "Well, I guess that's it," she said when she returned to the truck. "Thanks for your help with this, Bret. I hope Clancy works until he pays you back."

"Me, too. Time will tell." Bret pulled onto the two-lane highway and headed toward The Crooked Spruce. Neither of them spoke as the truck navigated the twists and turns to Hickory Mountain. Dorie thought about the previous day, her last full day on the mountain. Once the excitement about the Shelton brothers had calmed down, she'd stained shelves Bret had built to display the merchandise he would soon offer for sale. The soft walnut color blended nicely with the log-paneled interior of the lodge. Then, using her culinary experience, she'd made a list of food items Bret might need to fix meals for as many as a dozen people at a time.

She'd even convinced Bret to let her walk with Luke to the beginning of the old Timber Gap Trail. They hadn't been permitted to wander out of Bret's sight but still, she'd been encouraged because Bret had trusted her to go alone with his son. Maybe in the past three days he'd come a long way in accepting that she was a good person.

They drove through the arched entry to The Crooked Spruce, and Dorie took a good

long look at the lodge building. Bret had
completed staining the eaves and gutters a
dark green, and the matching trim Dorie had
applied around the door and screens made
the building appear fresh and new. She tried
to shake off a feeling of loss at leaving the
camp. Ironically, just when Bret was learning
to trust her, she was leaving. He'd kept his
word to her, and she'd probably never have
a reason to come back.

She got out of the truck. "I'll just pack up
my things and get going," she said.

"No hurry," he answered. "Do you want
something to eat?"

"No. I'll grab a snack on the road."

He nodded, followed her inside. Clancy
came out of the kitchen with a mug in his
hand. "Everything go okay?" he asked.

"It's taken care of," Bret said.

"I'll pay you back every cent, son," Clancy
said.

"We'll talk about it later."

Dorie hoped that at least in this instance,
Clancy would be a man of his word. She certainly didn't want to be out five thousand dollars, but she knew risking that amount was
a hardship for Bret, too. She went down the

hall to the storage room. In a few minutes she had her few belongings stuffed into her duffel bag. She slipped her cell phone into her pocket, grabbed her jacket and walked back to the main room. Bret and Clancy were seated at the picnic table.

"I guess that's it, then," she said. "You know, despite the reason that brought me here, I've really kind of enjoyed myself."

Bret's eyes widened. "Really? You enjoyed all this work?"

She smiled. "Maybe *enjoy* isn't the exact right word. But it's been different and peaceful, and I haven't minded helping out." She shrugged. "I like to keep busy, and since I lost my old business, this has been almost like therapy."

Clancy grinned in that way he had of warning folks that he was about to say something outrageous. "Did you think scrubbing the walls of the Crab Trap was fun, too? Because if you did, maybe we ought to reevaluate our deal."

"Don't push your luck," she said. "Besides, that money is probably already in a mail truck heading across the state." She slung her pack over her shoulder. "So, this is goodbye, gentlemen. Best of luck with your camp, Bret. I hope it's a success."

"Thanks." He looked as if he was going to say something else. His mouth opened for a second, but then he just cleared his throat.

"Something else on your mind?" she asked.

"I was just wondering…what will you do when you get back to Winston Beach? You have a job waiting for you?"

"Not a specific job, no. But I can always wait tables, and it's almost tourist season. I'll find something, if not in Winston Beach then up the road in Nag's Head or Kill Devil Hills."

"I suppose that's true," he said.

She looked from one man to the other. When neither spoke again, she headed for the door. "Take it easy." She stuck her hand in the pocket of her jacket and pulled out the can of mace she'd brought. "Want me to leave this for you guys in case any other troublesome women show up?"

Bret smiled. "No, thanks. My skills with troublesome women aren't so good as it is. I don't think spraying that stuff will improve my rep."

In the three days, Dorie had forgiven Bret

for all his suspicions about her motives, but she recalled that she hadn't been nearly so understanding that morning in the kitchen when he'd insinuated that she needed the money for illegal reasons. That day she'd thought him a judgmental cop who drew conclusions without knowing the facts—facts he didn't really have a right to know as far as his father's debt was concerned. They'd both learned a lot about each other since then. And now, as she was going out the door, she was genuinely sorry to be leaving.

She forced one more smile she didn't feel and went to her vehicle. Luckily the truck started up with the first turn of the key. She didn't think she could take going back inside again. She'd come to like The Crooked Spruce more than she could have imagined. This setting would make a nice retreat. Whoever stayed here would experience nature and peace not found at many places.

But it was the owner of the property she was thinking about when the lodge building disappeared from her rearview. When the first curve took The Crooked Spruce from her sight, she concentrated on turning her thoughts to home, Jack and the problems that hadn't gone away during her time in the mountains.

When she reached the end of the winding path, she braked at the gravel apron where a worn stop sign indicated the entrance to the more heavily traveled road. She scanned both directions and was about to pull out when a horn sounded behind her. A glance in her mirror revealed Bret's truck bearing down on her. He pulled up behind her, spitting gravel dust from his big tires.

"What on…?" She didn't dare let her mind wander to reasons why he might have followed her. Still, the thought that he might want her email address or contact information made her heart race. "Don't be silly, Dorie," she said to herself. She put her truck in Park and got out. Bret walked to the front of his vehicle.

"Did I forget something?" she asked.

"I don't think so."

"Did you forget something?"

He looked down, reminding her of a kid who was checking to see if his shoelaces were tied. This uncertain demeanor was a new side to Bret Donovan. "Sort of," he said.

"Okay. What is it?"

He looked up at her. "Well, I was just wondering…"

She waited, raised her eyebrows. "Yes?"

He coughed lightly into his hand. "What will you do if you don't find a job?"

"I'll find one. I always do."

"I don't know why you're so sure. The economy is still pretty bad."

She flattened her palm over her pounding chest. She wasn't used to someone actually seeming interested in her future, no matter how misplaced that concern might be. Bottom line, why should Bret care at all about what happened to her?

"I'm not looking for a CEO position, Bret. I can live on a waitress's salary. Besides, I don't know why this should bother you. I've been enough of a problem, haven't I?"

"Well, yeah, in a way, and I've noticed that you can probably take care of yourself."

"Exactly. I can."

"But I just started thinking after you left."

"And?"

He leaned back against the hood of his truck and stuck his hands in his pockets. "Here's the thing, Dorie. You don't really have to go back right away, do you?"

"I have a lot to take care of at home," she said. "I have to make sure the attorney is doing his job for my brother."

"You can't do that by phone?"

Yes, she could she supposed. But why would she? She had nowhere else to go but home, nothing to do but get a job and worry about Jack. Her instincts warned her not to let some crazy notion that Bret might be offering her another option cloud her common sense.

"I can do some things by phone, sure," she said, determined to remain cautious. "But if I don't go home and water my plants, they'll die."

He smiled.

"And of course, there's Jack. He counts on me for moral support."

"I know that. But your responsibility to him is financial as well as emotional, right?"

"I think we've already established that fact." She leaned against her truck door and crossed her arms. "What's going on, Bret?"

He took off his ball cap and scratched his nape "You've seen enough of The Crooked Spruce to know that I could use some help. I've got to get the camp up and running by May first, only four weeks from now. Pop and

I can handle the maintenance stuff, the painting, repairs and so on. But I need supplies, merchandise on my shelves. I need to build a website, advertise on social networks. I need someone to answer questions and man the phone."

"I didn't think you even had a landline."

"I don't, but I'm going to get one."

"Probably a good idea." She tried to hide a smile. Poor man. "You'd better get busy with that list then," she said. "You wasted about fifteen minutes already chasing me down the mountain."

"Come on, Dorie, you know what I'm getting at. I was going to hire someone from town to do this stuff, but you need a job, and I know you'd be capable."

A job. Here on Hickory Mountain. Could she actually let herself consider it? "How do you know I can do all those things? Some of your list requires computer skills."

"I know a little about computers. Don't you?"

"Some." She didn't admit that along with nutrition classes to benefit her picnic company at the local junior college, she'd also taken some graphic design courses. She could handle most computer programs.

"I figure between the two of us…and a fairly bright ten-year-old, we can cover the bases," Bret said.

She knew she could do the job. She could design a functional website for his business, and she'd done all the advertising for Clancy. A bit of research would lead her to social and business networks populated with Bret's target customers. But did she really want to stay on Hickory Mountain?

"I still have some meager reserves, so I'll pay you, of course," he said when the silence had stretched to nearly a minute.

She let out a long breath. "How much?"

"Minimum wage at least."

She narrowed her eyes. "That doesn't even match my tips at a good restaurant."

"Okay. Ten bucks an hour. That's the best I can do."

She tapped her foot on the gravel and chewed on her bottom lip. She thought of that cozy room in the lodge, the one filled with rolls of paper towels. She thought of the gorgeous views up the mountain, the cool breeze whispering over the porch swing. She thought of the gruff but kind man in front of her and the sweet, funny little boy who'd already begun to capture her heart. She should probably run in the other direction, but she couldn't help being drawn to them and to this place.

"I guess I could stay a couple of weeks. As long as I'm home in time for Jack's trial."

His shoulders relaxed. "Sure. We can accomplish a lot in two weeks."

"You'll need to get that phone put in. And arrange for an 800 number, too. Cell service is terrible up here. I have to be able to contact the lawyer, and we can't communicate with potential clients for The Crooked Spruce via a ham radio."

"I'll call the phone company today."

"We should both turn our trucks around, then," she said. "Unless you can back up to the lodge the whole way."

He settled the cap back on his head and opened his truck door. "I'll follow you out to the road and pull a U-turn behind you. And Dorie?"

"Yeah?"

"You're going to be a big help to us. I underestimated the length of time I needed to get the place open." He got behind the wheel and shut the door. Before she got in her own truck, he leaned out his window. "I'm glad you're staying."

She gave him a little wave, got in her truck and pulled onto the road. *So am I, Bret,* she thought to herself. But the truth was, she didn't know what had gotten into her. She should be heading back to Winston Beach and the troubles that waited for her there. But she couldn't deny the tingle of excitement that surged through her at this moment. Maybe she didn't deserve this escape from her life, but she was going to take it. And even if it was only two weeks, she would make the most of it.

But then what? She'd have to go back to Jack, to her little bungalow, her job hunt, her bills—she hoped her neighbor wouldn't mind bringing in the mail and watering her plants. She'd have to leave all this behind. She'd have to leave Bret. And Luke. But she had two weeks, and a lot could happen in fourteen days.

THIRTY MINUTES LATER, Dorie sat at the desk in front of Bret's computer. Her mind buzzed with ideas, and this machine was just waiting and willing to accept what her brain told it to do.

"There are six cabins out there," Bret said, leaning over her right shoulder. He seemed relaxed, almost as if her decision to stay had lifted some hidden burden. He hadn't warned anyone to be cautious about the Shelton boys in hours.

She jotted down the number of cabins Bret wanted finished and tried not to notice his clean, woodsy scent. "Okay, six cabins," she said, focusing on the task at hand. "And how many beds in each one?"

"Right now, eight. Four sets of bunks."

"So forty-eight beds altogether."

"Yeah, but since they are left over from the Boy-Scout days, they aren't in the best condition. We're going to eliminate the top bunk on each, and Pop's working on adding slats to the frames so the beds will support full-sized men. All of the mattresses need replacing, too. We can't expect anyone to pay money to sleep on the old cotton ticking ones out there now. I'll need you to research and find the best prices. I want firm, serviceable beds but not fancy. And naturally money is a consideration.

"I'll be satisfied if we have three renovated cabins with four good beds in each," he added. "I don't think we'll have more than twelve guests at one time for this first season."

"So the remaining three cabins will stay as is for now?"

"Yes, until I build up some capital. But I need one more ready with only one bed. It's for the guy who's coming here to help with security. He's got to have a place to live."

Remembering Julie telling her about Bret's friend from his academy days, she said, "Good idea. Those execs can be pretty dangerous. I doubt one ex-cop can handle all the mayhem by himself."

"Okay, you laugh, but I don't want to leave anything to chance. We're remote on this mountain, and anybody could come on the property without being seen. Matt's competent, but it could take a while for him to get here if there was a problem."

"I suppose." She referred to her list again. "And what amenities do you want in each cabin?"

He chuckled. "Amenities? *Necessities* is more like it. I'm catering to executives participating in a wilderness experience. I wouldn't want to insult their machismo with track lighting and indoor plumbing."

She smiled to herself. "That reminds me," she said, turning to look up into his face. "What facilities do you have? Will the men need to come into the main building here to shower?"

"They can. They're welcome to, but I plan to fix up the old bathhouse out behind the cabins. It already has plumbing, and I've got a couple of commodes and two showers to replace what's in there. It's on my list of things to update before May first."

"What about electricity?"

"There are two outlets in each cabin. I've already had an electrician check out the wiring. We'll be able to provide for a lamp and the opportunity to recharge cell phones and iPads. I figure these guys won't want to completely give up contact with the outside world."

"So we need one lamp per cabin, and maybe a basic desk for each, which we can order from a wholesaler and assemble here."

She finished making her notes and said, "What about windows?"

"What about them?"

"How many are there in each cabin?

"Two. Why?"

"Don't you want curtains or blinds for privacy?"

He pulled up a chair and sat beside her. His shoulder practically touched hers. "These are guys, Dorie. Guys don't worry about stuff like that. If we get female guests, I'll reevaluate. But for now, the only creatures that might look in the windows on our execs would be a bear or a moose, and that would only add to the wilderness experience."

"So you're not worried about Sasquatch?"

He grinned. "I want these travelers to tell a few ghost stories, roast a marshmallow or two and go to bed early. Then they'll get up with sun, eat a hearty, expensive breakfast, buy gear they probably don't really need and get on their way."

She shook her head. "Pardon me. I temporarily lost sight of your primary goal, which is to make money."

"Money is important to all of us. Even you. That's why you're here, isn't it?"

She stared at him. "Of course, I'm here for the job. Just the job." She almost choked on the words. There were jobs on the Outer Banks. Yet she'd stayed here for this one.

His brow furrowed. "I never thought otherwise."

She led the conversation back to business. "As far as sheets for the beds, I would suggest flannel. They're inexpensive, easy to wash, pretty much wrinkle resistant and most in line with your back-to-nature theme."

"I'll leave that up to you. Just show me some price comparisons before you put in an order. I don't like surprises."

"And yet you've had to deal with two big ones recently. Clancy and now me. For a man who doesn't like surprises, we must have really upset the normal flow of your life."

"Pop upsets my life whenever he appears. But right now I'm looking at you as a good surprise. I wouldn't have thought I'd say this a few days ago, but I'm glad you showed up."

He stood, walked to the coatrack and took down his mackinaw. "I'll leave you to do your thing. Pop and I will be outside working on the cabins." He stopped at the door and grinned at her. "No ordering pillows for that swing. There are no women here, you know."

She affected a wounded look.

"I didn't mean to exclude you," he said. "You're a temporary woman. I know that."

"Sorry, but I plan to keep this gender permanently."

The smile stayed in place as he opened the door. "I've got no objection to that."

Did he even *think* of her as a woman? She glanced down at her worn jeans and baggy sweater. Did *she* even think of herself as one lately?

He went outside and Dorie considered making a trip into the little town of Mountain Spring. There must be a Goodwill store with nice used clothes or a pharmacy where she might buy a bit of makeup. What if Bret actually did recognize her feminine qualities beyond innocent flirting? And if he did suddenly notice her, what then? Would that change anything? No. Jack would still be in jail, and her problems in Winston Beach would still be waiting for her.

CHAPTER TEN

BRET'S TRUCK IDLED at the bottom of the mountain as he waited for the school bus to round the bend in the road. He laid his head against the backrest and let the cool breeze from the open window wash over his face. He'd accomplished a lot today on the property. Having Dorie inside the lodge taking care of details that normally fell on his shoulders had lightened his load considerably.

But just because he hadn't seen much of Dorie after giving her a few instructions earlier, didn't mean he hadn't thought about her. While he added weather stripping to the cabin doors and windows, he'd remembered standing behind Dorie that morning and how her blond hair waved softly to her shoulders. He recalled her slender fingers, the nails blunt and painted with clear polish, gently tapping the keyboard as he went outside. He especially remembered how her eyes, intensely blue and alert, had focused on his as if she found everything he told her enormously interesting. And all he'd been talking about was camping gear and supplies for the lodge.

When he'd come outside and told Pop about Dorie staying, he'd experienced a flush of warmth throughout his body. But when Pop had commented again about Dorie being a good worker, Bret had merely said he believed she could help them get set up. He hadn't let Pop know that she had other qualities that had been occupying his mind over the past three days.

Bret no longer viewed her as a damsel in distress, and even if he believed that she was down on her luck, he wasn't the "knight in shining armor" type. Dorinda Howe was nobody's charity case, and he wasn't her savior. No, his attraction to Dorie was simple and elemental. He trusted her. She was kind to his son and even Clancy. She seemed to fit into the lifestyle he'd established on the mountain.

Since there was no point in denying the truth any longer, he readily admitted to himself that he was glad she was staying. But he'd do well to rein in whatever effect she was having on him. Her time at The Crooked Spruce was temporary. She would leave. And once again he would be the same man he was before she came. Alone with a son who needed him and a father who tested his patience. Normal would be normal again. But for the next fourteen days, what would be the harm in imagining the possibilities?

Bret's eyes blinked open when he heard the school bus stop in front of his truck. He sat up and watched the doors open. He knew Luke would be the only kid who got out. Most of the other riders had been dropped off already. Luke's was nearly the last stop. At the door, Luke turned and waved to someone still on the bus. Then he bounded down the two steps and ran to the truck.

"How was your day?" Bret asked him as he got inside.

"Good."

"Did your teacher give you a quiz on that book you were supposed to read over the break?"

Luke smiled. "Nope. He gave us a couple more days to finish."

"Lucky for you, eh?"

"I'm almost done."

They started back up the hill. After a moment Bret asked who Luke had waved to when he was leaving the bus.

"Some kid in my class."

"A friend?"

"I don't know. Maybe."

This seemed like a good opportunity to talk about Luke's social skills, or ones that had lay dormant since they'd moved to the Blue Ridge.

"You know, Luke," Bret began, "you can ask kids over to the camp whenever you want. After school or on Saturdays. I'd be glad to talk to their parents and pave the way. And I could take your friends home after if that would help."

Luke stared out the front windshield. He didn't respond for a while until finally he said, "I don't know, Dad. Most of the kids in my school live in town and they already have friends that live close."

"Doesn't mean they wouldn't like a new friend." Luke didn't speak so Bret pursued the subject. "Maybe some of the boys in your class would like visiting The Crooked Spruce. Lots of space to roam, cabins to explore."

Luke frowned. "There's nothing cool around here, Dad. No place to go for burgers or video games. No basketball net. Nothing. Guys like to do stuff, you know."

"Like all the stuff you did in Atlanta?"

Luke shrugged.

Times had sure changed from when Bret was a ten-year-old. Back then he would have loved leaving his cramped apartment with Pop and Maisie to hike among the trees and encounter wildlife. Today's kids wanted techie activities, sports arenas, fast-food joints. He'd probably been foolish to think that Luke would adapt naturally to this new environment after living in Miami. Or maybe he'd just hoped beyond what was practical.

"I could mount a basketball net on the shed," he said. "Larry Bird learned to play with a simple hoop on the outside of his barn in Indiana."

Luke stared at him. "Who?"

Bret sighed. "Never mind. I'll put up the net. I promise."

"Okay." They approached the last curve before the lodge and Luke said, "Is Grandpa still here?" His voice was hopeful but uncertain. Not unusual when asking about Clancy.

"He is. He's not going anywhere for quite some time."

"Okay, good. I'll probably miss Dorie, but maybe Grandpa and I can work on the puzzle if you're busy."

"I don't think you're going to miss…"

"That's Dorie's truck!" Luke hollered when they drove under the archway to the camp. "She's still here!"

"Yes, she is. She's decided to stay a couple of weeks to help us out."

Luke had his door open before the truck had come to a full stop. "Why didn't you say so, Dad?"

Yeah, why hadn't he? Bret didn't want to admit he was jealous, but there it was again— that pang in his chest at Luke's reaction to someone else in his life. Both of them were glad Dorie was still here. Even Clancy was if he'd actually admit it. But Bret couldn't allow himself to act like a ten-year-old and jump out of the truck and run into the lodge as if the moon would rise tonight because Dorie Howe had decided to extend her stay.

After taking his time, Bret entered the lodge, saw Luke's backpack on the floor and the kid in the chair next to Dorie's. Normally he would have made Luke pick up the pack and take it upstairs, but he didn't think acting like a disciplinary jerk was the right move at this moment. Luke laughed out loud at something Dorie was pointing to on the computer monitor.

"What's so funny?" Bret asked, hanging his jacket on the coatrack.

"You should see these sheets Dorie found," Luke said. "They've got bugs all over them so it looks like you have bugs in your bed. Bed bugs, you know? What if one of those rich guys staying here pulled down his sheet and saw all those things? It would be hilarious."

"Not so hilarious in my opinion," Bret said. There was something about seeing Luke and Dorie together that made his chest squeeze almost as if he was having a heart attack. Dorie, with her fair hair and slender figure, was nothing like Miranda in appearance. Luke's mom had been a voluptuous Latin beauty, olive-skinned, with dark hair and eyes. More than one of the guys in Bret's precinct had told him he was a lucky man.

Still, there was a chilling similarity in the scene. Miranda had made Luke laugh, too, in

the same natural, effortless way over something basically silly.

"I think your dad's right," Dorie said.
"Probably not a good idea to order these
sheets. How about we look at other possibilities?" She scrolled down the page.

"Stop there," Luke said. "Dogs. That would
be great, wouldn't it, Dad?"

"Do you like dogs?" Dorie asked him.

"Sure. I've always wanted one, but Dad
says I have to be more *responsible*." He
said the word as if it were a curse and Bret
cringed.

"A dog isn't out of the question," Bret said.
"Especially now that we're living in a place
where it can run."

Dorie smiled up at him. "So, what do
you say, Dad? You want to look at the dog
sheets?"

He ambled over to take a look. "I'm thinking we should stay with simple," he said.
"Pick a solid color and we'll go with that."

Even though he was pretty much being a
stuffy old grump, Dorie let him off the hook.
"That's fine," she said. "Luke, you can pick
the color."

Luke picked a dark green flannel and

seemed content to have been included in the decision. And then the most amazing thing happened. Luke got up, retrieved his backpack and headed for the kitchen and the stairs to the second floor. "I'm going to do my homework so we can work on the puzzle later," he said before disappearing from the room.

Was Luke remembering the rules because he wanted to impress Dorie? If so, that was a good thing, right? Nothing to be jealous of. Except…

He was glad when his cell phone rang and he could turn his attention to answering it. "My sister," he said when Dorie looked at him. "I've got to take this."

"Of course," Dorie said. "I'll show you these prices when you're done talking."

Bret pressed the connect button. "Julie?" He went into the kitchen to keep his conversation private.

"So, what's going on, Brat?" his sister said.

"Nothing new," he answered. "Pop and I got quite a bit done today."

"I called to tell you that I talked to Mom."

That wasn't a big surprise. The two women kept in touch almost daily. Bret hardly ever called his mother, and she rarely called him. But they had Julie to keep them connected so it was all right.

"What did she have to say?" he asked.

"She had plenty to say when I told her Pop was staying with you. You'd have thought they were still married, the way she carried on."

"What do you mean? She knows Pop shows up whenever we least expect him."

"This was different," Julie said. "Mom knows how important The Crooked Spruce is to you and she doesn't want Pop interfering. Mom and I think alike on this subject. We both want you to find some peace after Miranda's accident and the shooting last year. She's smart enough to realize that you probably can't if you have Pop to worry about."

"Put her mind at ease, Jules. Pop and I are getting along okay. It's working…for now."

"That's good, but something in Mom's voice hinted that there was more on her mind. She asked a lot of questions about Pop."

"They were married for a long time, Julie. Maybe she's developing a soft spot for the old guy again." Bret wasn't much for gabbing on the phone, especially when work still waited for him outside. To cut the talk short, he said, "I've really got to run, Jules. Dorie's waiting to show me some prices…." He stopped and pressed his lips together. He'd just opened a door he knew Julie wouldn't let him close.

"Dorie's still there?" Julie said. "I thought she was leaving this morning."

"Yeah, well, she was supposed to, but she's agreed to stay on a few days and give me a hand."

"Oh, really?"

Bret recognized the "I know what's really going on" tone his sister had perfected many years ago.

"How long is she staying?"

"A couple of weeks tops."

"Ah, ha…" That tone again.

"Julie, don't read anything into this. Dorie can use some extra money. I can use the help. That's all there is to it."

"Sure. I believe you."

He could sense her sly smile over the phone.

"I think that's great," she said. "You men need a woman around that place…for lots of reasons. And I like her. She's sensible and helpful. Easy to get along with. And she's cute and single. She's perfect for…"

"Jules…" He had to stop her now.

"I was going to say, perfect for The Crooked Spruce."

He frowned. "I've got to go."

Julie added one final jab. "And she'll be a good influence on Luke."

His sister's interference had just reached maximum overload. "Don't go there, Julie. Luke is fine. We're fine."

"I know you are. Luke adores you. And you're a wonderful father. But I see the way he is around me. He tries to act like a little man, but there's still some cuddle left in him. And, face it, Brat, as a cuddler, you're less than ideal."

"I can cuddle," he argued, and then felt like a petulant child. "But I'm not going to have Dorie cuddle Luke. My son will adjust. Don't get me wrong, his time with you is helpful, Jules. But he's got to come back to this testosterone world and learn to live with it."

"I understand that, but soft is good, too. And you don't do soft well. And that's okay. You're still healing, dealing with your own loss."

"Stop the psychobabble Julie. I'm healed. At least mentally." Sure he was. Would he ever be? "And I'm doing better every day physically. I can raise my son. I don't need a part-time mother to take on the job."

"Whoa, Bret! Where did that come from? I never said she was trying to be Luke's mother."

He wished he could take back what he'd said, but it was out there. "No, you didn't."

"I've made you angry," Julie said. "And I certainly didn't mean to. I love you. I worry. That's my job."

The anger flowed out of him. "I love you, too, Julie. You know that."

"I do. You tell Pop to behave himself. And you might warn him that I told Mom he was with you. Maybe you both should be alerted to a possible phone call from her."

"Wonderful. I'll tell Pop and see if the mention of her name gives him the same romantic tingle from twenty years ago."

"You laugh, but Mom did seem relieved that he was okay."

They disconnected, and Bret tucked his cell phone into his shirt pocket and went into the living room. He still had prices to look over. And he was probably going to be working on a puzzle later.

Had he done the right thing by asking Dorie to stay? Would Luke get attached to her? Would he? Life was full of risks, like opening an outfitter's store. But he'd decided when he moved up here that he was going to avoid as many emotional pitfalls as he could.

And yet he'd invited a very big pitfall into his home. And now he was looking forward to sitting beside her and discussing the prices of sheet sets. As risks go, not a good sign.

CHAPTER ELEVEN

DORIE HAD NEVER avoided hard work. She'd run her own company, kept her house reasonably in order, raised her younger brother and even attempted to get an education. By Friday morning, working steadily except for when she was spending time with Luke, she had arranged to have a phone installed and placed orders for all the supplies Bret would need to have his cabins ready. She'd equipped his kitchen with the extra utensils and cookware he would need. With Bret's input, she had arranged payment and shipment of dozens of items to stock his shelves—everything from prepackaged dehydrated meals to portable heaters and down-filled sleeping bags.

Now all she had to do was finish his website and wait until the shipments started arriving. She expected to have cartons stacked ceiling high by the first of the week. She would then display, store, price and itemize the complete inventory.

But this was Friday morning. Luke was in school and, unless she wanted to join the men and help with the outside projects, she had the entire day before her. An inspection of the kitchen convinced her that she could offer the most help by restocking Bret's personal pantry. The men were out of many staples, so she told Bret she would go to the market in Mountain Spring and pick up what they'd need to get them through the next week. He gave her two hundred dollars and the liberty to buy whatever she wanted.

She rolled down the windows on her truck, tuned the radio to a country station and zipped along the two-lane highway to the center of Mountain Spring. The supermarket was busy with shoppers obviously planning for the weekend. On the way back to the truck with her full cart, she passed a local pet adoption group just setting up a pen in the parking lot. She stopped to pet a few of the dogs. One in particular caught her eye mostly because he seemed to pick her out of the onlookers.

The dog jumped at the fencing, trying to

get her attention. She scratched his chest and a sloppy pink tongue poked out to lick her hand. She didn't know what breed he was, but despite his dubious pedigree, she was taken in by his curly blond fur and floppy ears.

"You want to take this one home?"

The voice came from behind her, and Dorie turned to stare into the kind gray eyes of a volunteer wearing a T-shirt that said *Find-a-Home Adoptions.*

"I wish I could," she said, knowing now was not the time to add to her responsibilities or expenses.

"He's been neutered, and he had all his shots," the woman told her. "And he has a microchip implanted to identify him in case he gets lost. Plus, you can see he has a really nice disposition."

Oh, yes. Her damp hand was proof of that. "How old is he?" she asked.

"We think about four. He was living with a lady out in the county who had more than forty dogs. That violates not only the laws of humane treatment, but criminal statutes, as well. She had to get rid of thirty of them. This little guy was one."

"Wow. He doesn't act like he's been abused in any way." The dog continued to leap happily at the fence.

"No, I don't think he was. I think he was just ignored." The lady smiled. "I come from a family of six siblings, so I understand how lonely you can feel in a crowd." She reached over the fence and picked up the dog. "Here, hold him. He's only fourteen pounds."

Don't do it, Dorie. The voice of reason echoed in her brain at the same time her hands reached out for the dog. He immediately put his paws on her shoulders and lapped at her chin. She laughed into the fur of his neck. "What's his name?"

"King," the woman said. "Although his royal lineage and bearing don't really support that title." She rubbed behind King's ears. "We have a special today. You can take him home for only fifty dollars."

Dorie had that much left from the grocery fund, although technically the money belonged to Bret. But she was getting paid today. No, she couldn't possibly....

You can't do this, she said to herself. There was no way she should give up her earnings for five hours of work to buy this dog. Plus, did she really want to commit to additional expenses of ownership? Granted she loved dogs. She and Jack had lost their dog a year ago, and they often talked about getting another one. But she already had enough going on in her life without adding this...adorable, friendly, needy little creature.

She started to hand the dog back, but his golden eyes locked on hers and she held him just a moment too long. Maybe this wasn't the right time, but this definitely was the right dog. She heard her voice as if it was coming from someone else, someone who made rash decisions based on temporary insanity. "I'll need dog food," the voice said. "And a leash and a toy or two."

"Got it all right here," the woman said. She slipped a nylon leash around the dog's neck and set him on the pavement. Then she handed Dorie a bag imprinted with *Find-a-Home Adoptions*. "There's a chewy bone and a squeaky toy in there to get you started and a five-pound bag of kibble. There's also a one-page info form we'd like you to fill out. Mostly it says if you can't keep the dog for any reason, you'll give him back to us."

Dorie tried to steer her thoughts in the

right direction, but with King's paws scratching lightly at the knee of her jeans, the only message that came through loud and clear was, *We need each other, King.* She fished in her pocket for the extra fifty, handed it over and quickly filled out the form.

"I know he's found a fine home," the woman said.

"I'll take good care of him," Dorie promised, knowing that the dog's "fine home" might not be a reality for his first week in Dorie's life. Somehow she'd just have to convince Bret that this addition wouldn't cause the least bit of trouble. As she walked to the truck, pushing the grocery cart and leading her new dog, Dorie leaned over and said, "You will behave yourself, right, King?"

His tongue lolled to the side and his eyes sparkled. If a dog could smile, King was grinning like he'd just been given his very own canine empire.

"Oh, boy," she said as she started the truck. "Enjoy the ride, little guy, because we don't know what the rest of the day will be like." King stuck his head out the window and did what she told him, as if he was exactly where he was meant to be.

When she reached the road to The Crooked Spruce, Dorie saw Bret's truck parked at the school-bus stop. She quickly tugged King onto the seat and held him down beside her. "Stay," she said to the dog. "Let's wait for the right time to reveal your existence." She had no idea when the right time would be though.

Bret honked, held his hand out the window. She had no choice but to stop so she did, as far away from his truck as possible. "I'll help you unload the groceries as soon as the bus comes," he said.

She inched forward with only one hand on the wheel. "No problem. I can handle it."

She drove up the mountain in record time for her laboring old truck, looked around for Clancy and unfortunately saw him coming off the porch. She got out of her truck and set King on the ground.

"What's that?" Clancy asked.

"It's called a dog," she said.

"I know that, but what's it doing here?"

"I don't have time to explain. Just promise me you'll let me tell Bret in my own way."

"Bret doesn't want a dog."

"I know that."

"Well, then, I'm happy to let you tell him

you brought one here. I certainly don't want to." He scratched his stubble of beard. "Funny-looking thing."

Holding the leash, she started jogging around to the back of the cabin. "That's what he just said about you," she shot back.

She scrambled in the garden shed for a length of rope and tied the dog to the door knob. "That should hold you for a while." She filled a planter with water from the spigot and set the bowl beside him and started to walk away.

When he realized he wasn't going to get to follow her, King let out a sharp bark.

"Quiet!" she said, her hand in the air near his face.

The dog sat back on his haunches and, amazingly, didn't make another sound.

Dorie smiled. "You're a really good little thing, aren't you?"

She ran back to her truck, grabbed Clancy and said, "Help me unload this stuff. I've got ice cream."

They'd just gotten the bags inside when Bret pulled up with Luke in the truck. The boy ran into the lodge and called Dorie's name.

"We're in the kitchen," she said.

Both Luke and Bret came in and started fishing items from the grocery bags and putting them in the pantry. Dorie hurried. If she got everyone out of the kitchen, maybe King wouldn't blow his cover.

Unfortunately King didn't cooperate. Sensing new humans around, he let out a few enthusiastic barks.

Bret stopped loading groceries onto shelves. "Is there a dog in our yard?"

"I'll go look," Luke volunteered.

"Don't bother," Clancy said, passing a quick glance at Dorie. "I was just out back and I heard a dog, too. You know how these mountains can distort sounds. With the echo factor, that dog could be two miles away."

"But I've never heard it before," Luke said. Before Dorie could think of a way to stop him, he ran to the back door. "There he is!" the boy cried. "It's a dog, and he's in our yard."

Dorie had thought she'd tied a strong knot in the rope, but apparently King should have been named Houdini, because he had freed himself from the tie. He was running around the yard, stopping occasionally to bark at the house. Poor thing was obviously starved for attention.

"I'm going out," Luke said.

Bret stepped between him and the door. "No, you're not. We don't know anything about that dog. He could be mean or rabid. You could get bit." He grabbed a dish towel... a dish towel? And opened the door a crack. "I'll go out and run him off."

"No!" Dorie said. "You'll scare him. He's probably not mean. Let me go."

But he was already in the yard and slowly approaching a dangerous animal whose tongue hung from his mouth in a panting, happy grin. King jumped at the totally non-threatening dish towel and ran in circles around Bret.

Bret snapped his weapon like he was in a football locker room. "Go on, get out of here."

Dorie caught up to him. "This dog is not a danger to anyone." She grabbed the dish towel from his hand. "I know the animal. I've seen his papers. You can let Luke play with him."

He stood for a moment, glancing from Dorie to the dog. His gaze finally settled on the length of rope hanging ineffectually from the shed door. "What's going on?" It was a question, but it sounded like a threat.

"I brought the dog here," she said.

"You what?"

"I can explain…"

His eyes glittered with fury. "How could you do this? If anyone is going to get my son a dog, it will be me! And I'm not ready to do that. We're all just getting used to living here. I've got a list a mile long of jobs I have to accomplish in a short period of time. Luke isn't old enough to take on the responsibility of a dog."

"Would you just calm down a minute?" she said.

"No, I won't. I can't take on the job of caring for another living thing around here."

His words stung. And anger boiled inside her just looking for an escape. "Oh, I get it," she said. "You have far too many living creatures sucking off your kindness at this place already. And I'm well aware that I'm one of them! Well, you invited *me*, remember? I was ready to go and you followed me down the mountain like some crazed maniac."

"I wasn't crazed. That's ridiculous. And I didn't mean you."

She'd been ready to tell him the dog was hers, but his self-righteous fury stopped her. Let him stew, she decided. She didn't care. If he was so anxious to take out his anger on everything around him, then let him. She picked up King and tied him to the rope again. "I'm going in the house now," she said, trying to keep her voice even. "I'll finish putting the groceries away, and then I'm packing up and getting out of here."

"And take this dog with you!"

"Oh, I will! I wouldn't leave a sweet, innocent animal anywhere near you!"

She started back to the house, and Luke came outside. "Can I play with the dog? Can I?"

Dorie looked at Bret. He scowled back at her.

"Dad?"

"Okay, play with him. But don't get attached. He's not staying."

Luke ran to the shed and began fussing with Dorie's knot. "What? Why not?"

"He's got an owner...somewhere. He's going back where he came from." His glare stayed fixed on Dorie. "Or going to wherever he'll end up...I don't know!"

Luke crouched down and rubbed the dog's back. "You're a great dog," he said. "Isn't he, Dad?"

"His name is King, Luke," Dorie said.

"Come on, King." The dog trotted beside Luke, his tail wagging. "Hey, Dorie, can King have a hamburger? You said you were fixing hamburgers tonight."

It was true. She'd promised Luke burgers and fries. She'd have to keep her word and stay until after dinner. "Maybe a bit of one," she said. "Dogs are meant to eat dog food. I brought him some, and you can give it to him."

Luke lay in the grass letting King lick his face. "Cool," he said between bouts of laughter.

Bret, who'd been witnessing the whole get-acquainted ritual, glared at Dorie. "Great, this is just great," he said. "I knew I'd end up the bad guy."

Ignoring him, Dorie went into the house to put the kitchen in order.

DURING DINNER, KING remained obediently curled under the table. Only Luke mentioned his presence, retelling details of the couple of hours they'd shared in the backyard. Bret responded with grunts. Clancy gave mono-syllabic reactions. Dorie, alone, engaged the boy in conversation. Having a dog on the property was a big deal to the kid. She wasn't going to let his father's grumpy attitude spoil it. Especially since she and King were leaving in a short while.

By the time the dishes were washed, darkness had nearly descended over the mountain. Bret paced in the kitchen while Dorie put everything in cupboards. After she was finished, he said, "Isn't it time you told me what this dog is doing here?"

"I adopted him at the supermarket."

"*You* adopted him? So he's yours?"

"Yes, and I'm taking him with me when I leave."

He pulled out a chair and sat heavily. "Don't you think that might have been a vital piece of information you could have told me earlier?"

"Yes, it might have been. And I would have told you if you hadn't gone ballistic over one little fourteen-pound animal."

"I didn't go ballistic over the dog. Not exactly."

"Oh?"

"I was upset that you were making an important decision for my son without consulting me."

She smirked. "For an ex-cop, your skill at asking questions to get the right information is a bit weak."

His sullen expression told her he was considering what she'd said.

"But no problem. I'm going to pack."

"Wait."

She turned back to him. "What?"

"You can't go tonight."

She stared at him a moment. "You have a thing about darkness, don't you?"

"Not a thing. Like I said before, I just don't think it's a good idea to navigate the mountain at night. If you're determined to go, then wait until daylight at least."

She was exhausted, and she didn't want to spend her hard-earned cash on a motel. "Thank you. I will." She hung the dishrag over the sink divider. "I'll stay out of your way tonight. But please tally up my hours and write me a check, minus the fifty dollars I gave the adoption group."

He nodded, mumbled something she didn't quite understand. "What?"

"I said you've been a big help."

"Oh. I thought maybe you said you were sorry for acting like a jerk over one little dog."

"I'm not sorry. You shouldn't have brought a dog here."

She tried to think of a sharp response but none came to her. He was right, she realized. She should have asked him first—this was his home, after all. But that didn't make his harsh reaction hurt any less. She took a book from the library of a few dozen titles she'd set up in the lodge's main room, called to King and went onto the porch to read. The wall-mounted fixture provided ample light, so she sat on the swing and opened the cover. King jumped up beside her and curled into a ball at the end of the blanket she'd brought from her room. A plump pillow she'd found among the storage supplies cushioned her back.

Before starting the first page, she pulled the blanket to her shoulders and let the swing adapt to its natural rocking in the breeze. She listened to the night sounds of mountain creatures. At bedtime the first night she arrived at The Crooked Spruce, those sounds had seemed alien. Now they were as common and comforting as the waves washing onto Winston Beach. She reflected with a sad smile that almost any place could be home once you let its familiarity get under your skin.

She'd read about an hour when Bret came onto the porch. She looked up, met his gaze and returned to her book.

"You look cozy," he said.

"I am."

He went to the screen and stood looking out. "What are you reading?"

"A mystery."

"Oh." A minute passed. "We finished the puzzle without you."

"Just as well," she said, not looking up. "I was the weakest link in finding pieces, anyway."

"Pop and Luke are upstairs watching a movie."

She nodded, kept her eyes on the page.

After another long moment, he said, "You know, Dorie, I feel like I should explain."

She turned a page, looked up at him

briefly and found his gaze intent on her face. "Go on."

King yawned, stretched and emitted a squeak of comfort. Bret almost smiled. "Maybe I was little over the top about the dog."

She set the book beside her. "Okay."

"I thought you brought the dog here for Luke, and I considered that, well, inappropriate."

"Yes, it would have been."

"I know he wants a dog, but it's a decision I will have to make if and when the time is right."

"Now you know I got the dog for me, Bret." She reached over and stroked one of King's floppy ears. "We seemed like two of a kind, this dog and me."

"You do have the same hair color."

She smiled and watched his shoulders relax. "I will admit that bringing the dog here was an imposition, even if only for a week. I probably should have checked with you before signing the papers."

"That would have been nice. I could have prepared Luke."

"Prepared him for what? An abundance of doggie licks?"

"No. Prepared him that the dog wasn't his, that it wasn't staying."

That stopped her. Bret was right. She'd risked giving Luke the wrong impression, and she certainly hadn't intended to let him hope for something that wouldn't happen.

"I'll talk to Luke," she said. "I'll explain again that I picked King out for myself. I think I can make him understand. And, anyway, the dog and I are leaving tomorrow."

"Right, tomorrow." He paused. "There's still more to do," he said after a while.

"The ordering is complete. I expect shipments to start arriving by tomorrow. The three of you can stock the shelves and put things away. And I can email you a file for the finished website from Winston Beach."

"I suppose."

"I'll be up early," she said. "You needn't bother to get up. It's Saturday and Luke doesn't have school. Give yourself a break for a change and sleep until a decadent eight o'clock. I'll be gone by the time you have your coffee."

He nodded. "Well, good night, then."

A small tingle of panic settled in her chest. She didn't want to say those two words back to him, knowing that good night meant good-bye. At this moment, he looked so much like his son. Vulnerable, uncertain, shy. And in the soft light, so very handsome. He was tall and strong, his limp seemingly nonexistent. The sun-streaked strands of his hair seemed almost golden. She cleared her throat and when she determined she was in control of her emotions she said simply, "You, too."

He headed for the door but stopped before going inside. His head dropped, his lips thinned.

"Is there something else?" she prompted.

"Dorie..."

"Yes?"

"Don't go."

"What?"

"Don't go. Stay for the time you promised."

She sat up straight. The swing lurched in an awkward motion. The book fell to the floor. "I don't know, Bret."

Suddenly he was standing right in front of her, his knees touching hers. He reached down and cupped her cheek. She was thankful she was sitting because she didn't trust her legs to hold her. His touch was sweet and warm and she couldn't help pressing her cheek into his palm.

"There's something happening here," he said softly. "I don't know how to explain it. Even when I'm angry with you…"

"What are you saying?"

"I'm not sure. But I don't want you to go."

A choking cough filled her throat. She swallowed, took a deep breath. His fingers trailed down her face, her neck before he dropped his hand. What should she do? Follow her instincts or her common sense? She should go. Every logical thought tried to convince her of that. But this was turning out to be a day of illogical decisions. Her heart begged her to stay, to give whatever this was a chance.

She felt her head nodding almost as if of its own free will. "I'll stay, then."

"Good." He smiled. "Dorie, I'm glad I'll be seeing you tomorrow." With a last look, he went inside.

CHAPTER TWELVE

BRET WENT STRAIGHT to the kitchen and leaned against the counter while he turned on the faucet. Taking a deep gulp of air, he cupped his hands to catch the cool water and splash it on his face. The temperature in the cabin was comfortable, but suddenly he was burning up from the inside out.

He grabbed a dish towel and dried off, leaving a little dampness along his neck to cool it. What was happening to him? He'd gone out on the porch hoping she'd tell him she wanted to stay, but he hadn't expected what he found. She'd looked so serene, so beautiful sitting on the swing.

The glow of the single bulb shining over her shoulder complemented her rosy cheeks, the gold of her hair. She looked as if she belonged in this world, in his life. He wanted nothing more than to join her, to put his arm around her and feel her curl into his side.

When he finally worked up to the nerve to say what was on his mind, he hadn't been able to use more than two words. *"Don't go."*

A week ago Dorinda Howe had come to him like a lost waif, determined and desperate, but never needy. But now, in only seven days, he was close to admitting that he needed her. She had begun to fill a hole in his life, one left by multiple tragedies, and one he'd tried to ignore for so long.

He was in trouble. He couldn't afford to lose sight of his goals. She was leaving. She had problems he couldn't tackle right now. He had a vision for his life with his son that he couldn't, wouldn't abandon.

Bret filled a glass with water and gulped it down. He didn't hear Luke come into the kitchen.

"Dad, are you okay?"

He was trembling, so he set down the glass and clenched his hands. "I'm fine. Is the movie over?"

"Almost. I paused it to come down and get popcorn. Grandpa and I want some."

"Did Dorie buy it at the store today?"

"Sure. She said every cool night needs either popcorn or hot chocolate."

"She's a smart lady," Bret said. He found the box of microwave popcorn in the pantry and handed Luke a pouch. "You know how to make it?"

Luke gave him one of those looks, the kind a ten-year-old would give a clueless adult. "Dad, it's microwavable."

"Go for it, then."

While the machine hummed and the corn began popping, Luke turned to Bret and said, "Oh, I forgot to tell you. Bobby Callahan from my class is coming over tomorrow to hang out."

"Really?" Bret couldn't believe his son had waited until this late hour to spring this important bit of news. "That's great. Should I call his mother?"

"Don't have to. I saw her after school in the pickup line. I told her I had a dad who would be here all day and a sort-of mom, too."

"A 'sort-of mom'? You're referring to Dorie?" That was the second time the word mother had been used in reference to Dorie lately. "How did Bobby's mom react to that?"

"She was cool with it. Why wouldn't she be? Three adults here. That's enough to watch out for us."

"True. What time will Bobby get here?"

"About eleven. I said you'd take him home."

"Okay."

"We'll play with King. Wait till Bobby sees I have a dog now." The popcorn was finished, so Luke grabbed the bag from the microwave. "Where is King, by the way?" he asked.

"Out on the porch with Dorie. But he'll probably smell the popcorn and follow you anywhere."

Luke laughed. "Yeah, he likes to eat." He left the kitchen calling King's name.

Bret's anxiety faded. This scene he could handle. It was the normal, natural play of a family, the way a family should be. And his son was having a friend over. Suddenly Bret was encouraged about his son's happiness...

Feeling back on track, he decided to take one day at a time, keep his thoughts in check, not expect too much or get his hopes up that the future held more than a few more days of Dorie Howe. He could live in the moment and handle his feelings.

"Don't forget, the contents of that bag are hot," he hollered to his son.

He heard King barking just before Luke said, "Sheesh, Dad, I'm ten years old. I can read."

THE SUN ROSE with a cool, blinding light on Saturday morning. All occupants of the lodge were up and bustling by 8:30 a.m. Bret poured cereal for everyone. Clancy made coffee and burned the toast. And, while feeding charred crust to King under the table, Luke talked about his plans for spending the day with his friend.

"I promise there'll be something better for lunch," Dorie told Luke. "Non-scorched grilled cheese is on the menu."

"That'll be cool," Luke said. "Yours has to be better than the cafeteria's."

Dorie tried not to look at Bret in too-obvious a way, but she had lain awake last night thinking about their cryptic conversation on the porch. She couldn't imagine two syllables affecting anyone more profoundly than the words *don't go* had affected her. He'd also said he suspected something was happening between them but he wasn't sure what. He'd wait a long time if he expected her to end his confusion. On that point they were on the same page—equally confused.

All she knew for certain was that something was definitely happening to *her,* and whatever it was, it was unexpected, scary and ill-timed. A group of people who a week ago had been completely dissimilar now gathered around this table as if they were a family. Add to that a dog and the promise of grilled cheese sandwiches, and it was almost eerie. And Dorie didn't know what to make of it. She just hoped she wouldn't regret her decision to stay.

Bret and Clancy went outside to work on one of the cabins. Luke took King out for a run. And Dorie stayed inside to clean up the dishes. She expected her first delivery to arrive by truck today, and when it did, she'd be busy organizing and storing.

She'd just finished putting the last of the silverware away when her cell phone rang. Knowing she could lose reception in the lodge, she quickly answered, "Hold on." She ran outside and partway up the mountain path before she returned the phone to her ear. "Sorry about that. Just trying to make sure I have cellular service."

A male voice said, "Is this Dorinda Howe?"

"Yes. Who's this?"

"This is Eric Henderson. I'm the attorney with Grant Schreiber's group who was assigned your brother's case."

"Oh, Mr. Henderson! I'm so glad to hear from you. Have you seen Jack?"

"I drove down to Broad Creek yesterday and we talked for about an hour."

Her hand trembled. This phone call was so important. "What did you think? You believe him don't you?"

"Unfortunately whether I believe him or not isn't the central issue."

She didn't want a lawyer defending Jack who didn't believe in his innocence. "But you have to be on his side in court."

"Of course, and I will be. That's what you're paying me for, Miss Howe. I've already come up with a strategy that hopefully will work in front of a jury."

"Jack didn't know about the gun that night, Mr. Henderson…."

"Eric, please."

"All right. Eric. Anyway, he didn't. He would never have agreed to go in that convenience store if he'd known Vince had a weapon."

"That sounds good, Dorinda…I can call you Dorinda?"

He was testing her patience with his pleasantries. "Yes, of course."

"But the other two boys haven't recanted their stories. They both say Jack fired the weapon and drove the getaway car."

"It wasn't Jack's gun! He would never have a firearm."

"You do know, Dorinda, that Jack's fingerprints were all over the weapon."

She'd been through all this with the state-appointed attorney. This wasn't news to her. "Jack took the gun after the shot had already been fired. In a panic. He wanted to be sure no one else would get hurt, but he dropped it in the backseat of the car the minute they were outside. He didn't have time to realize that Vince was setting him up to take the blame."

"It's his word against theirs, and unfortunately, with their extensive rap sheets, none of these kids is a credible witness." He sighed into the phone, and Dorie's heart sank.

"And the one man who could identify the killer is dead," Eric added.

Dorie felt her throat close up in an effort to hold back tears. Why did this attorney have to sound as hopeless as the last one? "But…" She swallowed and spoke slowly. "You said you have a strategy?"

"That's right. Jack's record, since it only consists of smaller crimes, gives me an opening. I can work on the jury's sympathies using Jack's background, the abandonment issue."

"Being abandoned doesn't justify murder!" she said. "A jury won't excuse the charges because of that."

"No, and I'm going to have to ask you to downplay your role in raising Jack. You have to come across as far less attentive to him than you really were. Make it sound like your brother practically raised himself."

She knew she'd tried to be there for Jack every step of the way, but she was willing to minimize her role in his life if it would help. But she didn't believe it would. "I see what you're getting at, but won't the jury conclude that Jack still made a decision to do the wrong thing that night?"

"If I can paint Jack as the poster kid for abandonment and hard luck, it could be very effective in getting us a decent plea-bargain agreement."

"A plea bargain isn't an acquittal. I want Jack acquitted. That's why I hired you. Mr. Schreiber said…"

"He said I'm good, right?"

"Yes."

"I am, so you've got to trust me. I said this is just the beginning of what I'm hoping to do. I have other angles to pursue. I want to talk to the district attorney and see what his agenda is. There's a lot of work to be done yet."

She forced a breath from her constricted lungs. "Okay."

"But I wanted to touch base with you today, explain what's going on, tell you what I need from you as his sister."

"All right. One more thing…"

"Yeah?"

"How was Jack? How did his mood seem? In our phone conversations, he tells me he's holding up, but I can't tell."

"Truthfully, Dorinda, the kid is wound pretty tight. I detected anxiety in his words and his body language. He's a kid in a fairly grim adult world. It's not easy."

She closed her eyes and tried not to picture Jack's face—this was not the time for tears. Her breathing was short and shallow so she simply said, "I understand."

"But that reminds me. I'm pulling some strings to get Jack transferred to a new cell block, one with fewer violent prisoners. He could be in his new cell by tomorrow."

"That would be a relief."

"And even if he's convicted, I'm pretty sure I can get him transferred to a juvie facility while we work on appeals. That will make big sis feel better."

"Big sis" knew that only an acquittal would make her happy.

"I'll keep in touch as often as I have news," Eric said. "Until I talk to you again, keep the faith."

She disconnected and sat heavily on the ground. Bracing her arms on her knees, she dropped her forehead to her crossed wrists. Okay, this lawyer seemed more competent than the last one. He was trying lots of angles. Still… "Poor Jack," she whispered,

"How did this happen to you? Where did I go wrong?"

She looked up when she heard the rumble of a truck engine down the mountain. The first supply order for The Crooked Spruce would be here in a few minutes. But she had enough time to make one call while her cell was working.

She dialed the number to Broad Creek and waited a short time to be connected to Jack. "I heard the attorney, Mr. Henderson, was there to see you," she said when he came on the line.

"Yeah, he came yesterday."

"How are you feeling about his visit?"

"To tell you the truth, Dorie, I don't think he's going to be able to do a thing for me."

This desperation in Jack's voice was exactly what she didn't want to hear. She'd hoped the attorney would have made Jack feel more positive about the outcome. "He told me he's working on some things, like getting you moved to a less violent cell block."

"I guess he is, but bottom line, my fingerprints are on that gun. He can't erase those.

And he can't make Vince and Tony change their stories."

She waited for a bolt of inspiration to come to her, something that would console her brother, but the truth was the truth. "So how are you doing?" she said.

"All I can think about is spending the rest of my life in this place."

She swallowed and prayed her voice wouldn't crack. "You have to hang in there, kiddo. We will keep trying."

"Look, sis, maybe it's time we stopped believing in miracles. Henderson is welcome to do his thing, but even he doesn't think it will be enough."

"I'm so sorry, Jack."

"It's not your fault."

Maybe, maybe not, but it didn't matter whose fault it was.

The boy she'd tried to raise, the one family member she had on this earth, was depending on her, and her heart was breaking to think she would let him down now. Sure Jack had made some mistakes and traveled paths he shouldn't have. But she should have tried harder to guide him in the right direction.

There were times when she'd probably

been easier on Jack than she should have. She'd known he'd snuck out of the house at night, but she hadn't wanted to smother him. She should have insisted more forcefully that he stay in school. She'd let her desire to protect Jack, to be his friend rather than a disciplinarian, blind her to the depth of his problems. "I'll be home soon," she said. "Friday or Saturday."

She didn't trust herself to speak again, so she pressed the disconnect button on her phone. After gathering her strength, she stood and went back down the mountain. A UPS truck had arrived at the lodge, and she had a lot to do.

CHAPTER THIRTEEN

"WHAT ON EARTH is in all these boxes?"

Bret stood in the doorway between the main room and the kitchen, his hands on his hips, his eyes wide.

Dorie, stooped over in the middle of several stacks of cartons, peeked around the tallest one and said, "Don't worry. You personally approved everything that arrived today."

"And exactly what did arrive and why did it take so many boxes to get it here?"

She tore the packing tape on the nearest carton. "This is stuff that doesn't compact well." She motioned him over. "We've got twelve sets of sheets, twelve mattress pads, twelve blankets—thermal, of course—sixteen pillows so we'd have extras. We have towels and soap and…"

"Okay, I get it. Enough to stock the three cabins I'll have ready by the opening." He

studied the number of boxes again. "Obviously sixteen pillows take more boxes than
sixteen napkins."

She smiled, something she hadn't done
since hanging up with Jack.

"What are we going to do with all this stuff
until the cabins are finished?" Bret asked.

She looked toward the hallway that led to
the storage room. "I guess it will all have to
go in my roo…" Realizing what she'd been
about to say, she changed gears. "The spare
room."

"There goes your bed, Dorie," Bret teased.
"You'll be in a room filled with bedding
without a place to sleep." His brow furrowed
in mock horror. "Oh, the irony!"

She crossed her arms and surveyed the
chaos. "Could happen, I guess. But I'll manage. I've slept in worse places than on the
tops of boxes."

His jaw dropped. "What? You're kidding,
right?"

She laughed. "Of course I'm kidding."

Despite her morning, Dorie was enjoying
this side of Bret. His good mood was infectious, as good for him as it was for her.

"You know," he said, rubbing his chin, "I

shouldn't have let Luke have a friend over this morning. He should be in here helping you."

She took pillows from a box and squeezed one. "Absolutely not! I want Luke to have fun and so do you. I like Bobby. He's a nice kid."

"Yeah, he is."

"What did you think of his mother? I thought she was nice." She pressed the pillow to her chest. Why in the world had she said that? What did it matter that she liked Mrs. Callahan? It's not as if she was going to have any say in discussing the families of Luke's potential friends.

"She's a mom. Looked like she needed a good night's sleep." Bret reached for the pillow. "Let me hold this thing. I want to see what my money paid for."

"Soft, isn't it?"

"Well, it's a pillow. Oh, and by the way, Dorie, I think Bobby was allowed to come over here because Luke told Mrs. Callahan that we have a 'sort-of mom' here at The Crooked Spruce."

Dorie thought about that comment for a moment. A couple of hours ago, when she'd talked to Jack, she'd thought of herself as a failure as a sort-of mom. Now, knowing Luke thought of her that way, she rather liked the term. But she didn't let on. Instead, she smiled and said, "Really? Is that how Luke thinks of Clancy?"

Bret grinned. "Yeah. We all do."

"Tell you what," she said. "I'll make those grilled cheese sandwiches. You let the boys play and send that old codger 'mom' in to help me with this stuff. We'll have it all sorted and inventoried by this evening."

"Deal. And Dorie?"

"Yes?"

"Thanks for everything you've done."

Bret left and Dorie got to work. She'd once told Bret that she liked to keep busy. It was true. Using her hands to accomplish something made her feel vital, even if the effort was for someone else. She'd get through this next week and go home knowing she'd done everything she could to keep Jack's defense on track. And in the meantime, she'd help turn The Crooked Spruce into the best executive outpost it could be.

THE SUN SET that night on a picture-perfect spring evening in the mountains. After Bret took Bobby home, the four residents of The Crooked Spruce sat in front of the big-screen TV and ate pizza Bret had picked up. They watched a PG movie about two zany step-brothers with Will Ferrell as the star. About halfway through the movie, the lodge phone rang.

"Must be Julie," Bret said. "I don't think anyone else has called us on that number."

Luke paused the movie and Clancy got up first to answer. "You all stay seated. I'll take it." He glanced at the caller ID screen and cringed. "I'm not answering this."

"Why not?" Bret asked.

"It's Maisie."

"Grandma!" Luke shouted.

"She must have gotten the number from Julie," Bret said. "You have to answer it, Pop."

"Nah. We're in the middle of a movie. Let it go to voice mail."

Bret started to rise. "But it might be an emergency."

Clancy waved him back down. "Okay. Okay. I'll take it, but I'm turning on speaker so you all can hear. Any time I talk to this woman I need witnesses."

Bret settled back on the sofa. He wondered if Julie had told Dorie anything about his parents' strange relationship. She was smiling, so he figured she had. And he wondered how long it had been since Clancy had spoken to Maisie.

Clancy cleared his throat before pressing the speaker button. "Harpy."

The responding voice was clear and almost melodic, as if the person on the other end were in the next room. "Buzzard."

Bret frowned, folded his arms over his chest. "How charming. Button your seat belts. Here we go."

Luke giggled. "I think they really like each other," he told Dorie.

"Sounds like it," she said.

"You want to talk to Bret?" Clancy asked her.

"In a minute, maybe," she said. "Actually I called to talk to you."

"I'm warning you, Maisie. You're on speaker. Don't say anything you don't want repeated in a court of law when I'm forced to sue you for slander."

"I'm not worried, old man. Anything negative I'd say about you is only half as bad as the truth, anyway. How's my grandson?"

"I'm fine, Grandma," Luke hollered.

"That's good, sweetie. Grandma misses you." She paused. "Now, Clancy, I want to know what you're doing at Bret's place. What's going on? Julie told me what she could, but I suspect she doesn't have all the details."

Clancy glanced over his shoulder at the others. "Hold on a minute, Maisie." He picked up the receiver and pressed the speaker button again. "Nobody but me can hear you now." He tried to muffle his voice, but Bret could still hear. "You got a problem with me visiting our son?"

That question must have opened a can of worms because Clancy didn't say anything else for several minutes. He just shook his head once in a while and grunted. Finally he said, "No, don't do that. I hate when you make threats."

Another pause. "Bret and I are getting on fine, so don't go manufacturing trouble between us. He doesn't have any problems, and I only have one, and I'm talking to it."

Bret held his breath until Clancy spoke again.

"I've got to go, Maisie. We're doing stuff here. Important stuff." Another minute passed. "Don't do it, woman. No need. You'll only be wasting money, and we all know how you like to hang on to every dime." He made chomping motions with his fingers and thumb to sign to the others that Maisie was talking his ear off.

"I'm hanging up now," he said. "Sure, I'll let you know where I go next. Nice talking to you."

He put the phone back on its cradle and ambled toward the couch.

"What was that all about?" Bret asked.

"The usual." His voice rose to mimic his ex-wife's. "Tell Bret and Luke I love them."

"That can't possibly be all she said," Bret responded.

"She thinks I'm taking advantage of you. She always thinks that."

"Gee, where would she get an idea like that?"

"Apparently Julie has a bigger mouth than I thought. She couldn't wait to tattle on me.

But here's the worst part. Maisie's actually threatening to fly out here."

Luke jumped up and raised his arms. "Yay! Grandma's coming! She never goes anywhere."

Bret dropped his head to the back of the couch and covered his eyes with his arm. Great. The Crooked Spruce was opening in just weeks and someone else was coming to upset the flow of his preparations.

"Just our luck she picks North Carolina to visit out of all the fifty states," Clancy said.

Bret kept his eyes closed. "What a coincidence." As if Clancy hadn't done enough already, now he was responsible for bringing Maisie.

He sensed Dorie sliding closer to him on the sofa. She whispered in his ear and he caught a whiff of that shampoo she used. "First me and now your mother," she said. "Clancy is the gift that just keeps on giving."

He smiled. He was beginning to realize that one of Clancy's gifts, the one sitting next to him now, was becoming pretty important to him.

CHAPTER FOURTEEN

THE AIR WAS still and cloudless, allowing the stars to shine down through budding leaves. The temperature was just right, in the low sixties. Cool enough to light a fire in the chiminea on the porch and bring a throw to Julie's swing for added comfort.

Dorie didn't read her book. Instead, surrounded by the flicker of a few hardy early spring fireflies, she let the swing lull her and King into a sense of peace. Despite her phone conversations this morning, she, along with the inhabitants of The Crooked Spruce, had enjoyed a nice day. Luke's friend had stayed for hours and seemed to not want to leave. Bret and Clancy now had two cabins ready for occupancy. And Dorie had inventoried the supplies and stacked them in the storage room, even leaving space for her bed.

She'd nearly dozed off when Bret came onto the porch. Hearing his footsteps, she became instantly alert. She sat straight, tucked the throw around her legs. "Is it quiet inside?" she asked.

"Sure is."

"It must ease your mind that we haven't heard anything about Dabney Shelton lately."

"Yeah, it does, but I'm not letting my guard down."

"Where are Luke and Clancy?"

"Both asleep and I can't tell who is snoring the loudest." As was his custom each night, he walked to the screen and looked out. "You like it out here, don't you?" he said to her.

"Sometimes I think I could sit here on the swing forever and just watch the seasons change. Like now. The trees are just getting leaf buds. That's a change since I got here. It's almost as if the trees have personalities…."

She cut herself off. Though she would love to stay, her time here was drawing to a close, and they both knew it. "Anyway," she added, "I don't see the seasons change much in Winston Beach. This is nice to experience."

"I know what you mean. Miami is just hot, except for the summers when it's hotter."

She smiled. "So you're glad you moved here? No regrets?"

His profile reflected worry lines at his temple. His eyes narrowed. "I can't imagine anyone but a fool claiming to have no regrets," he said. "I worry about Luke fitting in. I miss some friends in the force. But I'm closer to my sister now, and that's a plus."

"And the mountains? You prefer height over sea level?"

"No question. Give me boulders instead of beach and waterfalls instead of waves any time."

She nodded. "Until I came here, I can't recall a day in my life that I didn't come home and dump sand out of my shoes." She set the swing in motion again. "Now I get acorn pieces caught in my socks."

He turned then and gave her a long appraising stare. "Earlier, when you came down the mountain path, you seemed upset. I could see you on your cell phone. Did you get bad news?"

She wondered how much to tell him, but decided to take a chance. "Yes. Jack's new lawyer called. He didn't sound very encouraging about Jack's chances in court. I think he's going to suggest a plea deal."

"Really?" Bret walked over to her and motioned to the swing. "May I?"

She slid over, giving him room to sit next to her. King shuffled his position along with her. "Of course."

"We haven't talked much about Jack," he said, leaning back and crossing his arms on his chest. "What kind of a case do they have against him? Any solid evidence?"

She told him about the fingerprints on the gun. "He did handle the weapon," she said, "but only after one of the other boys had shot the clerk. It was then that Jack took possession of the gun so no one else would get hurt."

"I'm sure he explained that to the police who investigated," Bret said.

"Yes, but they didn't believe him. Both Vince and Tony claimed Jack shot the clerk. And the other boys made Jack drive away from the scene."

"In Jack's car?"

"That's right. But Vince was threatening Jack the whole time."

Bret's eyes reflected his interest, but otherwise, his face revealed nothing. Dorie decided he must have been a top-notch interrogator himself.

"How about the other boys' records? I know Jack has a rap sheet…."

"Only minor offenses," Dorie said. "Vince and Tony's crimes are pretty similar. Some vandalism, petty stuff."

Still that composed face. Dorie wanted more. Bret had been a cop. He must be thinking something. After a moment she spoke the words she hoped she wouldn't regret. "So what is your professional opinion? Does Jack have a chance?"

He dropped his hands to his knees and stared at her. "Honestly? It doesn't seem particularly promising to me. The facts are certainly stacked against him."

"But he's innocent," Dorie said. "He can't spend the rest of his life in jail for something he didn't do. What kind of a justice system would allow that?"

His answer was swift and cutting. "One that usually works, Dorie."

"But if a jury finds Jack guilty, this would be a monumental failure in the system. Surely you can see that."

He clasped his hands between his knees and looked down at the floor. He didn't speak.

"Well, out with it," Dorie said. "Obviously you want to say something."

His hands clenched tighter. He raised his eyes to the ceiling. "I'm not sure I do. Anyway, what I think isn't really important."

"What? Of course it's important!"

"I don't want to get into this, Dorie...."

"You asked me what was wrong. I told you. And I asked for your opinion. Now you don't want to give it?"

He sighed, stared hard at her. "Okay." He looked as if he might change his mind, but then continued. "I'm just wondering if you might be a bit naive about the whole thing."

Naive? Of all the things he could have said, this was perhaps the most inaccurate. Lately she hadn't had room in her psyche for naïveté.

She swallowed her first reaction and said calmly, "What do you mean?" There was a chance she'd misunderstood his intention.

"You obviously love your brother. But your ability to see things clearly might be influenced by your emotions. Can you really be certain that Jack didn't shoot that clerk? All the evidence points—"

She didn't let him finish. "Of course I'm certain. He's my brother, my family. I know he isn't capable of such an act."

"Clancy is my family, too," Bret said. "I would never knowingly cheat you out of a dime, but the same isn't true of my father. Just because someone is family doesn't mean they share the same principles as you. They may be capable of doing things you wouldn't imagine."

Her eyes filled with tears, and she struggled to hold them back. Bret reached for her hand. She snatched it away and fisted it over her chest.

"I'm sorry," he said. "I shouldn't have said anything. I don't even know Jack. I'm just looking at this from the perspective of a cop, one who listened to dozens of suspects proclaim their innocence over the years."

She wiped the moisture from under her eyes and took a deep breath. "But he can't be guilty," she said.

Bret spoke so softly she could barely hear him. "Dorie, he can be. I hope, for your sake, he isn't, but…"

"No, that's not it," she said. "He can't be guilty because he's all I have. I can't lose him, not after all I've..." She was about to say *all I've done to raise him, all I've given up.* But she knew that was selfish, almost as selfish as admitting that without Jack she didn't know how she would go on. She'd focused so much energy, attention and emotion into doing what was right for Jack, she'd let her own life slide by. And now it could be too late to get it back.

"I can make some calls, Dorie, talk to someone in the Winston Beach department. Maybe they'll let me in on the progress of the investigation."

And reinforce your opinion with even more certainty? Dorie's inner strength, her instinctive protectiveness, returned in a rush of adrenaline. Once again she was the fighter she'd always been for her brother. "No, I don't want you to do that." She thought about leaving the porch, putting distance between them. For some reason she stayed.

"I don't want your charity," she said after a minute. "You've made it clear what you believe, and frankly, I don't think you'd be any help."

"I don't know what I believe." His voice was low and hoarse as if he was uncomfortable with this level of emotional turmoil. "I'm just sensing that you don't *want* to believe that the police could be right."

"Of course I don't! And you don't want to admit they could be wrong!"

"They usually aren't."

She placed her hands on her knees, looked out at the trees, the insects swirling in the dark night. Needing, right or wrong to lash out at him, she said, "That sounds pretty cut-and-dried coming from the most conflicted man I've ever met."

He pulled away from her and cleared his throat. "What do you mean by that?"

"Look, Bret, you moved up here to get away from the memories of your wife, and yet, your guilt over her death is with you every day, every minute. You say you don't want to have anything to do with your father, and still you help him every time he messes up. You don't want me to stay one minute. The next you do…."

He leaned toward her, and King jumped to the floor. Bret cupped his hands over her upper arms. "You're wrong. I've always wanted you to stay."

"You say that now…"

"Yes, I said it out loud just now, but inside, it's always been true." His eyes glittered intensely into hers. "When you drove down the mountain and I chased you, I was nearly frantic. I didn't know how I would convince you to stay, but I knew that I had to try."

Her resolve melted with an involuntary sniffle. "Okay, maybe that's true. Maybe I can believe that."

"You should believe it. But you're right. I am a conflicted man. I'm very conflicted right now, but it has nothing to do with my former wife or my father."

"Then what are you conflicted about?"

"About knowing that we've just had a major disagreement and yet I still want to kiss you more than I've ever wanted to kiss any woman. And I know my timing probably stinks."

She didn't trust herself to speak. She had been thinking of the same thing for days. She looked into his clear eyes, let her gaze fall to his full lips and hoped he could read her mind. One kiss, how could it hurt?

"I suppose a gentleman would ask permission, especially under these circumstances, but I'm not going to do that, Dorie. I'm beyond asking." He pulled her to him, wrapped his arms around her back and settled his mouth over hers. The kiss was hungry, needy, almost desperate and yet the sweetest, most honest one she could remember. When it ended, Dorie lowered her forehead against his chest and breathed in the musky pine scent of him.

He released her and stood. The swing pitched at the change in weight, leaving her even dizzier. "If I crossed the line, I'm sorry," he said, then added, "though maybe that's not quite true." He smiled slightly, then turned and went into the cabin.

BRET COULDN'T HAVE planned the opening scene of the next day of his life any better if he had been a professional director. It wasn't enough that he had been thinking of Dorie all night, but she was the first person he saw when he came into the kitchen at sunrise. As he walked in from the hallway, she came through the back door, King trotting beside her.

They both stopped, looked at each other.

She coughed into her hand before shrugging out of her jacket. He rubbed his neck while his gaze lingered on the light pink-and-white checks of her blouse. The pink was the exact shade of her lips, the lips he'd kissed. The same ones he wanted to kiss again.

"What's going on with you two?" Clancy said from the kitchen table. "You both look like you've seen ghosts."

Bret blinked hard. "Pop. I didn't see you there."

Dorie scurried to the counter. "Everything is fine, Clancy. Thanks for making a whole pot."

Bret and Dorie each reached for a mug and then simultaneously grabbed the coffeepot handle. She jerked her hand away. "Sorry. You first."

She wouldn't touch him this morning? He'd been afraid of this. He'd spooked her last night coming on so strong after disagreeing with her about her brother. He'd said too much. He'd done too much. They would have to talk, and soon.

When all three adults were settled around the table, Clancy looked from his son to Dorie. "Kind of quiet this morning, isn't it?"

"Why would you say that?" Bret asked, too loudly.

"Takes me a while to wake up," Dorie said, covering what looked to be a fake yawn.

"So what's on the docket for today?" Clancy asked.

"We can work on the last cabin so all will be ready for occupancy." Bret waited for someone to comment. When no one did, he added, "Dorie, can you come up with a list of contacts for corporations that sponsor employee retreats and camping stores that might let us advertise The Crooked Spruce on their bulletin board or website?"

Staring into her cup, she nodded. "Sure."

"Are you kidding? It's Sunday!"

King gave a loud yelp and scrambled to the door where Luke, in his pajamas, had just entered. He reached down to scratch the dog before going to the refrigerator. "You don't work on Sunday, Dad. We're supposed to do stuff."

"Oh." Bret thought about that. "Didn't you do stuff yesterday?"

"Not with you. Today I figured we'd go to Mountain Spring Park. All of us."

"Why the park?"

Luke poured a glass of orange juice and took the last chair at the table. "Hi, Dorie. You'll love this idea."

"I will?" She twisted her hair to one shoulder while she took a sip of coffee. "Why is that?"

"They're having Poochpalooza today."

"Pooch what?" Clancy asked.

Bret just stared. If this activity had the word *pooch* in it, he didn't think he was interested.

"Poochpalooza. They have it twice a year. It's like a big fair for dogs. People tell you how to take care of your dog. They give stuff away free, like treats and Frisbees. And your dog gets to meet other dogs. I've got a flyer in my room I brought home from school."

Bret leaned back in his chair and refused to look at Dorie. Luke was right. She would love the idea, and if both of them worked on him, he'd have to give in. "Luke do I have to remind you that we don't have a dog?"

"I know. But Dorie does. We'll all go for King. We'll be his family."

Bracing his hands on the table, Clancy rose. "Tell you what. I think I'll take a pass on this. I can get started around here and maybe squeeze in a nap while you guys palooza all around that park."

"Dad? Dorie?" Luke's smile was infectious, as was the hope in his eyes. "We can go, right?"

Dorie waited until a slight shrug of Bret's shoulders must have told her he was putty in his son's hands. Then she said, "I'm game."

He didn't stand a chance. His day was obviously going to be filled with barks and tennis balls and watching where he stepped. But then again, there probably was nothing like a few dozen dogs to cut the tension around here.

CHAPTER FIFTEEN

TWO HOURS LATER, surrounded by more than two hundred dog-happy people and half again as many people-happy canines, Bret pointed to a plus-sized furry creature with huge paws. "I thought they only allowed dogs here, not bears."

Dorie smiled. "That's a Leonberger, a large breed from Germany. A friend of mine had one."

"A large-breed bear?"

"No. A large-breed dog, of course. They were bred to look like lions and actually look like a cross between a lion and a bear. But they are very gentle and adapt well to families."

"I would think the biggest concern would be the opposite, the families adapting to them."

"Come on, nature man," she said. "You're not afraid of a dog, are you?"

"I guess you didn't read *Cujo*."

They walked the gravel pathway, following Luke and King, who was sporting a new retractable leash since arriving at the dog fair. He trotted along with an inspired gait, as if he believed he were the best dressed dog around. Bret stopped next to a German shepherd. "Now at least this is a dog I'm familiar with," he said, dipping his fingers into the thick hair at the dog's neck.

"Naturally," Dorie said. "Cops know shepherds."

"And poodles and Yorkies," Bret added as they hurried to catch up with King who had stopped to enjoy a dog biscuit from a pet-sitter's booth.

"You're familiar with those two dogs?" Dorie asked.

"Sure. Every senior citizen in Miami who ever called 911 had either a miniature poodle or a Yorkie, or as we cops call them, ankle biters. I've been mauled by them on many occasions."

Dorie laughed. "I'll just bet you have." She automatically slowed her pace when she saw him rub his thigh. "Let's take it easy. There's still a lot to cover and I don't think Luke is going to want to miss a single giveaway."

Bret didn't argue. He measured his walk carefully. "It's funny. I can climb up and down a ladder all day, but get me walking a half mile and I give out pretty quickly."

"You might consider exercise," she said. "You should start taking short but aggressive walks on a daily basis. You'll gradually notice you have your strength back. I've heard that movement is the best cure for stiffness."

"Yeah, so I've been told. But it's hard to work exercise into my schedule."

"Don't think of it as a chore. Call it an exploration of nature trails. Luke would be happy to walk with you. So would I." Then realizing how their time was limited, she said, "For the days I'm still here, anyway."

He gave her a sideways look. "Nature walks, eh?"

"Hey, Dad!"

They hurried to catch up. "What is it, Luke?" Bret asked.

"Can I take King on the small dog obstacle course? If he makes it to the end, he wins a package of poop bags."

"Boy, King will love those." Bret looked

at Dorie. "What do you say? Can King strut his stuff?"

"Absolutely. Good luck, King."

Luke patted the dog's head. "He could handle the large dog course with no problem, but I don't want to stress him out."

"Good idea," Dorie said. "Start small and work your way up."

Luke and King ran across the yard to the obstacle course where they met up with Bobby Callahan. Now King had two people in his cheering section.

"He's going to miss that mutt," Bret said.

"And the mutt will miss him." Spying bleachers used for spectators during ball games, Dorie said, "Why don't we sit awhile, rest your leg? I brought a couple of bottles of water in my backpack."

Bret readily agreed. He followed her to a bench three rows up where they could keep an eye on the boys and took the bottles she offered him. Unscrewing the cap, he handed the first one to her and opened the second for himself. "Cheers."

They guzzled their water and watched the activity in comfortable silence until Bret said, "That dog's lucky day was when he met you."

She paused, the bottle halfway to her lips. "I think you just said something sweet."

"It can happen."

She sipped. A few minutes passed before Bret said, "I suppose we should talk about what happened last night."

"Or about what's happening right now," she said softly.

"What's happening now?"

"Well, we've been sitting here for almost ten minutes, our shoulders touching, our hips connected at the denim seams. I haven't moved. You haven't moved. So I'm going to conclude that we're finding this closeness less than awkward for once."

His eyes narrowed. He took a long gulp of water. "I'm experiencing something completely unlike awkwardness."

"Oh, really? What?"

He rolled the bottle between his hands. "Hard to describe, but basically, if we weren't in the middle of dozens of yapping dogs and hundreds of prying eyes, I would have my hands locked on either side of your face, and I'd be kissing you like crazy right now."

His words warmed her deep inside while a delightful shiver ran down her spine. "Hmm.

In that case, I'd say the time for talking about what happened last night is over. We should maybe talk about what might happen in the days to come."

"I have a better idea," he said. "Remember your high school days?"

"It was a while ago, but yes."

"Good. I'll meet you under the bleachers in ten minutes."

She laughed. "Bad timing. We're kid- and dog-watching, remember?"

"Okay. We'll behave for now, but the next time we meet on that porch swing, things could get interesting."

Just when he was allowing his mind to wander in a most pleasant manner, Dorie gripped his wrist. She pointed toward the horizon. "Look. Do you see smoke?"

Bret tensed in every muscle. He stood, shielded his eyes from the sun. A steady plume of gray smoke rose from the trees some distance off. And he knew exactly where it originated. "Let's get Luke, King and go," he said. "It's coming from Hickory Mountain."

Dorie was down the bleachers a couple

of steps ahead of him. She ran to the doggie obstacle course and called Luke's name. By the time they all reached Bret's truck, sirens could be heard heading out of Mountain Spring.

"Pop hasn't called," Bret said. "I'm assuming that means the fire isn't at The Crooked Spruce. But I'd wager it's close."

He stepped on the accelerator, pushing the speed limits of the mountain roads. When they arrived at The Crooked Spruce, red lights could be seen up the mountain, thankfully beyond the outpost. Bret screeched to a halt in front of the lodge.

Clancy was waiting for him on the porch. "It's okay, Bret. The fire's about a half mile from us. The sheriff's car veered left at the fork and headed west."

Shouting orders, Bret jumped out of the truck. "Luke, in the house. Dorie, you, too."

"Do you think it's Dabney?" she asked as she ran inside.

"I do." His mind had settled on the most logical explanation for the blaze. Shelton had been at it again. Luckily the smoke had diminished, indicating the fire trucks had gotten there before the fire could spread to other properties. Studying his key chain, Bret followed Dorie inside, found the key that opened his rifle case and grabbed his .22. He wasn't about to take a chance that Shelton would try anything at The Crooked Spruce. He headed for the back door.

"Dad, are you hunting for someone? I want to go with you."

"Absolutely not. Stay inside with Dorie and Grandpa." He gave Dorie a quick glance and was rewarded with her nod. She would keep his son safe.

Bret raced for the nearest trail that headed up the mountain and crouched among the low brush. His hunch that the Sheltons would be escaping down the mountain and not up proved correct. He heard a rustle in the trees just seconds before two figures darted out of the brush several yards in front of him.

Bret stood and immediately swung the rifle to rest against his shoulder. "Hold it right there," he hollered.

Both males paused long enough to consider the threat facing them. A large man with his head shaved, obviously Dabney, turned suddenly and ran back into the trees. The younger one, Leroy, started to follow.

Bret couldn't fire. He knew his advantage over the two was just bluster, one he'd hoped would work. Despite a dull throbbing in his thigh, Bret advanced on Leroy. "Get down!" He said. "To your knees."

Leroy dropped to a kneeling position and followed Bret's command to thread his hands behind his head. Fear bright in his eyes, he said, "Who are you?"

"A concerned citizen," Bret said. "One who doesn't want to see the properties on this mountain scorched to the ground."

"You don't need to shoot me," Leroy said. "I didn't have anything to do with starting that fire."

Bret lowered the rifle. "Sure you didn't, kid. That fire just started itself."

"I tried to talk…" He stopped, bit his lower lip.

"You're going to have plenty of time to say whatever you want," Bret said. "So start thinking of a good way out of this."

He lifted Leroy to his feet and followed him back to The Crooked Spruce. Clancy waited by the closest cabin.

"Get some rope," Bret said. "I'm thinking this boy won't appreciate our hospitality."

Within minutes Leroy's hands were tied behind his back and he was safely secured to a kitchen chair in the lodge. Clancy stayed in the kitchen to guard the prisoner while Bret went outside to call the sheriff on his cell phone.

"Matt? Bret Donovan. I've got a Shelton tied to a chair. You want to come get him?" Once the details of the capture were explained in detail, Bret reentered the house and went upstairs to check on Luke. The boy was fine, waiting anxiously to hear what had happened. But Dorie? She was nowhere to be seen.

DORIE OPENED THE kitchen door as quietly as she could and peeked through. She saw two males. Clancy, who stood with his arms folded over his chest, his gaze fixed on the second person, a youth who appeared younger than Jack. This boy was tied to a chair, his arms bound behind him and his feet roped together.

Determining there was nothing to be frightened of, she walked into the room. Both men stared at her. She tried to see into the younger one's eyes, but his hair, long and unkempt, fell well below his eyebrows. He jerked his head back, flinging dirty strands away from his face.

"Who is this?" she asked Clancy.

"Bret caught one of those brothers who have been causing all the trouble around here," Clancy answered.

"I didn't do anything," the boy said.

"Then why are you tied up?" she asked, suddenly realizing that she was close to jumping to the same conclusion as the police would.

"You tell me and we'll both know," he snapped back. "Some wannabe cop threatened to shoot me in the back if I didn't cut short my walk through the woods.

Clancy scoffed. "You're talking about my son, and he's no wannabe anything. He used to be with the Miami Police Department. And that wasn't any walk you were taking. You were escaping the police."

The boy snorted. "Everybody around these parts seems to draw conclusions without having any proof."

Dorie couldn't help imagining a comparison between this young man and Jack. Both in trouble, confused, defensive. Both having taken wrong turns in their lives.

"You'd do well to admit whatever you were involved in," she said. "It will go easier for you."

He looked at her with deep blue eyes that melted her heart. "Lady, I'm not lying to you. I didn't start that fire. I know who did, but it wasn't me. And I didn't want him to do it."

"But you didn't do anything to stop him."

"What could I do?" He stared down at the kitchen table, shutting down.

Clancy grunted. "Don't pay any attention to this mongrel, Dorie. He'd lie as soon as take a gold filling from your tooth."

The boy sat straight. "I'm not lying. I didn't start the fire."

Dorie turned to leave the kitchen. "Good luck. I hope you are telling the truth." She thought of Jack again, and a familiar pain squeezed her chest. "And I hope someone believes you."

She stopped at the door when he called out to her. "I'm thirsty," he said. "Hungry, too. I know I can't eat with my hands tied like this, but I might be able to drink some water if you have a straw."

She went to the cupboard and took out a glass and a straw and filled the glass with water. "Here you go."

He gulped the whole thing and slumped back in the chair. "Thanks."

His eyelids slid down over those blue eyes. He was tired. Standing at the kitchen door, Dorie ached for him. What if he was telling the truth? What if his brother's reputation had carried over to him? She remembered Bret telling her she was naive. Maybe she was, but Jack was in prison for associating with bad people. Maybe deep down, this boy, this Leroy Shelton, could be saved.

She paused at the door for another minute before coming back into the kitchen. "I'll fix you a ham sandwich," she said. "Maybe the sheriff will let you eat it."

"That'd be real nice of you, lady," he said.

She finished making the sandwich and wrapped it carefully in waxed paper.

"It looks good," he said.

"It will stay fresh."

She slid the sandwich across the table at the same time a booming voice said, "What's going on in here? Have we started a take-out business for vandals?"

Dorie turned to stare into blazing brown eyes. Bret strode into the kitchen, picked up the sandwich and dropped it back to the table. "Why don't you add a pickle and some pudding for dessert?" he said. "I'm sure Leroy has a sweet tooth. Never mind that he just about burned down a property a half mile from here."

Dorie reined in her temper. "The boy's got to eat," she shot back. "He looks like he hasn't had a meal in days."

Bret's voice kept the sharp edge. "And that's your problem because…?"

"Because he's just a boy and he's hungry. He should be everybody's problem."

Bret stared hard at the boy. "How old are you, Leroy?"

"Fifteen."

"Too old to coddle," Bret said.

Dorie didn't trust herself to speak. Making one sandwich wasn't exactly coddling a criminal. While she waited for what else Bret would say to chastise her, anger built inside her looking for a way out.

When Bret spoke again, his voice was low. She strained to hear him. "Let it go, Dorie," he said. "The sheriff is on his way. He'll take care of Leroy. It's not our responsibility."

"Fine." She left the kitchen without another word. The only sound she heard was Leroy's voice. "Thanks for the sandwich, lady."

CHAPTER SIXTEEN

THE SHERIFF CAME and picked up Leroy. Before leaving, he told Bret that Dabney had not been caught yet, so all the residents of The Crooked Spruce should keep watch for him. For the rest of Sunday the lodge was quiet. Dorie roasted a chicken, though her efforts were rewarded with very little enthusiasm. After dinner, she sat on the porch alone while Bret helped Luke with his homework. It seemed the promise of more meetings on the porch swing had been forgotten.

Monday Luke returned to school and Dorie stayed busy building a database of contacts for The Crooked Spruce. Bret worked outside and Clancy helped him between naps. King slept at Dorie's feet under the computer with his head on his paws.

At nine o'clock Monday evening, Dorie went out on the porch, settled on the swing and waited. For what, she couldn't say for certain, but the anticipation was unlike any-thing she'd ever experienced. Would Bret come out to be with her? She didn't know what to expect, They'd had the argument over Leroy, but Dorie now realized that she prob-ably shouldn't have interfered to the extent she had. Now her heart hoped Bret would come to the porch.

With only four more days left at the out-post, her thoughts tumbled to a variety of topics, each one important in its own way. How was Jack holding up? Could she possi-bly extend her stay and see what developed between her and Bret? Did Bret even want her to after she'd been kind to Leroy? She felt consumed with so many new and unex-plored feelings, all based on one kiss. One in a million, but still, only one.

When the door to the lodge opened, her gaze fixed on the person coming outside. Bret wore a plaid shirt and low-slung, well-worn jeans. Her heart lurched in her chest. She'd seen him a dozen times today and still, when he came onto this porch in the nighttime, with the soft light burnishing copper streaks in his hair, he was utterly and completely the most handsome man she'd ever known. She forgot she'd ever been angry with him.

Four days left at The Crooked Spruce. She was in such trouble. Four years, forty years wouldn't be enough.

He approached the swing.

She said, "I'm sorry."

Not missing a beat, he answered, "Me, too. It was a stupid argument. You were just being compassionate." He smiled. "It's not like I didn't know that about you."

She smiled back. "But this is your home, and you used to be a cop. I should have checked with you before interfering."

He sat next to her, crossed one leg over his knee and folded his hands on top. "So, that's out of the way. I don't want to spend one minute of the next few days arguing about anything."

"That sounds good to me." Still, it was comforting to know they could have an argument and come out of it unscathed.

"And here we are," he said.

"Yes, again."

"How are you feeling tonight, out here, just the two of us?"

"Curious. A little scared. Mostly anxious. The usual girl-boy middle-school stuff."

"I hear ya."

"Luke in bed?" she asked.

"He's reading, but yeah. Pop's watching a game inside."

She'd thought she heard a sports reporter's voice, hoped someone had just left the TV on. But no. Clancy was just a few feet away on the other side of the wall.

"Makes a serious discussion a bit difficult," she said.

"Yep. Makes most everything difficult." He turned toward her. One hand came up to cup her nape. He pulled her to him and kissed her softly. A low moan from his throat indicated it had been too soft. And too short. "But not impossible," he said when he drew back.

"Where should we start with our talk?" she asked.

"I think we should start by making a pact not to mention anybody else for at least a half hour. Not Luke, Pop. Not your brother, Jack. This is about us."

"That sounds wonderful, but don't you

think there is one person we absolutely must talk about?"

His brow furrowed just a bit. "Who's that?"

"You know that Julie told me about Miranda and how she died," she said. "I'm so sorry."

Bret's eyes shuttered. "I don't like to talk about that time," he said.

"Any of it? I can understand not wanting to relive the day it happened. I don't blame you, but the rest of it… You loved her. I want to know about her. If you don't want to tell me, there's always going to be a hole in our history too big to fill with chatter."

He pinched his lips together and considered her words. "Okay. What do you want to know?"

"Tell me about her. What was she like?"

He sighed. "She was beautiful."

Dorie waited for him to say more. "That's a start," she said. "At least we got the man-stuff out of the way."

He smiled, and she relaxed against the back of the swing. "Now more."

She knew words didn't come easy to him so she accepted that a little might be all she'd ever get.

He raised his hands, forming a ball with his fingertips together. "She was like this core of energy," he said, rolling his hands. "Always doing something, always thinking, planning, reacting to the world around her. I never knew from one minute to the next what she would say or do."

"Must have made for an interesting life," Dorie said.

"Oh, yeah. She didn't seem to have any boundaries, at least for herself. There wasn't anything she wouldn't try. She'd taste the most awful foods just to experience them." He laughed softly. "I think part of it was her upbringing. She came from a rich Argentinean family. She wasn't denied much when she was growing up. And she wasn't willing to give up much when she was an adult, even when she decided to marry a policeman with a modest salary. She savored life, both spiritually and materialistically."

Dorie remembered the details Julie had given her of the wave runner incident. Bret hadn't wanted his wife to get the machine, but Miranda's desires had won out, and she'd let her father buy it for her. That had to have been a slap in the face for a man like Bret, a man who obviously wasn't a taker, a man who worked to provide for his family.

"We had some fights in our ten years of marriage," he said. "Some real doozies. The sad thing is, we would have had another one the day she died. I was itching for a fight." He glanced at Dorie. "I guess I'm glad Julie told you about the accident."

"It must have been horrible."

"Did she tell you that Miranda's father gave her the watercraft when I refused to go along with the purchase?"

"Yes."

"I paced along the shore while she took that machine out. I was worried for her, and I was mad. She had ignored my wishes, and I wondered if I'd ever forgive her for it. The seas were rough, but that only seemed to inflame her determination. It was a weekend, and there were so many people trying to get in a morning of thrills before the weather got too bad. I kept repeating in my mind the words I would say to her when she got back to shore."

"And you never got to say them," Dorie added.

"No. They weren't kind words. It's hard

for me to live with the knowledge that the last thoughts I had for Miranda were ones of anger and hurt pride. And guilt for not stopping her."

"Could you have stopped her?" Dorie asked.

"I'm bigger and stronger, so yeah, I could have bullied her into staying on shore. I could have kept her with me if I'd used more than just stupid words. I could have dynamited that blasted Sea-Doo into a hundred pieces, but I didn't." He expelled a long breath. "Though if I had, I don't think the argument would have been any less explosive that night. We were pretty well matched when we argued. She shouted in half English, half Spanish. I placated with my own brand of common-sense mumbo jumbo." He chuckled. "Must have been a sight, the two of us."

She expected him to say something about how they made up after the fights. He didn't, and she was relieved.

"There is one thing I will always be grateful for," he said after a while. "She listened to me when I said she couldn't take Luke on the back of the craft. If she had done that... No, I would have stopped her. I'm certain of it."

She covered his hand with hers. "And now, when you think back on your time with Miranda?"

"Now the arguments seem silly, a waste of time mostly. Nearly every argument is like that, when two people love each other." He stared off into space a moment before concentrating on Dorie again. "But you asked me what she was like. I think now you know. She was a woman who did as she liked, and she had the misfortune to marry a man who wanted to protect her from everything. She was like a fire, always bright and burning with intensity. And I ran around beside her with a garden hose, frustrated as heck most of the time."

She left her hand covering his and let his image sink in. "You know," she began, after the silence had stretched into minutes, "I think we can learn something even from life's biggest tragedies."

His mouth curled up at the edges. "Yeah, like follow your instincts and don't let people you love do something stupid."

"Ah, no, I don't think that's it. You see, if that's all you learned, then you'll go on forever blaming yourself for what happened. And, Bret, you just can't do that."

He turned his hand up, entwined his fingers with hers. "Then, please, tell me, what should I have learned?" His voice was earnest, almost pleading.

"Well, I'm not the smartest person in the world, but I'd say you should have learned that you can't make other people's decisions for them. You can't force them to do what you think is right. Miranda made her decision that day. You need to let it go."

He squeezed her hand. In the low light she watched moisture gather in his eyes. "I don't know..." he said before his voice hitched.

"You can't protect the people you love from everything in life," she said. "There's just too much out there. Too many influences, too many bad people, too many stubborn ones."

He rubbed his thigh with his free hand. "The night I was shot...I couldn't even protect myself, and I was in the business of keeping people safe."

"And I tried to be a mother and protect Jack, and I failed at that too many times."

He twisted around until he could see

clearly into her eyes. "And now I have Luke, and I'm sure I'm not half the parent I need to be. Sometimes I think I'm smothering him. Truth is, I don't know how to back off."

"That's understandable," she said. "There are different rules for kids. You have to protect them until they are old enough and wise enough to recognize the pitfalls for themselves. And, Bret, you're doing a great job. He's a happy, well-adjusted boy. Sure, he's known sadness but he's come back, and he has only you to thank for that." She smiled. "You shouldn't sell yourself short. You know what it is to be a parent. Thank-yous from kids are rare and special, and Luke may not say it to you in so many words."

"It's okay. I get all the thanks I need when I see his steps to normalcy again. When he complains about homework and bedtime and doing chores. When he starts making friends. Those things are my thanks."

He rubbed the tips of her knuckles with the rough callous of his thumb. She felt a tingling energy go all the way to her shoulder. Instinctively, she pressed her body closer to his.

"Now you," he said, smiling down at her.

"Me?"

"Yeah. I've talked a blue streak. It's your turn."

"There's not much to say. I've pretty well detailed the past few months of my life. You know where I've been, what I've been doing."

"True but stuff must have happened in your life before you got messed up with Clancy. I want to know about your business, your house, your dreams and goals, your friends."

"Wow, that's a tall order," she said.

"Okay, let's start with something easy. Mostly I want to know if you have a boyfriend."

She chuckled. "I'm temporarily unencumbered."

"Good. I don't think any guy is worthy of you."

"So that's the most important question you wanted to ask?"

"Yeah. None of the rest of it matters so much. I say we table all discussion for a while. We don't want this swing time to go to waste."

He reached out and hit the switch to the light, put his arm around her and gathered her close. *He might not think he's a worthy protector,* Dorie thought, but she had never felt so sheltered in her life.

He kissed her while he set the swing in motion. She snuggled her head against his shoulder and let him press gentle kisses along her temple, her cheek.

"What are we going to do when this week is over?" he said, breaking the magical spell of the silence and darkness that surrounded them.

She looked up into his eyes. "We don't have to think about that now, do we?"

He kissed her lips and said, "No, not to-night."

CHAPTER SEVENTEEN

"WORK IS A PRIVILEGE. Don't abuse it. Work is a privilege…" The warden's words kept repeating in Jack's brain. He supposed in a way it was true. Being on a grounds-maintenance work detail at Broad Creek, meant a prisoner could get outside, breathe fresh air, without having to interact with cellmates the way he would if he were assigned to the laundry or cafeteria.

He picked up a rock and tossed it into a wheelbarrow before resuming his raking duties. He'd cleared his section of fence, making it possible for the mowers to cut a clean sweep all the way to the cement blocks holding the heavy-gauge chain link. The fencing and concrete went several feet underground, prohibiting inmates from tunneling under the barrier. At the top of the fence, ten feet up, razor wire discouraged prisoners from attempting to climb over. The yard at Broad

Creek was like every prison Jack had ever imagined—stark, bleak and impenetrable. He'd just never imagined living in one.

The guard walked by on his leisurely stroll. "How are you doing, kid?" he asked.

"No problem." Jack would have said he was doing okay even if he'd been bitten by a rattler. Being in the yard was so much better than being inside. Especially since he was basically on his own.

"This is a sweet-cake assignment," the guard said. "You must know somebody high up."

"Don't know anybody," Jack said, resting on the rake handle. That wasn't exactly true. Eric Henderson had pulled a couple of strings. Jack was now in a different cell block. His roomie, Barry, was a twenty-four-year-old man who'd been convicted of doping horses at a track in Charlotte. Barry was bitter and determined to get out. He wasn't interested in striking up any kind of friendship with Jack, but at least he wasn't violent.

The guard wandered off and Jack got back to work.

He was beginning to resign himself to the possibility that he'd never get out of Broad

Creek. His sister was doing all she could, but she couldn't change the facts. She couldn't work miracles. He was going to trial, and the prospects of getting off were grim. Maybe he'd have to accept a plea deal, admit to a lesser charge. He looked up at the sky, so blue and clear. At least if he copped to manslaughter, a big "if," maybe he could see the sky from the other side of this fence someday.

He heard the rumble of a large vehicle, one of those big dump trucks, no doubt, loaded with stone and concrete scraps to be used as fill. The sound of a big engine was not unusual on the dusty, unpaved road that ran along the back of the prison. Some sort of project was under construction a half mile or so down the road. He'd heard a do-gooder organization was building a state supported housing facility for families suffering financial troubles.

There would be training programs for parents looking for work, activities and tutoring for teens on the verge of quitting school, baby-sitting for little kids who needed day care.

That was okay. Let the charities save the people they could. It was too late for him.

He shielded his eyes as the big truck rounded a bend and came into view on the other side of the fence. The huge monster was rolling, kicking up clouds of dust and gravel from its back tires. "What's the hurry?" Jack said to himself. "They can't build nothing till you get there."

Ignoring the truck, he continued raking and tossing rocks into the wheelbarrow until a loud explosion made his whole body tense. The tire on the front right side of the truck blew, spitting rubber shards all over the road. The vehicle swerved toward the fence. Jack dropped the rake and stumbled over the rocks he'd just unearthed. Unable to get away, he crouched as low as he could.

It all happened in the blink of an eye. The truck careened in Jack's direction at high speed. He was grateful for the ton of cement and wire that would keep the vehicle from invading his space. Better in prison than dead. But his gratitude was short-lived. The truck barreled into the fence, splitting the chain link as if it were made of pipe cleaners.

Jack sprawled flat to the ground and crossed his arms over his head. In one breath-stealing glance, he watched the massive tire gyrate on its bent axle as it passed just inches from his skull. A little closer and his brain would have looked like cream cheese. He pulled his arms and legs close to his body, crawled over the concrete abutment and rolled once, ending up beneath the middle of the truck's undercarriage. The vehicle continued to rumble over him, tearing wire and splintering cement in a path of destruction.

Jack heard the guard's voice issuing orders. "Get in one line! Back to the cell block!" The hiss and sputter of the truck engine mingled with the cries of fellow inmates and the thunder of his own heartbeat in his ears. Dust filled the area occupied by his trembling body. He coughed, tasting cement, and fought for a full breath.

And then, in moments, the dust started to clear. Jack looked beyond the shelter he'd been forced to take under the truck and saw daylight. Just across the road, a few yards away, was forest, thick and green and beckoning.

He started to crawl, as low to the ground as a snake. He wiggled to the other side of the truck and into the road. Just a few feet and he was in the scrub at the side. Weeds covered his head. He grasped handfuls of root and vine as his knees bit on solid ground and propelled him forward.

"It's fate," he said through the dirt caking his lips. "This is a sign." About a hundred yards into the trees, he stopped slithering and assumed a crouch. Looking back at the prison, he saw his cell mates being herded into the building. No one even called his name. Ha! They didn't know he was gone. Bent nearly double so he couldn't be seen from a distance, he ran through the woods.

CHAPTER EIGHTEEN

THURSDAY MORNING WAS gray and overcast, a fitting environment for Dorie's next to last day at The Crooked Spruce. When the skies opened up, she went to the front porch and took a few moments to listen to the rain gushing in rivers down the old Timber Gap Trail. Overhead, fat drops pattered on the tin roof of the lodge. Dorie breathed deeply, filling her lungs with moist, cleansing air. To her, the rain refreshing the mountain in spring was as much a small miracle as the sun shining through the new green leaves.

She'd come to love Hickory Mountain with its variety of temperatures from crisp, clear nights to sunny, warm days. The animal sounds she listened to each night were now as soothing as music. And today was special, too, as the waterfalls swelled and the flowers were coaxed to bloom.

She and Bret had enjoyed two more evenings on the swing. Meeting there at the close of their busy day was natural and comforting, and Dorie didn't want to think about having to abandon this precious time. For long spells they sat in easy silence broken by minutes of spontaneous chatter about their pasts, their fears, their hopes.

And on Wednesday night Bret had news. He'd heard from the sheriff that Dabney Shelton had been captured. The police were working on their case to accuse him of the arson crimes. But today was Thursday, and Bret hadn't asked Dorie to stay at The Crooked Spruce for a longer period. And on Saturday morning, even if he had asked, she would have to go. She'd made a promise to Jack.

And Bret hadn't said that he wanted to explore the feelings they shared more deeply. Did he see a future with her as a possibility? Dorie wanted to tell him that he'd come to mean everything to her. But she'd stopped before spoiling what they had with an admission that might be too soon or too one-sided. Besides, her life was too complicated for this man and his son right now. She needed to fix her own emotional house before she could fully be a part of a family struggling to fix theirs.

The outpost was nearly ready for hikers who wanted showers and a night in a warm bed. Dorie had answered internet questions about the camp from interested hikers. The website she'd designed was scoring more hits every day. The pictures she'd added of the cabins and the lodge made The Crooked Spruce look rustic and inviting. The bunk houses were painted and spotless with new mattresses and fresh linens. The bathhouse was functional and gleaming. The Crooked Spruce and its owner were ready to open their doors. Only Dorie was far from ready to let the door close behind her.

The school bus brought Luke home a little after noon. Pine Crest Elementary was having a teacher planning session, which meant early release for the students. When Luke asked her to go pick pinecones for the fireplace with him and King, Dorie said yes. The threat from Dabney Shelton was all but forgotten, and every minute with Luke added an indelible memory she would take with her.

"You and King go on outside and wait for me by the cabins," she told him. "I need to respond to one more email from a potential guest, and then I'll be along."

Luke grabbed a bucket to hold their loot and ran outside. Bret and Clancy had made a trip into town for hardware supplies and would be back soon. The property was peaceful and quiet. Outside the lodge, the trees rustled gently in the wind. Dorie was finishing her email when she heard King's frantic barking.

She hurried out the back door and ran toward the sound. She found Luke and the dog standing about fifty yards from one of the guest cabins. The hair on King's back was standing up. His legs were stiff and straight, his head down. He inched forward, growling at the bunk-house door.

Dorie put her arm around Luke. "What's wrong? Are you all right?"

"Yeah, but Dorie, I think there's someone inside that cabin."

It was possible. King was definitely in protection mode. Had Dabney escaped? No, surely not. But if he had, he very well might have considered The Crooked Spruce and its owner his next target.

"I saw a shadow move across the window," Luke said.

"You go back to the house," she said. "Go inside and lock the doors. Don't open them to anyone but me or your dad or grandpa."

"I'm not leaving you here by yourself," he said. "Let's just call out and see if someone answers us."

She spun him around and looked into his eyes. "No! I told you what to do. I've got King here. I'll be fine. In fact, with all his barking, I wouldn't be surprised if whoever was in there hasn't gone back into the woods."

Finally Luke obeyed and ran to the house. Dorie held King by his collar and hollered, "Is someone there? I'm calling the police."

With her heart hammering against her ribs, she did a quick survey of her surroundings and picked up a tree limb to use as a weapon. But she hoped she wouldn't need it. Perhaps Luke had been mistaken. At any rate, she couldn't just let someone ruin the work Bret had done in the cabin. A stern warning might make an intruder run off. Or…

She backed toward the lodge. "I'm dialing

911!" she called. A false threat. She hadn't brought her cell phone.

"Dorie!" The word cut through the air as a harsh whisper.

The recognition of her name penetrated the rush of blood in her ears. "Who's there?" she called again.

"It's me, Dorie. It's Jack!"

She dropped the limb and charged the door. Her brother's head popped out. He looked around and retreated back inside. When she reached the door, he grabbed her arm and pulled her over the threshold.

She struggled to catch her breath. "Jack, what are you doing…? How did you…?" In the dim light of the cabin interior she could see cuts and bruises on his face. He wore an embroidered Outer Banks sweatshirt with the sleeves pushed up. Below his elbows, his arms were scratched. She placed her hands on each side of his face. He winced.

"What happened to you?" she said.

His arms came around her, and he buried his face against her shoulder. She wrapped him a hug and listened to him draw deep gulps of air. "Jack, just concentrate on breathing. It's okay. Whatever it is, we'll figure it out."

After several minutes he'd calmed enough to back away from her. He half stumbled to a cot and sank down onto the mattress. She sat next to him and examined his cuts. They were all surface injuries. He'd suffered worse skateboarding with his friends, but for some reason, these made her heart ache more than the wounds of a little boy.

"Who did this to you, Jack?" she said. "Did someone abuse you at the jail?"

He shook his head without speaking.

"Then what? Did you do this to yourself?" A terrifying thought came to her. "Oh, Jack, did you escape?"

His indrawn breath quivered. "I had a chance, Dorie. One chance in a million and I took it."

"What did you do? How did you get out? Was anyone besides you hurt?" She prayed he hadn't injured a guard or another inmate. She looked around the cabin. Every inch of the small space was visible. They were the only two people inside, but still she said, "Did anyone escape with you?"

Breathlessly he began recounting his adventure from the day before. She had trouble following his story. His facts seemed jumbled, the time line inaccurate. How could the truck accident, his reaction and his escape have happened in what he called a few seconds? He'd had no time to think, he said, to consider the consequences. He'd just seen an opportunity and acted.

She took a deep breath. "So you crawled through the woods until you thought no one could see you?"

He nodded. "A mile, maybe more." He pointed to the scratches on his arm. "I couldn't even feel all this at the time. I just kept moving."

There was still so much to ask, but her instincts took over. "I've got to get soap and water and some antibiotic ointment," she said. "You wait here. I'll be back in a few minutes."

He wrapped his hand around her wrist. "Don't go, Dorie. I don't know if anyone's out there. I think I heard another voice, and I can't be seen."

Luke. Her mind scrambled to come up with a solution. She couldn't hide Jack forever. And Luke was already aware that someone was on the property. But Jack needed time. She needed time to decide what to do next. "Okay," she said. "But I can at least get water from the shower room next door."

She rushed out and returned less than a minute later with soaked paper towels. Jack was sitting on the edge of the bed where she'd left him, his face buried in his hands. She began washing his cuts.

"What am I going to do?" he asked.

She had no idea. This had happened so fast. It was all she could do to concentrate on the here and now, her brother's immediate needs. "Have you eaten anything since yesterday?" she asked.

He nodded. "I found half a box of breakfast bars in a Dumpster outside a 7-Eleven," he said. "I ate those."

He'd foraged through a Dumpster? She didn't need to think about that now. "Have you slept any?"

"Yeah. I came up on an old camper in a parking lot. I guess it was stored there. And it wasn't locked. I slept inside with the window open so I'd hear if anyone came along. No one did, so I got two or three hours' sleep."

"And those clothes?" she said.

He plucked at the trousers he was wearing. "These are prison issue, but since they're just blue, I didn't worry about them. I got the sweatshirt from a dryer in a laundry place."

He continued answering her questions, explaining how he'd remembered the name of the camp and how he'd hitched a ride with a trucker who dropped him in Mountain Spring. He'd walked the rest of the way, the journey taking almost six hours.

"You can't stay in this cabin," she said. "You were right about hearing another voice. The little boy who lives here saw someone inside. It's only a matter of time…"

Jack stood and started pacing. "Why didn't you say so? It's been at least fifteen minutes. He'll bring his parents."

"His father's not here right now, but he'll be back soon. We've got to move you somewhere else until I can think."

"There are other cabins," Jack said.

"They will all be searched," she said. "I don't know…"

She never finished. Voices from outside broke into her thoughts.

"It's this one, Dad," Luke said. "I saw Dorie go inside."

Bret's voice drowned out his footsteps. "Dorie, are you okay? Answer me."

Under other circumstances, the sound of concern in Bret's voice would have comforted her, but not now.

Jack stopped walking and froze in the middle of the room. "Who's that, the father?"

"Yes," Dorie said. She leaned against the door. "I'm fine, Bret," she called. "There's no problem in here."

She didn't expect him to believe her. He would know something was wrong.

"Dorie, I'm coming in!" Bret hollered. "Stand back."

"Stop him, Dorie," Jack said. "If he sees me…"

The door flew open, and Bret came inside with a rifle pointed. He aimed the weapon around the room, seeming to take in everything at once. "Get down on the floor," he hollered at Jack.

"Put that thing down," Dorie said, stepping in front of her brother. "There's no need for it."

His eyes narrowed. He stared at her, then looked past her to see Jack's face. He slowly lowered the rifle. "Dorie! What's going on?

I thought Dabney had escaped and had you for sure." He stared at Jack. "Who is this?"

She thought about trying to make the situation seem less dramatic, but realized the futility of that plan. Jack had escaped. Bret was an ex-cop. This was truly drama at its worst. "Bret," she said, moving away so Jack was fully revealed, "I'd like to introduce you to my brother. Jack, meet Bret."

THE RIFLE HUNG at Bret's side as he stood rooted to the wood plank floor. He stared at the kid in front of him, trying to make sense of the situation. The teen had Dorie's deep blue eyes, her slim build and firm, often stubborn chin.

"How did you get here?" Bret asked. "Did they release you?"

"No," Dorie said.

"Not exactly," Jack said.

"Then how…?"

Luke ran in the door panting with excitement. "Dad, did you shoot somebody?"

"No. I told you to go back to the house!"

Luke stared at Jack. "I always have to go to the house! I want to know who this guy is."

"I'll talk to you later," Bret said, holding

the barrel of the rifle and balancing the butt against the cabin floor.

Luke didn't move, so Dorie said, "Luke, this is my brother, Jack. He…ah…he came for a visit."

Luke grinned. "Oh, cool. Hi, Jack."

Jack opened his mouth to respond.

"He's not staying," Bret said, interrupting him.

Luke approached Jack, and every muscle in Bret's body tensed. "Stay next to me," he ordered his son.

Luke stopped. "What happened to your face and your arms?" he asked Jack. "You been in a fight?"

"Naw," Jack said. "Nothing as exciting as that."

Dorie cringed.

"Everyone okay in here?" Clancy came through the door wielding a shovel.

"Yes," Bret said. "You can put that down. You won't be clobbering anyone."

Clancy glanced at the rifle. "I guess you've got things covered."

"This is Dorie's brother, Grandpa," Luke said. "He's visiting. Isn't that neat?"

Clancy gripped the shovel more tightly and

took a step back. "Your brother? The one that's been at Broad…?"

"Yes," Dorie answered quickly, interrupting him. She gave a sideways look at Luke, warning Clancy to skip the details.

"Pop, take Luke back to the house and keep him there. I'm going to be here awhile with Dorie and Jack." He tried to sound normal for Luke's sake, but no one would miss the edge of severity in his voice. He didn't want anyone to misinterpret his intentions right now, and it was just as well that Luke knew it.

"I don't want to go," Luke said. "Jack probably knows how to play video games, and I figured…"

"You figured nothing," Bret said. "Pop?"

Clancy turned Luke around and pushed him toward the door. "Come on, kid. We can use this shovel to dig a hole or something."

"I don't want to dig…"

Further complaints were drowned out when Bret closed the door behind them. When just the three of them were alone, Bret looked at Dorie. "Did you know this was going to happen?"

Her mouth dropped open. "No! How could

you think that?" She gave her brother a sideways glance. "As a matter of fact, Jack, why didn't the prison call me? I should have been the first person they notified when you went missing."

"I don't know," he said. "Maybe your cell phone wasn't working."

"It often doesn't up here," she admitted.

Bret kept his features still. Maintaining the typical cop stance that let all perps know he wasn't kidding around, he said, "Jack, if you want to say anything, now's your chance, but make it quick."

"Okay," Jack said. "I'll start at the beginning which was about twenty-four hours ago."

Dorie's eyes were wide on Bret as if she couldn't believe he had assumed the role of law-enforcement officer. "Wait a minute, Jack," she said. "There's something you should know before you speak."

Bret snapped his sternest gaze on her, surprised she would caution her brother about anything. "What should he know, Dorie?" he asked.

She kept her attention on her brother. "Jack, this man is an ex-cop. You should keep that in mind when you tell the story about how you got out of Broad Creek. And anything else you might feel inclined to reveal."

Bret leaned toward her. "What's this, Dorie? You're drawing lines between us? After everything that's happened?"

"He should know who he's talking to," she said. "He has a right to the truth."

"Don't we all," Bret said. "Start explaining, little brother, and despite what your sister said, I suggest you don't leave anything out."

CHAPTER NINETEEN

JACK TOLD HIS story again. The details were the same as when he told them to Dorie. He ended with, "I could have been killed, but instead I got a break."

"You got a break all right," Bret said. "Bottom line, you broke out of prison. There's no other way to look at it."

"Yes, there is," Jack said. "You can look at it the way I see it. I got this work detail for being a model prisoner. It's like I was meant to be in the yard yesterday when that truck came by." He paused before adding, "And there's no other way I'm ever going to get out of that place."

Dorie didn't buy the whole fate, right-place, right-time theory. She knew Jack shouldn't have run. But she didn't blame him. She might have done the same thing knowing she probably wouldn't have a future outside of Broad Creek. An innocent boy in prison is driven to do foolhardy things. At this point she could only hope that Bret would see Jack's side of the story and give them a little time to figure out what to do.

Bret's tone was harsh as he summed up the situation. "You are in jail on a murder charge, kid. And you broke out. That's a criminal action and you can't talk your way around the truth."

Jack started to argue, but Dorie raised her hand. "I think we all need to take a step back. Jack's cuts need attention. He's hardly eaten. I've got to get him some food. After we've all calmed down, we can discuss this further."

Bret's eyes narrowed. He rubbed his nape. Was he debating his response to her? How could he? Jack was practically a boy, only six years older than Bret's own son. And Bret was having a problem with Dorie tending his cuts and feeding him? She was beginning to question whether this ex-cop had a heart. She'd believed he did. But now…

Finally, Bret said, "Okay, you can go up to the house and get what you need. Jack and I will stay right here. But then we're settling this according to what's the right thing to do."

The right thing to do? What did that mean?

Dorie took Jack's arm and tried to be encouraging. "Everything's okay, Jack. I'll get food and bandages and come right back."

When she returned, Bret remained vigilant while Dorie put ointment on Jack's scratches. She brought him a meal which he wolfed down in just a few minutes. Bret seemed to be studying Jack from every angle. Dorie only hoped he was seeing her brother as a human being and not a convict. A boy who needed help. Since Bret had discovered Jack in the cabin, all she'd seen was that there was still too much cop left in the owner of The Crooked Spruce.

After Jack was finished eating, Bret said, "I'd like to talk to your sister now, Jack. You stay right here with my father." After a pause, he added, "He'll have the rifle, so…"

"He's not going to run," Dorie said. "He's injured."

Bret called for Clancy, and as soon as he appeared, Dorie nodded at Jack, letting him know he should do what Bret said. Clancy stood guard while Dorie followed Bret to the next cabin. She knew Jack would be okay, and she understood Bret's behavior. Still she was hurt. Couldn't Bret at least consider her feelings?

"Sit down," Bret said when they were alone. He pointed to one of the cots, and he took another one.

She immediately took the offensive. "You don't have to worry. I know Jack better than anyone. He wouldn't hurt you or Clancy or Luke. And he won't run. I'm all he has."

"Your loyalty is fine," Bret said. "But I've had a lot more experience with these kinds of…" He paused, not finishing his sentence.

"You were going to say these kinds of *kids,* weren't you?"

Bret remained silent.

"He's my brother. I think I have more experience with him than you do."

He placed his hands on his knees. "I'm sorry, Dorie, but the fact that he's your brother is exactly why I have to make the right decisions here. I can't let emotions influence what has to be done."

She began to tremble with fear and disappointment. This was going to turn out badly for everyone. The maternal instincts she'd nourished for years kicked into overdrive. "Why do you have to make all the decisions?" she challenged. "He's my brother. My responsibility."

"In case you've forgotten, this is my home. I used to be a cop. I think that entitles me to weigh in on an escaped murder suspect showing up here."

"That's all you see when you look at Jack, isn't it? A murder suspect. Even after I've told you he's innocent, you refuse to see him as a boy who's been railroaded by the system."

"I don't know that!" Bret said. "And I happen to believe in the system. Is it possible it didn't work this time? Sure, anything's possible, but nothing so far has convinced me of that."

"You don't have to act like a cop all the time, Bret," she said. "Can't you find some sense of humanity somewhere in that playbook of rules you follow?"

"What exactly are you asking me to do, Dorie? Look the other way?"

She took a deep breath to calm her nerves. "You would never do that, would you?" she said after a few moments. She already knew the answer.

The muscles worked in his jaw. The

creases around his eyes deepened. "Besides everything else, I have a son to think about," he said.

She wasn't going to change his mind. Ultimately he would do what a cop had to do, and that meant if they stayed, even for a little while, he would turn Jack in. She leaned forward on the cot.

"Look, Bret, let me make this easy for you. Just give me the money you owe me for working the past few days, and Jack and I will leave. Once we're gone you won't have to make any decision at all. You can build a moat around your outpost and keep all the evil Jack Howes away from your precious camp."

His lips formed a thin line. His chest expanded and held until he blew out a long breath. "Fine," he said. "You're owed the money. When I get back to the house I'll leave a check for the full amount on the counter."

"Thank you." She stood and walked to the door.

"Dorie, wait."

His words stopped her. She turned. Hope flared in her heart. "What?"

His face sober, his voice hoarse, he said, "I can't let you leave with Jack."

For seconds she could only stare at him. She'd been afraid it would come to this all along. But she was going to make him say it even if he choked on the words. After the kisses on the porch, the sharing of their pasts, the closeness, she was going to make him utter his total betrayal. "Why not?"

"He's an escaped convict, Dorie. I can't let him walk out of here."

The words cut straight to her heart. "Don't do this, Bret. Let me take care of this. Don't let the man you used to be rob my brother of his future."

"The man I used to be was a law enforcement officer, plain and simple. I upheld the law. And I exist today, here, in this place, because that former job still pays me a monthly stipend. I can't just forget everything I believed in before I was shot. There is still right and wrong."

"I happen to believe there are many other options in between right and wrong," she said. "Jack is innocent. What about that? That should count for something, Bret. It matters."

"Jack will be tried in a court," Bret said.

"If he's innocent, the system will work, and he'll be acquitted."

Her eyes burned. Through the blur of unshed tears she saw the hard planes of his face. "Now who's being naive?" she said. "If you send him back, especially after what happened yesterday, he won't stand a chance."

The muscles in his jaw clenched. "It's the right thing…." He paused as if knowing that phrase would only inflame the situation more. "I'm sorry, Dorie. Really, I am, but the law can't work any differently for Jack just because he's your brother."

"I'm not talking about the law here, Bret. I'm talking about you and me, and the past two weeks. Stop being a cop for one minute and think about what is the decent, humane thing to do. Be the man who talked to me on the porch for hours, the man who held me, who told me his regrets, his hopes." She came toward him, her hand outstretched, but he didn't take it. Dorie refused to let his cold demeanor stop her. She knew what she was asking him was hard. She knew he'd have to compromise his principles for her. But what else could she do? Jack's future, maybe his life, was on the line.

"Be the man I knew on that porch," she said. "The man who, underneath all his unwavering ethics and sense of morality, is a caring person."

The small cabin room was eerily quiet for several agonizing seconds until Bret slowly shook his head. "I can't, Dorie. I'm going to call the sheriff and tell him Jack is here. I have to. It's who I am as much as I'm that man who sat on the porch with you."

Panic flooded her body. She felt the blood rush from her head and didn't trust herself to stand. Her hands shook. Deep down she knew what she was asking of Bret was unethical and beyond his capacity to give, but she had to fight for Jack. She'd always fought for Jack. She was his only chance. She couldn't let him down.

Bret stood and walked to the door.

"Don't! Not yet," she said. "Hear me out. I have an offer to make."

He stopped, faced her.

"I'll take Jack back myself," she said. "Let me at least do that. It will go easier for him if he returns on his own."

He rubbed his forehead, slowly shook

his head. He didn't believe she would keep her word.

"I mean it, Bret. I swear. I'll take him back. We'll leave now." She was telling the truth, but didn't know how to make him believe her. He should trust her. After all this time together, he had to know she wouldn't lie to him.

"Don't test me, Dorie. Yes, I have ethics. And I struggle with them every day. But I have to…"

"Trust me," she said. "You can trust me." Both hands reached toward him, but he was too far away to touch. "Please, Bret."

He couldn't look at her so he stared at the floor. He was going to deny her even this.

Desperation made her attempt one last plea. "Get Clancy. Go back to the house. Leave Jack to me. We'll be gone in ten minutes. Then give us an hour. After that, call anyone you want, the police, the highway patrol. I don't care. Tell them whatever you want. We'll be partway across the state. I'll take Jack directly to Broad Creek. You have my word." She waited. He didn't speak. "Please Bret. I swear I'm telling you the truth."

He kept staring at the floor as if looking

at her were unbearable. Then he said, "You have ten minutes to pack your stuff. Jack stays here." He turned and strode from the cabin.

A FEW MINUTES LATER, after Dorie had tossed her belongings into her duffel, she and Jack stood in front of the lodge with Clancy nearby. "Are you crazy?" Jack said. "This place is perfect. No one would ever find me here."

"No. We can't stay." She slung her pack over her shoulder and headed to the truck. She intended to keep her word. Bret was upstairs with Luke and probably watching the clock.

"Why not? Can't you convince Bret to give us at least a few days?"

She paused to glare at him. "You saw how he reacted to you, Jack! And besides, do you think this is what I want? Do you think this is easy for me?" She huffed a deep breath. "For that matter, have you thought at all about how this is affecting me?"

"No offense, Dorie, but you're not the one going back to Broad Creek."

She threw her bag into the truck. "I'm not

talking about this anymore. We don't have time."

"I can't go back there! They'll add years onto my eventual sentence for escaping. I'll never see daylight."

Her nerves were frayed to a breaking point. If Jack said one more word, she was afraid she would start yelling at him and wouldn't stop. She'd given up everything for him. She was still giving up everything, especially that man upstairs who was cutting them a break they probably didn't deserve. "Get in the truck, Jack."

"I'll go, but we're not going to Broad Creek," he said. "I can't do it, Dorie. I can't believe you're even suggesting it. Do you realize what I went through to get out of that place? I wasn't kidding! I was almost killed."

"I know that, and I'm sorry, Jack. I'm sorry for everything you've been through, but you have to know that running for the rest of your life is no life at all. We'll call Eric Henderson on the way and ask him to meet us at Broad Creek. We need his advice on this. We're out of time. Go."

"I'm not letting up on this, Dor. I'm getting in the truck because it's apparently the only option we have, but I'm not through trying to talk sense into you."

"You know what, Jack? I'm frankly sick of everyone thinking they're going to talk sense into me. You, Bret. I'm done. We are going to do what I believe is right from now on. But at least we'll do it on our own terms. You don't know how lucky you are that Bret didn't call the police immediately and turn you in."

"Lucky? You call that lucky? I was starting to think you and this guy had something going, but apparently I was wrong. He wouldn't do anything for you if he won't at least give us some time to sort this out. He's done nothing but threaten since he saw me!"

"Don't you see, Jack? You are a threat. To Bret's life here, to his son, his dad. To Bret you're a criminal who presents danger to the people he loves."

"But I'm innocent! I wouldn't hurt his kid."

"He doesn't know that. And you don't know him. He's lost a lot in his life, and so far as he knows for sure, you're an accused murderer who's escaped from jail. I said it before, but you're lucky he didn't take you to the police himself."

She paused, took a deep breath. Where

had all that come from? She was actually defending Bret to her brother. Well maybe he deserved it. Letting them go had to be one tough step for him. She'd seen how protective he'd been when Dabney was a threat. Letting a convict stay around his son was impossible. She consulted her watch. "It's time. I don't want to test him. Let's drive."

Dorie assumed Bret had told his family something about her sudden departure. She hoped he hadn't given Luke a bad impression of her. No, he wouldn't have. He believed as she did that there was no reason to inflict hard truths on kids when they couldn't do anything about them, so she was sure he'd come up with a convincing story.

She whistled for King and the dog bounded after her. She and Jack got in the truck. She did a three-point turn and headed down the drive. Before going under the archway, she looked in the rearview mirror at the lodge. She saw Luke upstairs in his bedroom window. His face was pressed to the pane. He waved at her. She stopped the truck, got out and blew him a kiss. And then she choked back tears when she drove away. She needed to put in a lot of miles in one hour.

"You did this," Luke said. "You made them go away."

Bret sat next to his son on the porch swing and set it rocking in a slow, easy motion. He knew exactly why that swing provided a sense of calm. He'd spent the happiest moments of his recent life in that swing, a piece of furniture he hadn't even thought he needed, but one that had made such a difference in his life. But he wouldn't be sharing that swing with Dorie tonight, or maybe ever again, and now he had to convince his son that he wasn't a coldhearted monster. Maybe he even had to convince himself.

"No, I didn't make them go," he said. "Dorie just had an emergency and she had to leave. You know how it is. Sometimes things just come up." Luke sniffed, and Bret put his arm around him. "But her decision had nothing to do with you, son."

"She didn't even say goodbye."

"I know. She thought it would be easier this way."

"And her brother. I just met him. We didn't even get to play a video game."

Being reminded that Jack probably still enjoyed video games didn't make this any easier for Bret. Six years. That was all that separated Jack from Luke. Six years and a very different upbringing.

"I don't know that he would have played any with you," Bret said. "It's hard for you to understand this, Luke, but Jack is in trouble. He's had a tough life."

"How could he? He's got Dorie, and she's the nicest lady I know."

Bret took a deep breath and swallowed. "Sure, she's nice. But they were raised without a dad around. And when Jack was about your age, his mom left. Dorie did all she could, but Jack grew up a little too fast and did some things he shouldn't have."

"You mean he's a delinquent?"

"Well, sort of, yeah. He's been in trouble with the police a few times."

"So that's why you made them go? Because Jack got in trouble that way? You could have helped him!"

"No, I couldn't. I gave up that life when I got shot, remember? Now my life is all about you and this place. But I still know what a kid like Jack needs. He has to face up to what he's done and hopefully come out the better for it."

"What did he do that was so bad?"

There was time enough for Luke to hear the true answer, so Bret avoided giving it to him right now. Besides, there was still some doubt about Jack's crime, right? "I think mostly minor things, but he has to pay for hurting people. You understand that, Luke."

"And Dorie took him back to where he did that stuff?"

"That's right." Bret was as miserable as he could ever remember being. But he was sure of one thing. Dorie had told him the truth. She was returning Jack to Broad Creek.

"Will Dorie come back here after she gets Jack home?"

Bret gave his son a little extra squeeze. Dorie had become such a vital part of their lives in such a short time. "I don't know. But I'm thinking we shouldn't count on it."

Luke looked up at him with moisture shining in his eyes. "Doesn't that make you sad?"

"Oh, yeah. It makes me plenty sad," Bret said. "But I'm just glad I have you to cheer me up. We'll do that for each other, okay, partner?"

Luke nodded and rested his head on Bret's shoulder just about where Dorie used to rest her head. Bret felt a catch of breath in his throat. She'd been gone three hours. He still hadn't made the phone call that would put the police on her trail. He didn't need to. In spite of what she must believe was his ultimate betrayal, he knew she would keep her word. She was that kind of woman.

CHAPTER TWENTY

"I'VE ALREADY ASKED for a medical evaluation from our firm's doctor," Eric Henderson said.

The lawyer had been waiting for Dorie and Jack at the prison when they'd arrived around 8:00 p.m. that night. Dorie had called him when they were about an hour away and he'd driven down from Wilmington. Now they were seated in the visitor's room, Jack on one side of the table and Dorie and Eric on the other. Two guards stood outside the door when only one was customary. Obviously the prison authorities were taking precautions to assure that Jack wouldn't run again.

"Why did you order a medical evaluation?" Dorie asked the attorney. "Jack is fine."

"No, he's not," Eric said. "Trust me on this, Dorinda. We need our own personal physician to come in and check him out. Jack has enough scratches and bruises to prove that his ordeal yesterday did some real damage."

He gave Dorie an intense stare. "And that's not even taking into account the emotional scars."

"I don't have any emotional…"

"Stop right there, Jack," Eric said. "You're paying me to handle this for you. Let me do my job. Unless you want ten years for escape added on to whatever sentence you may get." He switched his stare from brother to sister. "Our one chance of mitigating this escape is to plead that Jack was hit so hard by that truck, he was dazed. He didn't know what he was doing and just wandered off into the woods. Hours later he realized what he'd done and panicked."

"And that's why he came to me?" Dorie said, appreciating the lawyer's skills even if Eric was bending the truth a bit.

"Exactly. Jack is still a teenager. It's logical he would go to the only source of support he's known…." He leveled a knowing look at Dorie. "Even though your mothering talents were sorely lacking during his formative years. Remember? We already established that fact."

"What are you talking about?" Jack said. "Dorie has been great to me. She's been better than my real mother was or ever would have been."

Dorie tried to calm him. Once they'd gotten on the road, Jack had settled down and accepted that a return to Broad Creek was his only option. "It's okay, Jack," she said. "This is all part of Mr. Henderson's strategy. I've agreed to downplay my role in your upbringing."

"No way," Jack insisted. "I'm not going to let you lie about all you've done for me. You'll end up looking bad to the jury, and I don't want that."

"You'd better start listening, kid," Eric said. "Your sister knows this is what we have to do to get you a plea deal. You've got to come across as abandoned and pathetic. We need the jury's sympathy if we're going to get a lighter sentence."

Jack looked as if he was going to argue, but Dorie just held up her hand. "I've agreed to this, Jack, and I'm okay with it. What do I care what that jury thinks of me as long as you get out of this place sooner."

He bit his bottom lip and stared at the tabletop.

Eric relaxed. "All right, then. I'll speak to

the warden one more time, tell him we want our doctor to take a look at Jack. The warden conceded that the accident could have left you confused and might even have caused a temporary loss of memory. And, lucky for us, the truck driver caught a glimpse of you when he crashed the fence. He thought he'd run over you. So, for now, because you came back on your own, you can return to your cell block with no further punishment at this time." Eric grinned. "Although I doubt you'll be allowed on grounds maintenance again."

Dorie stood. "I can't thank you enough, Eric," she said. "I can only imagine the trouble Jack would have been in without your influence."

"It's what you're paying me for, Dorinda. Oh, and by the way, I've gotten a trial date. Two weeks from Monday we have jury selection if we haven't cut a deal with the District Attorney before then."

"Did you hear that, Jack?" Dorie said. "Only two more weeks until the trial."

The guard opened the door at Eric's signal and motioned for Jack to leave the room. "I'll come see you tomorrow," Dorie said. "Just try to rest." She watched until Jack was no longer visible.

Eric took Dorie's elbow. "I'll walk you out." He pulled back the cuff on his oxford shirt and glanced at his watch. He was dressed casually in a plain blue shirt and perfectly creased chinos that probably cost more than Dorie made in a week waiting tables. Eric made a good first impression. She hoped that carried over to a jury.

"It's early still," he said. "Only nine o'clock."

"I appreciate you coming here on a Friday night, Eric. I'm sure you had better things to do. Maybe you can catch up with your plans and save some of the evening."

He pushed a shock of blond hair off his forehead. She noticed his hair was a perfect length, just long enough to brush his collar, the style handsomely boyish. All in all, there was a sense of competent success about him, one she'd noticed as well in their only phone conversation.

"Actually I don't have any plans," he said. "I was thinking maybe you and I might go out for a drink."

She stared up at him, uncertain of what

he was suggesting. A date? More strategizing? She was dressed in the jeans and the T-shirt she'd put on that morning. She hadn't combed her hair or put on makeup. She felt grimy, head to toe after driving for hours. Even her teeth were gritty. Surely he wasn't coming on to her.

"Or coffee," he said when she didn't respond. "If you'd rather."

"Do you want to discuss the case more?" she asked.

"Sure, if you'd like," he said. "And maybe other topics. Let's just see where this leads."

Oh, no. This was not going to happen. But she had to decline without offending him. "Well, thanks, but I'm exhausted to tell you the truth. This day has been, well, I don't have to tell you. Plus, my dog has been in the truck for over thirty minutes now."

"I'm sure your dog is fine. It's a cool night. Why don't you take him home and meet me someplace?"

"That's another thing…" Dorie scrambled for her next excuse. "I haven't seen my house in a long time. I have a lot to catch up on."

He smiled in a professional, practiced way.

"Okay, I understand. But don't think I won't ask again."

"Some other time maybe," she said, heading toward her truck.

She walked briskly across the prison parking lot, keeping her gaze focused on King's nose sniffing the air outside the passenger window. She didn't even turn around when she opened her driver's side door and slid inside. How could she tell this attorney her mind was three hundred miles away in the mountains of western Carolina? If she wanted to have coffee with anyone, it would be with Bret, and that wasn't likely to happen.

THE NEXT MORNING, Dorie sat outside with her brother. As was the custom, she was on one side of an aluminum picnic table, and he was on the other. His fine brown hair was mussed, falling into his eyes. He looked so innocent. How could anyone think this boy had killed someone? A guard stood nearby, just out of hearing distance.

"How did you sleep last night?" she asked, though Jack's red-rimmed eyes had already given her the answer.

"I couldn't sleep," he said. "Kept thinking about stuff."

"I hope you didn't worry about backlash from your escape. I think Henderson has covered you on that one."

"No, I didn't worry about that, although when sentencing comes down, I'm sure my little absence will be taken into consideration."

Dorie figured it would be. "Look, Jack, now that we have a trial date this will all be over soon. We'll know your future."

"Ha. I know it now, Dorie." He seemed to be taking in every detail of the yard. "I'm looking at my future," he said.

"Things can change, Jack. The truth about that night can still come out. Henderson can get the jury to sympathize with you because of your background. We have cards we can play."

"That's another thing," he said. "I don't want you lying about what you did for me growing up. You were always there for me."

"Don't worry about that. I'll be careful about what I say and how I say it. I know what's at stake for you, and I'm willing to let the jury think you were on your own much of the time. After all, it's true what Henderson says. Our mother did leave us, and..."

"But you didn't!" he said. "Anything bad that's ever happened to me is because I screwed up. Not you. I won't let you take any of the blame."

She wished she could take his hand, but the guard was watching every move. Jack seemed more upset than usual. "Calm down, Jack," she said. "It will be all right. Henderson hasn't even talked to Vince and Tony yet. He might get them to recant their testimony and tell the truth about who fired the gun that night. We've got two weeks. Let's give him the chance to make those guys do what they should have done weeks ago."

Jack's voice was so low Dorie had to lean across the table to hear him. "They won't change their stories," he said.

"They might. I have a hunch Henderson can be pretty persuasive."

"I can't do this any longer, Dor."

His voice was so pained. He seemed so fragile. "Do what, Jack? What can't you do any longer?"

"Vince and Tony won't change their testimony because they aren't lying."

His words were like a physical blow to her stomach. She almost doubled over, but flattened her palms against the tabletop to steady herself. "What did you say?"

"I did it, Dorie. I shot the guy."

She blinked hard trying to keep his face in focus. She had to have misunderstood. But his features were rigid. "No, Jack. You're confused. Maybe the truck accident really did injure you. You didn't shoot anybody."

His head nodded, just a slight up and down motion that challenged everything she'd ever believed about him.

"The clerk was like a crazy man," he said. "He came over the counter swinging that bat. Vince just stood there like he was dumb or something. He didn't move.

"I yelled at him, told him to duck. He didn't. He just started shaking. I grabbed the gun from Vince's belt, hollered at the clerk to stop. He landed in front of us. Vince didn't even back up. He just stood there staring."

Blood rushed into Dorie's head and pounded in her ears. Of all the confessions she could have heard about this night, this was the last one she'd expected. She felt as if her heart was being ripped in two. The words didn't seem to come from her throat when she said, "You have to stop talking, Jack. You don't know what you're saying."

"I have to tell it, Dorie. It's killing me. I only meant to shoot the bat, make the guy drop it, you know like they do in the movies. Then I figured we'd run. But my hand was shaking so bad. I'd never fired a gun before. I didn't even aim, Dorie. I just pulled the trigger. The guy fell back against the counter, clutching his chest."

Dorie's head dropped into her two hands. "Oh, Jack…"

"The guy would have killed Vince," Jack said. "And everybody would have called him a hero for killing the punk kid who was robbing him. I couldn't let that happen."

Dorie pushed herself up from the table. Her legs were trembling so violently she didn't think she'd be able to climb over the bench. For a moment she thought she might throw up. She had to get out of the yard, away from the ugly truth she'd just heard. "I…I have to go, Jack," she said.

He looked up at her, his eyes swollen, his cheeks puffy and red. He could have been eight years old again, this boy she had loved with all her heart. But he wasn't that boy. He had done a terrible thing and he had lied to her. At the moment she didn't believe she'd ever really known him.

"What's going to happen now?" he asked her.

She tried to think rationally, but her thoughts were in a jumble. She hardly trusted herself to speak. "I don't know. We'll tell Eric. We'll…" She couldn't go on. Her throat was closing with burning tears. For once she didn't have the answer. She turned and walked away. The last thing she heard was the guard, calling her brother back inside.

DORIE UNLOCKED HER truck and climbed behind the wheel. She tried to put the key in the ignition. After two unsuccessful attempts, she slammed her hand against the steering wheel. And there, in the prison parking lot, she finally let the tears fall. She was crying out her disappointment in Jack, her fear for his future, her guilt over not having all the answers. And she was crying because she desperately missed the family she'd come to care for so much in the past two weeks of her life. After a few minutes, she tried the key again and the trusty truck started. "You'll be okay, Dorie," she said.

But she wouldn't be okay. She'd lost everything that was important to her. Jack would be in prison for years. Bret had been right about him. She couldn't go back to The Crooked Spruce, and she didn't want to go home. But she didn't have anywhere else to go.

She pulled out of the lot and headed toward Winston Beach and the cottage she'd slept in last night for the first time in two weeks. The tidy little home she'd taken care of for years had changed, too. It seemed small and lonely. Hopeless.

Nothing will ever be like the days on Hickory Mountain again.

A half hour later she pulled into her driveway. In the daylight she realized how neglected her cottage seemed. Maybe in a day or two, she could turn her attention away from what she had lost and think about what she still had. King. Hopefully a job soon. This house.

The grass was long. She'd have to mow it. All the blinds were still drawn, a safety precaution she'd taken when she left to find

Clancy. She'd only planned to be gone overnight. How long ago that trip to the mountains seemed now. How desperate she'd been to get her money from Clancy. How hopeful she'd been that she would be able to get Jack out of jail. But that was when she'd believed in him.

She got out of the truck and went in the front door. King greeted her with tailing wagging and tongue hanging out. She scratched the top of his head before going into the kitchen to get a drink. Her refrigerator needed a good cleaning.

She got a Coke for herself and filled the water bowl for King. Through the kitchen window she saw her elderly neighbor, Mrs. Eisenberg waved. "You're home!" she called. Dorie waved back. "I've watched the house for you. And I got your mail like you asked me to when you called."

"Thanks. I'll pick it up later," Dorie said and went into the living room to drink her soda. King jumped onto the sofa beside her. She absently stroked his silky ears.

This little house had always seemed like her refuge, and it should have this morning. Physically her belongings were just as she'd left them. Her magazines were still stacked neatly on the coffee table. The wooden clock ticked comfortingly on the wall over the television. Before she left to find Clancy, she'd made certain that Jack's room was straightened up, his bed made and his clothes put away. She'd wanted the room to be perfect for him when he got home.

She wiped another tear from under her eye though she hadn't thought she'd be able to cry anymore today. But thinking of Jack again made her realize that days, maybe weeks would pass before her personal pain subsided. Her brother had lied to her. He'd let her believe in his innocence, that he was worth fighting for one more time. She'd given up so much. Her youth. An education, her business. And especially that man on Hickory Mountain who might have loved her as much as she loved him. Now she'd never know.

And for what? So she could come back to the home she'd made for her and Jack and face living alone, waiting, wishing for happiness that seemed never to be in the cards.

CHAPTER TWENTY-ONE

"GRANDMA ROSALITO'S SPAGHETTI," Clancy said, his sarcasm clearly indicating his opinion of the food container he was handling. "I bet if there ever was a Grandma Rosalito, she's rolling over in her grave right now."

Bret took the poly bag from him and examined the graphics on the front. A nice mountain scene under the words High Country Kitchen, and below that a steaming plate of pasta and sauce. "Looks good to me," he said, hanging the bag on its appropriate hook.

Clancy took another bag, one labeled *Green Bean Casserole* and hung it next to the spaghetti. "It's all freeze dried," he said. "You add boiling water and eat it right from the pouch."

"Pretty convenient, I'd say," Bret said. "No muss, no fuss, lightweight and easy to carry."

"And only $7.99 a serving!" Clancy barked.

"It's highway robbery. I tell you, son, I'd have to be starving before I'd eat any of this stuff."

"It's very nutritious, Grandpa," Luke said, handing the next pouch to Clancy. "I had one for lunch, the macaroni and cheese, and it was really good."

Clancy attached the pouch to the hook and took another from Luke. "Your son is eating all the profits, Bret. But I guess based on his recommendation, I might try this chicken Alfredo."

"Never mind, Pop. You can go into the kitchen and open a can of Chef Boyardee. We need to sell every one of these within the next—" he checked the packaging on a breakfast skillet meal "—seven years!" He grimaced. "This stuff must be made of iron filings and bird toenails if it lasts that long."

Luke dropped the next bag on the floor. "Ew, Dad! I was going to have one like that for breakfast."

"Maybe you'll think twice before wasting another $7.99 from now on," Bret said, and immediately regretted his sharp tone.

Luke stared up at Clancy with a shocked expression on his face. Clancy shrugged one shoulder. "In case you haven't noticed, your dad's been a little cranky lately," he said. "Cut him some slack, Luke. That's what I've been doing. Along with staying as far away from him as possible."

"But it's been five days," Luke said.

Bret knew exactly what his son was referring to, and the kid was right. Today was Wednesday. Dorie had gone out of their lives five days ago, and nothing had seemed right since. He should be apologizing to his son right about now, but instead, he snapped, "You can both go do something else if you want. I'll finish up here. I can handle hanging up some bags."

Luke handed him another pouch. "Come on, Dad. I miss her, too, but you don't see me going around biting people's heads off."

That wasn't exactly true. Bret had lost count of the number of times Luke had complained about having nothing to do since Dorie and King had left. He griped about the cooking, too, which was probably why he'd resorted to eating meals made with boiling water. Even Clancy had seemed out of sorts, although Bret wasn't sure if that was because Dorie had left or because Maisie was coming.

He didn't know when his mother would

arrive, but anticipating her appearance at any minute was like having a cloud hanging over all of them. Oh, he loved his mother, he guessed, even if long ago he'd stopped admiring her maternal skills. But he feared that Maisie, out of her tinkling-bell-canyon element, could be a force to contend with.

Bret hadn't heard from her since her call informing them she might come for a visit, but that wasn't surprising. Maisie was unpredictable. For days, he and Clancy had been living as if they'd heard a tornado warning, and yet the skies were still clear.

"Look," he said after a moment, "We've been at this for a while. Let's leave the food for now and switch tasks. Luke, you and Grandpa can stack those mylar blankets. Put a price of $5.99 on each one. I'll work on these aluminum pots. We'll have supper in an hour."

If he'd expected that announcement to cheer his crew, he was wrong. They all missed Dorie's cooking.

Luke and Clancy worked at one end of the shelving while Bret stayed at the other end. His family was right. He wasn't fit company to be around. He'd done a lot of soul searching in the past five days, trying to analyze what had gone wrong and what he could have done differently.

Dorie had been absolutely convinced her brother was innocent. The boy she'd raised couldn't possibly shoot someone. That kind of blind loyalty could be a good thing, but Bret had seen far too much during his days as a cop to buy into a theory based on instinct alone. Even after meeting Jack, Bret hadn't formed a rock solid belief about the kid's guilt or innocence. But one thing he was certain of—teenage boys went through skyrocketing testosterone as they navigated the waters between childhood and adulthood. He'd seen their tempers when confronted with challenges, heard their cocky denials when they were caught, their attempts to get out of trouble by blaming others.

Maybe Jack was innocent, but if hunches were worth anything, and they could be to an experienced, open-minded cop, Bret's hunch told him the boy was guilty of far more than he'd admitted to. And even now, after five days of going over the situation in his mind, Bret's opinion hadn't changed.

He had done what he had to do because he

had his son to think of. Luke was the most important person in the world to him. His son, his small family, they were the only people he had left. Or they had been, until that pretty woman armed with mace and undeniable grit had driven up his mountain and made him think about a future. But even for Dorie, Bret couldn't be someone he wasn't. His instincts told him to protect his son, and that's what he would do, even if it cost him the woman he loved.

The realization that he did truly love Dorie hit him square between the shoulders. He didn't think he would ever feel that kind of connection with another woman. Dorie had come into his life bringing sunshine, determination and compassion.

And now she was gone. He didn't even know her address or her cell number. Not that those details would be hard to find. Her brother was in lock-up. His address was public record, and a cop, or ex-cop, could get it easily. But even if Bret found out where she lived, what could he do? In Dorie's eyes, he'd betrayed her. She probably hated him.

He looked down at the price stickers he'd been putting on the aluminum pans he was displaying. For Pete's sake. He'd forgotten the first number on every price tag. If he didn't correct himself, he'd have to sell everything for ninety-nine cents! *Way to go, Donovan,* he said to himself as he picked up his pen to begin making adjustments. He had to shake off this funk he was in. He owed it to Pop and Luke. But how?

Inspiration suddenly hit him. He dropped everything and called to his son. "Hey, Luke. I'll pick you up at school tomorrow, so don't take the bus."

"Okay. Why you doing that, Dad?"

This decision had already lightened Bret's mood, but he kept his smile hidden and spoke as if what he were saying was no big deal. "I thought we might go down to the Walker County Animal Shelter and take a look around."

A grin spread across Luke's face and took more of the darkness from Bret's world. "Are you kidding, Dad? We can get a dog?"

"I'm thinking it might be time," he said.

FOR A MAN who'd moved away from Miami to avoid danger, stress and surprises, Bret had experienced more than his share of unexpected occurrences. On Friday afternoon he came around the side of the lodge trailed by the most recent surprise in his life, his mostly Labrador, seventy-pound black dog.

"Where is Luke, anyway?" he said to the energetic canine. *Probably in his room playing a video game.* And Skeeter, the dog, had obviously decided not to stay with him. "Do I need to remind you that, technically, I am not your owner?" he said. "Have you forgotten that ten-year-old human upstairs?"

Skeeter pretended not to understand a word, but his ears perked up when they both heard a chugging noise coming from down the mountain. Bret paused, peered through the archway, and Skeeter plopped down on his haunches beside him.

"What do you suppose that is?" Bret said just before catching sight of the tiny car when it crept onto the property, putting along like a super-charged golf cart. He was surprised the car had made it up the mountain, and he couldn't imagine who was driving it.

A woman got out of the car and ran toward him, her long, salt-and-pepper hair trailing in the wind behind her. "Darlin'!" she hollered. "I made it!"

Maisie's ankle-length skirt whipped around her legs. And she jingled. She always jingled. The small brass bells hanging from her belt contributed the happy sound today.

"Hello, Maisie," he said, allowing her to give him a monstrous hug and even offering a tentative one in return. After the age of seven, he'd never called her Mom, though Julie still did. Despite all her professions of love, Maisie had never felt quite like the moms his friends had. Maybe it was her complete lack of motherly instincts or her inclination to be a pal rather than a parent.

She'd never prepared his school lunch, never checked his homework and always let him miss school when he wanted to. Rules were made for everyone but Maisie.

"I wasn't sure you'd follow through on this threat," Bret said.

"That was the old Maisie," she said. "I always keep my promises now." She looked down at the dog. "Who's this? Don't tell me…"

"Yes, we got a dog."

She stuck her nose in the fur at Skeeter's neck and inhaled. Bret had no idea what she was testing for, maybe a new homeopathic canine potion. He didn't think she'd smell much. The rescue kennel had bathed Skeeter.

"Well it's about time," she said. "No boy should grow up without a dog."

"Ah, I did."

"That was different. We had your father to feed and bathe." She glanced around the property. "Where is the old snake-oil sales-man, anyway? And where is my grandson?"

"Luke's in his room. Pop's around."

"Probably napping if I know him."

Bret couldn't argue.

"Where did you get that car?" he asked.

"I rented it at the airport, of course. Only $17.95 a day." She gave him a coy smile. "I can stay a week or two at those rates." She checked the watch hanging around her neck. "Julie's not here yet I see."

"Julie's coming, too?" Another surprise.

"Well sure. What would you expect? She wants to see me."

"Naturally."

She pointed to the colorful automobile. "Get my suitcase, sweetie."

"Where is it? There's no trunk."

"There is, too. You'll find it, and show me to a room."

"A room? Maisie, this isn't a hotel."

She spied the cabins around back and clasped her hands in glee. "One of those places, then! Perfect."

"There's no heat in any of them," Bret said.

"So what? It's not cold."

"But it could be tonight."

She spun in a complete circle. "I want to see every inch of this place. Reminds me of a commune we have in the valley."

"It's not a commune. It's a business."

"Maybe you should rethink that. All these trees and rustic buildings. It's just perfect for the disenchanted, where they can commune with nature, and grow their own vegetables. Non-violent inhabitants only, of course."

His brow furrowed. She was the second woman lately to envision another purpose for his outfitter's store. "There are many reasons for people to want to commune with nature," he said. "I'm catering to men who want to explore their wild sides—in a civilized way."

She smiled. "Oh, goody. Wild men. I've come to the right place."

Thank goodness he wasn't open yet....

She tucked her arm through his. "Actually darling, I have a plan."

"Oh, no."

"You'll like this one. I'm thinking about taking your father off your hands."

"Really?"

"Yes. It's time I fixed the old dunderhead." She walked toward the cabins in back, pointing her finger in all directions until divine inspiration made her pick a spot. "This building, under that giant elm. This is the one I want."

He backtracked to get her suitcase out of the tiny hatchback compartment of the car and then followed her. They'd only gone a few steps when Clancy came out of the bathhouse, stopped cold and hollered, "Why didn't you warn me, Bret? I could have run off into the woods and hidden in the trunk of a hollowed-out tree."

Maisie planted her fists on her hips and laughed. "You're still welcome to do that, Moon Doggie."

"How long is she staying?" Clancy asked Bret.

"*She's* right here, Clancy," Maisie said. "So you can start talking directly to me."

"All right. How long are you staying?"

"As long as it takes, so get used to me."

Bret kept walking toward the cabin, rolling the suitcase over the dirt. He did not want to get in the middle of this. He'd been caught between his mother and father too many times when he was a kid. When he went inside, he heard his mother's voice.

"You don't look half bad, Clancy, considering you've been on your own for so many years. But I can still make some improvements."

JULIE, ALONG WITH her two boys and the usual cooler full of food, arrived around five o'clock. Luke was in heaven. Skeeter, barking and circling the new arrivals, was as close to doggie nirvana as a four-legged creature could be. Bret, as he'd been for more than a week, was still miserable, though he had to admit that the commotion was a distraction from missing Dorie.

After dinner, Julie and Bret cleaned the kitchen while the boys played in the dusk. Clancy and Maisie were temporarily MIA.

"I think it's going well," Julie said. "What do you think, Brat?"

"Nobody's killed anybody, so I'm optimistic," he said.

"Mom and Dad are really more alike than I remembered," she said. "Both of them look like flower children with their ponytails. Both of them are unapologetically unconventional. And they both use those stupid nicknames for each other, like time hasn't passed at all."

"Apparently nicknames run in this family," Bret said.

Julie grinned. "I can't imagine what you're referring to, Brat."

"Maisie said she's going to take Pop back to California with her."

"Yes, that's what she told me when she called last night. She thinks they can make a go of it this time."

"Stranger things have happened," Bret said. "I just hope she knows about his history from the past few years. He hasn't exactly become Mr. Responsible."

"No, and that's part of the reason she's willing to take him back. She hates that Pop keeps dropping into your life every time he messes up."

Bret wadded up the dish towel he was holding. "Now wait a minute. That's no reason for Maisie to take him on. She can't let

Pop become her problem just to keep him from being mine."

Julie put the last pot in the cupboard. "You need to let her decide that," she said. "I think she's regretting her lack of mothering where you're concerned, and she wants to make it up to you."

"Taking Pop off my hands would be a good way to start," Bret conceded. "But only if that's what she really wants to do. And I'm getting kind of used to the old guy. He's been a help around here. And he's working off a debt to me. I still wonder, though, when he's going to drop another anvil on my head."

"Oh, there's one other thing you should know."

"What's that?"

"Mom knows about Dorie. I told her everything."

Bret made a note to never tell his sister anything, ever again. "I don't know what you could have told her. I mean, you never even knew Dorie that well. And she's gone now, anyway, so what does it matter?"

Julie pulled out a chair and sat. "Now don't be mad at what I'm going to tell you…"

Bret hated any sentence that started out

with "Now don't be mad." Almost always when a person said that, Bret was mad before he could count to ten. "Oh, no. What now?"

"I'm a bit closer to Dorie than you might think. After you got the landline put in, we talked on the phone a few times."

Bret felt his muscles tense. Now his sister no doubt knew more about the woman he loved than he did. Sometimes he felt like an outsider in his own world.

"And I really like her," Julie said, oblivious to his discomfort. "I know I told you that before, but she's remarkable. She's so independent and strong. And she's very giving. And she really cares for you, Bret."

"Cared," he said. "She doesn't care so much now."

"Sure she does."

"You don't know how we parted. It wasn't pleasant."

"So? You can change that. You just have to try. If you want to reconnect with her, that shouldn't be so tough."

This was too much. Julie was about to get into an analysis of his feelings and he wasn't prepared for that. He'd done what he had to do when he'd threatened to turn Jack over to the authorities. And even then, he'd given Dorie a break when technically he shouldn't have. Ever since, his emotions had been playing havoc with his familiar feelings of guilt. The last thing he needed was his sister's amateur psychoanalysis.

"Don't go there, Jules," he said. "This is my problem and I'll handle it."

"By trying to forget about her? News flash, bro. That's not handling it."

"Neither is dissecting my psyche," he said and strode from the kitchen.

CHAPTER TWENTY-TWO

MAISIE FINALLY RETURNED to the lodge a little after ten that night.

Bret looked up from filling his soda glass when she came in the back door. "Where have you been all evening?" he asked her. "I was beginning to…"

She smiled and sat at the kitchen table. "Sit, okay?"

He did.

"Were you worried about me?"

He shrugged. "These are the mountains, Maisie. And you're hardly more than a quick snack for some of the creatures who live here."

"Well, I'm fine as you can see. I've spent the past two hours talking to your father. He's coming back to Nettles Canyon with me to help run my herb and aromatherapy business."

This was the biggest surprise of the day.

Bret took a long swallow of soda while he contemplated what to say, how to tell his mother that Clancy would never go back with her. "Are we talking about the same Clancy Donovan whose dependability quotient is hovering around zero?"

Maisie laughed. The sound reminded him of the tinkling bells on her skirt. "I convinced him, darling. I swear I did. He's going to quit gambling, involve himself in the shipping of my products and continue to pay you back."

Bret frowned. "Now I know I'm in an alternate universe." He regarded his mother's confident expression. "How did you manage it?"

"I reminded him of our good old married days, when he was irresponsible, unreliable, funny and kind, and never, ever boring."

Bret conceded her accurate portrayal with a nod. "I guess that's true."

"Of course it is," she said. "No marriage ends without some of the blame on both parties. We know your father's faults, but I had some, too. I was a nag and a dreamer. I stood in front of a justice of the peace and swore my fidelity to a man who by his very nature would never meet my ideal." She sighed. "I should have known I wouldn't change him until he was ready to be changed."

"And he is now?"

"I think so. Believe it or not, he really feels bad about what he did to you and that woman. It was low, even for him."

Bret couldn't argue that.

"Now I'm willing to take a gamble," she said. "On Clancy. My business is successful. My goodness, people in the urban areas love that natural aromatherapy stuff. I can't keep up with the orders. I can really use his help."

Bret studied his mother's still-youthful face and found much to admire in the fine lines of experience around her eyes. "I'm happy for you, Maisie," he said. "Seems like you have the life you always wanted."

"With the man I never stopped loving. Now if I can just get you to love me as much as you did when you were a little boy…."

She placed her hand over his and the years melted away. He felt like a boy again, one whose skinned knee had just been kissed and made all better. He cleared his throat. "Stranger things have happened, I guess."

"Oh, you bet, darling. The universe is full

of strange, wonderful, blessed things. Miracles big and small."

She stood. "Now I'm going to meet your father on the porch. I think it's past time that we sealed our deal with a kiss."

STILL NOT COMPLETELY convinced, Bret waited a few minutes and then ambled out to the main room. When he heard soft laughter coming from the porch he peered out the front window and saw his mother and father sitting next to each other on the swing. Clancy had his arm around Maisie's shoulder.

"So you sure about this, Tinker Bell?" Clancy said. "If I come back with you, I might overstay my welcome. I've heard I can do that."

"I'm sure. But Clancy, I meant what I said. If you so much as bet with a butterfly on the direction of the wind, we'll have a problem."

Clancy was silent. Bret held his breath. He wanted his father to take this offer. Not just because of his own history with Clancy, but because he figured it was time.

"Okay, you talked me into it," Clancy said. He put his other arm around her, leaned in and kissed her cheek.

Feeling like a voyeur, Bret looked down, giving them privacy. "What is it about that porch swing?" he said to himself. At one time, not so long ago, even a hard-nosed, wounded cop like himself had believed in its magic.

"TOMORROW IS SATURDAY," Maisie said to her son later that same night.

"Yeah, and?"

"Julie and the boys aren't leaving until the morning. I'm going to be here with Clancy for a few days, at least until Monday. Your camp opens next weekend."

It was late. Bret was tired. He'd just come into the kitchen to get a glass of water. He figured his mother and father would have already retired to their respective beds. Julie, Luke and his nephews were in cabin number two. The outpost was getting a good workout tonight and he wanted a good night's sleep.

He stared at this mother. "Maisie, did you come in here to give me calendar details or do you have something you want to say?"

"Julie told me about that woman."

"What woman?" Of course, he knew.

"Don't play dumb. We both know you're not. Julie really likes her."

"Yes, I know. She's told me so several times."

"And you like her, too."

Bret drank his water without commenting.

"All I'm saying is that there are plenty of people here to watch Luke if you decide to get up in the morning and take a little drive."

He set his glass on the counter. "Where would I go?"

"I was thinking the beach."

"Oh."

"I don't know who was at fault in that girl running off like she did," Maisie said. "I suspect it was partly your high-handed ethics that had something to do with it. You always were the critical one, Bret."

I grew up the son of a hippie canyon-dweller and a gambling conman. What in the world did I have to be critical about? Bret didn't speak his thoughts. He just stared out the kitchen window.

"It doesn't matter who was at fault, anyway," Maisie said. "I just think it's time you started living again. And if this young lady can help you do that, then I say go for it."

"I am living, Maisie," he argued. "I'm living my dream. This place. These mountains. My son…"

"None of those things keep you warm at night, baby."

"You're a fine one to talk," he said. "All these years who's been keeping you warm at night?"

Maisie actually blushed! Had he hit a nerve?

"We're not talking about me, young man."

He smiled.

She filled a glass of her own with water and headed to the door. "Now then, I'm going to bed. If you're gone in the morning, I'll know where you went. If you aren't gone, I'll find you wandering aimlessly under a dark cloud for another day. And I'll be disappointed."

Bret refilled his glass and climbed the stairs to his room. He probably wasn't going to get a good night's sleep, after all. Funny, all these years had gone by, and now, out of the blue, his mother had finally given her only son something really important to think about.

CHAPTER TWENTY-THREE

BY TWO O'CLOCK Saturday Dorie had decided it was time for her to accept Jack's role in the robbery. She loved him and couldn't abandon him now, so she would do her best to ensure he was treated fairly. That meant she had to find a job that paid well enough to support herself and maintain payments to Eric Henderson. She would have time to sort her feelings about all this, and Bret, later.

Wearing her usual beachside attire of shorts and T-shirt, she sat at the 1960s Formica-top kitchen table her mother had purchased from a secondhand shop. She sipped an iced tea while perusing the help-wanted ads on Craigslist. She was writing down a phone number for a waitress position in Nag's Head when a knock sounded on her door. King ran barking to the front room. Looking out the window she saw a fancy sports car, one she didn't recognize. She opened the door to Eric, who was dressed in what she assumed must be his typical attire of oxford shirt and creased chinos.

"Hi," she said. "What brings you here?"

"I just came from Broad Creek. Jack said he thought you'd be home so I decided to pop over."

"Okay." She held on to King and opened the door so Eric could come into her living room.

He looked around at her well-used, but meticulously maintained furnishings, which could be called vintage by today's decorators.

"Quaint," Eric said. Then he looked at King, who was eyeing him suspiciously and growling low in his throat. "You have a dog?"

"I do."

"Funny-looking little thing."

Dorie frowned. "Obviously you're not seeing his distinguished side." She motioned to a chair next to her fireplace. "You said you'd been to Broad Creek?"

"Oh, right. Had a talk with Jack." He sat, crossed his legs. "That was quite a bombshell he dropped on me this morning."

"Yeah, I imagine it was. I was going to call you later when I had a minute." She'd had plenty of minutes, truthfully, but was still dealing with the news herself.

"Jack's real involvement in this crime is something I need to know, Dorinda, as his lawyer." His voice was scolding, though calm.

"Yes, I'm sorry. I suppose that changes everything for Jack."

"Sure does. But we're not giving up. I've still got some angles we can play. The pathetic, confused kid protecting his friend, the overzealous clerk. We might still be able to get a plea deal."

"I hope so," Dorie said.

"I didn't ask for a continuance, so we still have the same trial date, and both sides will have this new confession to work with. But I'll keep digging."

"I appreciate that, Eric. I'm not counting on Jack being released anytime soon, but at least we can try to make his imprisonment as easy and short as possible."

He stood. "Well, then, I guess that's it. Except I have the rest of the afternoon free. How would you like to head up the coast for some R and R? I think we both could use a break from this case."

She wasn't even tempted. This wasn't the right man or the right time. "I'm sorry, Eric, but I'm in the middle of something. I have some job interviews later today."

He gave her a half grin. "I'm a hard man to discourage, Dorinda, so I'll keep trying. I think you and I can be on the same team in more than one respect."

"Well, anyway, thanks for the invitation."

He left and she returned to her computer in the kitchen. She hadn't lied to Eric. She needed to find a job and quickly. It wouldn't be long before she received another bill in the mail from the law firm. The five thousand Bret had sent was certain to run out soon.

She had completed a list of a half-dozen job possibilities when she heard another knock on her door. She looked down at King. "The guy is persistent, I'll say that."

King's ears perked and he galloped to the front door. This time his tail was wagging, and he yipped playfully. "Boy, you establish allegiances quickly," Dorie said to him. "A few minutes ago, you wanted to bite the cuff of Eric's fancy trousers."

She opened the door, but it wasn't Eric on her threshold. In jeans and a short-sleeved cotton shirt, Bret Donovan looked as if he'd just come down the mountain. And his mussed hair and tired eyes suggested he'd driven straight to Winston Beach. Her heart worked overtime to keep up with the blood that had suddenly rushed to her head. She gripped the door handle to steady herself. He looked so wonderful.

"Oh." The word came out as a breathless whisper. She didn't trust herself to speak again, but King covered any awkwardness when he charged out the door and jumped on Bret with unabashed glee.

"Hello, mutt," Bret said. He patted the dog's head absently while his gaze remained fixed on Dorie's face. "I guess he's forgiven me for threatening him with a dish towel."

"He has a short memory."

Bret smiled. "So, hi. How have you been?"

She blinked rapidly while trying to keep his face in focus. "How have I been?"

"I'm just asking because the past week I haven't been so great, and I'm wondering if the same is true for you."

"This hasn't been such a good week for me, either." She resisted every impulse to fall into his arms. She needed facts, details.

Lately she'd leaped to the wrong conclusions far too many times. "How did you get here?" she asked.

He jabbed his thumb in the direction of his truck in her driveway. "I drove."

"No, I mean how did you get *here,* to 1321 Winston Beach Boulevard?"

He looked down at his boots as if they had magically transported him across the state. "I can see how you might be wondering that. We didn't exactly exchange addresses, although you know mine." When he raised his eyes again, they were clear. The smile continued to play around his lips. "I stopped at Broad Creek and saw your brother. He told me where you live."

"You saw Jack?" She didn't know how to react to that. Did Jack tell him the truth? Had he come here to gloat? *Please, God, not that.*

"I did."

"Did he tell you the latest about his case?" she asked cautiously.

"That he did fire the pistol? Yeah, he told me."

"You should feel vindicated," she said. "You were right. I guess I was naive all along." She held her breath.

"I don't feel anything but regret, Dorie. There's no joy in discovering that someone you care about has to accept a difficult truth."

Someone you care about. Her chest squeezed with a comforting sort of pressure. "Thanks for that."

He peeked over her shoulder. "Can I come in?"

"Of course. I'm sorry." She held the door open and he walked in.

His gaze took in the cozy room. "Nice place," he said. "Kind of how I pictured a room you would live in."

His simple statement made her feel better than if he'd praised the room with false flattery. She liked that he saw the reflection of her personality in the home she loved.

"Would you like to sit down?" she said.

He chose a floral chintz wicker chair that she'd found at a flea market and had patiently restored.

She sat on the sofa, the coffee table separating them.

"So how did Jack appear to you?" she asked after a moment.

"Actually I think he seemed relieved. Telling the truth can do wonders for anyone's anxiety level. There's guilt for committing a crime, and then there's guilt in hiding it. I think the second kind can be the worst."

She smiled. "His confession didn't do much for my anxiety level."

"I understand, but Dorie, I learned something interesting from a friend on the force. He called before I left home this morning."

"You did? What?"

"The clerk who was killed has a rap sheet of his own. He's been arrested a couple of times for violent behavior. Seems he liked batting heads a little too much."

Dorie understood where this bit of information might lead. "That is interesting," she agreed.

"You might want to share this with your lawyer. I'm sure he can use it in Jack's favor. Coming at a kid with a bat is excessive even considering the circumstances. Jack claims the guy never saw the gun in Vince's belt and therefore had no reason to fear for his life."

"So maybe the jury will conclude that Jack was protecting his friend."

"Yeah, it could help a lot, though Jack was still in the store for an illegal purpose. This won't get him off completely, but his lawyer can argue for manslaughter."

Dorie sighed with pleasure. A day that had started out so badly now held an unmistakable ray of hope. Still she didn't know how she might fit into Bret's life. She leaned forward. "How is Luke?"

"He's okay. Misses you, though."

"I miss him, too. And Clancy?"

Bret chuckled. "Now that's a story.

"When isn't Clancy a story?"

"True. But this time is different. Do you remember me telling you about Maisie, my mother?"

"Of course. She was coming to visit you. I was there when she called."

"She arrived yesterday, and it seems she has a solution to Clancy's itinerant living conditions."

He explained Maisie's plan to take Clancy back with her to California, including Bret's observing them on the porch swing. "I never thought I'd see those two getting along so well," he said. "It was almost surreal."

"I think it's very romantic," Dorie said.

"I suppose you could say that. And, let me guess. You like romantic stories."

She did, but she'd never lived one of them herself. Having Bret in her home was about as close to a feeling of true romance as she could remember. She was almost ready to cross that line which would allow her to believe in possibilities again.

"I guess I still believe romance is possible," she said. "Although I must admit I didn't think it would be Clancy who convinced me of it."

He gave her a smile that seemed to hold a promise. She clenched her hands, her muscles suddenly tense.

"If you don't mind, I'd like to throw my hat in this ring."

Her breath caught. She swallowed and reminded herself that only one week ago she had left Bret without even saying goodbye. And he'd let her go. "You? Are you a believer in romance, too?"

"A few weeks ago I would have said no. Now I've changed my mind. If romance makes a guy feel as lousy as I've felt these past few days, then I guess I have to accept that it's still possible."

A warm, wonderful flush crept into her cheeks. She'd never been so happy to hear that she'd been responsible for someone's misery.

He stood, took a package from his back jeans pocket and brought it to her. It was about the size of an envelope and almost as flat. "Here, this is for you."

She took it, let it lie in her palm. It had substance, a weight of nearly a pound. A small store-bought bow was on top, smashed from being in his pocket. "A present?"

"Sort of."

"I can't imagine what it is," she said.

"Only one way to find out."

She took off the paper and lifted the flap of a sturdy cardboard envelope, the kind supplied by the post office for CDs and such. She slid a brass number from the envelope, turned it over and studied it from all angles.

"It's the number four," she said.

"It is. I've assigned each cabin a number and a name," he said. "Cabins one, two and three are named after members of my family."

"That's a nice idea."

"Pop and I have been working on the fourth cabin this week. This morning before I left to come here, I told Pop to leave all eight bunks in number four so it will accommodate more people."

"You're leaving it the same as when the Boy Scouts used it?" she asked.

"Yep. If everything goes as I hope it will, I'm ordering eight new mattresses as well as more of those flannel sheets you like."

She still had no idea why he'd brought her the brass number. "You're expecting that many corporate guests?"

"No. I probably won't ever have that many execs at one time. I'll be lucky to fill cabins one through three."

"Then why…?"

He sat beside her on the sofa, threaded his fingers together and let his hands hang between his knees. "I didn't sleep much last night. I had this idea that kept playing out in my mind."

"What idea is that?"

"One that originated with you actually."

"Me?"

He smiled at her confused expression. "Remember when you said that troubled boys need role models to fill a void in their lives? And I said the role model wouldn't be filled by me? And then you said the property had probably been a pretty good Boy Scout camp?"

Yes, she remembered saying that, but Bret had been so sure he wanted to cater to wealthy execs seeking a wilderness adventure. Had he suddenly changed his mind? "I'm afraid I don't understand what you're getting at, Bret," she said.

He took her hand, placed it on his thigh and covered it with his own. "There are about a zillion details I need to check out," he began. "But during my sleepless hours, I did some research. I discovered that the state of North Carolina has a special program, a rehabilitation course designed for adolescents and young teens who appear to be heading on the wrong path."

"Boys like Jack?" she said.

"Could be. Though the idea is to catch them before they break the law."

"I wish I had known about that program when Jack was younger."

"Yeah, it might have helped. Anyway, I made some calls, set up some appointments. I'm thinking of starting a facility like that at The Crooked Spruce."

Dorie gasped. Had she heard him correctly? He was smiling, so she knew she had. "Bret, I don't know what to say. You may not realize it, but you would be a perfect role model for these boys."

"I don't know about perfect, but I think I could stand in for a kid who has no dad at all. Plus, Jed Whitaker, my friend from my academy days is coming to live at The Crooked Spruce. He's a straight arrow, a good man. If we both check out with the authorities, I don't see why the state wouldn't approve us, at least on a trial basis."

He threaded his fingers with Dorie's. "I never would have thought of doing something like this if it weren't for you, Dorie. But it seems like a natural to me now.

"And here's another thing…"

A flood of happiness was seeping into Dorie's heart. She couldn't stop it and she didn't want to. "What?"

"I thought I might talk to Leroy and his family about letting him be a charter subject for the program. Matt released him without putting a blot on his record."

"That was kind of him."

"There was no real evidence to support Leroy participating in the fire. As a matter of fact, after talking to Matt, I'm convinced Leroy could have a future."

Dorie smiled. "I'm sure of it. Especially with the proper role models."

Bret's self-deprecating grin endeared him to her even more. "Right. Me, the role model," he said.

"So what else would you need to get this boy's camp off the ground?" she asked.

He slowly nodded his head. "I'm glad you asked that question. Jed and I were both cops, so I figure we should qualify as authority figures. I still need a counselor, someone trained in dealing with troubled kids."

"How will you pay for all this?" Dorie asked, knowing Bret had to support his family and keep things running somehow.

"I found some info on that, too. The state will subsidize the program if certain standards and codes are met."

Jack had missed out on a program like this. It was too late for him, but the possibility that other boys could be helped took away some of the hurt Dorie felt for her brother.

His enthusiasm evident in his voice, Bret continued. "Like I said, we'll start small. A few boys just for the summer. I'll have to hire a cook…"

Even though she wasn't involved, Dorie was already thinking ahead and giving her imagination free rein. "Maybe you could have some animals. Nothing inspires responsibility more than having to care for another living thing."

"I'm already one step ahead on that one," Bret said. "I am now the proud owner of a Labrador something-or-other…"

"You?" She couldn't help herself. She reached for him and wrapped her arms around his neck. Even if they weren't going to be together, she was so proud of him. "Luke must be absolutely delighted."

"He is." Bret looked down at the rug by the fireplace where King was curled into a fluffy ball. "But he still misses you-know-who."

She let the details of Bret's plan gel in her brain. But still she wondered how the teens would fit in with his plan for the executives. "What about your original idea to offer shelter to hikers on the trail?"

"I'm not giving up on the outpost idea. My shelves are stocked and I've had several requests for directions to the place from the old Timber Gap Trail. But I figure the execs might be a good influence on the boys. I'll tell the men when they show up that they will be sharing the property with the boys. And I don't expect any backlash. As for the teens, I figure the execs can offer a real-life picture of the way their futures could be if they straighten up."

She was thinking about the wonderful transformation she saw in Bret and was so pleased that she had contributed to it. The burden of guilt that he'd lived with for so long seemed to have been lifted. She concentrated on the brass number still in her hand. "Why did you give me this?" she asked.

"It's going next to the door on the fourth cabin," he said.

"The boys' cabin?"

"Yes. I've already named it. I'm calling it the Dorie Howe cabin. It's because of you that these kids will have a chance."

She didn't even know she was crying until one tear fell on the number. She wiped it on her shorts. "I'm going to tarnish the thing before it's even nailed up," she laughed.

"I sprayed it with non-tarnish shellac. It'll be fine for quite a while. And even if it rusts

I'll keep it on the door forever." He cupped his hand under her chin and lifted her face. "And I hope you will be at The Crooked Spruce forever, too."

"Me?" Pure elation sparked inside her, ready to burst out. Was she close to a future she had only dreamed about? Even if Bret was only offering her a chance to help mold young lives, to be part of something so worthwhile, it could be enough. She would have a life of purpose and stability. He didn't have to offer her that place next to him on the porch swing forever. She could take the happiness she felt right now and make it work for her.

He smiled. "Of course you. Who do you think I thought of immediately to be our meal-planner? You have the skills and the knowledge. You've cooked for large numbers of people."

Her eyes widened. "I could! I could do this. I could be perfect for the job."

He leaned over and kissed her. "Honey, you already are."

She smiled. "I have a hunch you guys have missed my cooking."

His features became soft and still. His eyes

locked on hers. "Don't you get it yet, Dorie? Yeah, I want you to come back with me and help these boys. Yes, I want you to have a permanent job at The Crooked Spruce. But, Dorie, that's just the beginning. I want you to share my life. I love you, and I want to marry you so we can all be together—you, me and Luke. King and that goofy animal I picked up at the shelter. Maisie and Clancy when they come to visit. And your brother when he's able."

His grin was so like Luke's that fresh tears gathered in her eyes.

"When I spoke to Jack I asked him if I could officially date you. I think we've missed the dating step somehow and we need to correct that situation. He gave me his blessing. Now all I need is yours."

She swallowed, blinked hard and tried to get a clear view of the man who'd made her happier than she'd ever hoped. "You want my blessing? Well, you have it. I will go out with you."

"That's it? You'll go out with me?"

"I'll probably accept that other offer, as well, the one where I marry the man I love. We'll see how the first date goes." She pulled his face to hers and kissed him with all the passion that had grown for him since that very first night on Hickory Mountain.

She looked around the comfy living room that had sustained her through the years. She would have to leave this cottage and that was a regret. But a girl couldn't have everything, not when she had so much. "If the date goes as I expect it to," she said, "I guess I could sell my house."

"Are you kidding? I don't think so. I've always wanted a beach place, somewhere to go when we're tired of plowing the snow. We're lucky here in North Carolina. We have the best of both worlds. Beach and mountain. I don't think we should give up either one."

"I don't, either," she said. "I'll be happy to be with you in both places."

He grinned. "So how long will it take you to pack?"

"I can't go now." She hoped he would understand. There was still so much at stake here. "I have to be at Jack's trial."

"I know. I expected that answer. But you won't be alone. I'm going to schedule conversations with government officials in Raleigh, but I'll come back and sit next to you in the courtroom. Jed will be at The Crooked Spruce by then and he can handle things."

"You would do that?"

"You're going to be part of my family, Dorie. There isn't much I wouldn't do for you."

She snuggled next to his chest and felt the comforting warmth of his arm around her shoulders. "I never knew I could be this happy."

She felt his smile. "And we have Pop's con-man antics to thank for it," he said. "Who would have thought that something that started out so bad could turn into something so good."

Who would have thought indeed.

TWO WEEKS LATER, Dorie was permitted to give her brother a big hug in the courtroom. He would be going to a juvenile facility where he could work toward his high school diploma. The verdict of manslaughter, so competently argued by Eric Henderson, assured Jack that he would have a future.

"Sorry it didn't work out between us," Eric said after the trial ended.

"You're a great lawyer, Eric," she said. "But there's someone else...."

He looked over her shoulder to where Bret sat. "I think I figured that out. Good luck to you, Dorinda. If you have any questions about Jack's progress, give me a call. I'll check on him often."

"Thank you, Eric, for everything."

She went to the parking lot, got in her truck and went home to get her packed bags and King. Once the cargo area was loaded, she headed to the highway and the roads that would lead her to Hickory Mountain. But this time was so different from when she'd traveled this distance before. This time she wasn't alone. She wasn't facing uncertainty, desperation and worry. This time a pickup truck driven by the love of her life was leading the way. This time she was happy to be following him to the Blue Ridge Mountains.

* * * * *

REQUEST YOUR FREE BOOKS!
2 FREE WHOLESOME ROMANCE NOVELS IN LARGER PRINT
PLUS 2 FREE MYSTERY GIFTS

☆☆☆☆☆☆☆☆☆☆☆☆☆☆☆☆☆☆☆☆☆

HEARTWARMING™

☆☆☆☆☆☆☆☆☆☆☆☆☆☆☆☆☆☆☆☆☆

Wholesome, tender romances

YES! Please send me 2 FREE Harlequin® Heartwarming Larger-Print novels and my 2 FREE mystery gifts (gifts worth about $10). After receiving them, if I don't wish to receive any more books, I can return the shipping statement marked "cancel." If I don't cancel, I will receive 4 brand-new larger-print novels every month and be billed just $4.99 per book in the U.S. or $5.74 per book in Canada. That's a savings of at least 23% off the cover price. It's quite a bargain! Shipping and handling is just 50¢ per book in the U.S. and 75¢ per book in Canada.* I understand that accepting the 2 free books and gifts places me under no obligation to buy anything. I can always return a shipment and cancel at any time. Even if I never buy another book, the two free books and gifts are mine to keep forever.

161/361 IDN F47N

Name	(PLEASE PRINT)

Address	Apt. #

City	State/Prov.	Zip/Postal Code

Signature (if under 18, a parent or guardian must sign)

Mail to the **Harlequin® Reader Service:**
IN U.S.A.: P.O. Box 1867, Buffalo, NY 14240-1867
IN CANADA: P.O. Box 609, Fort Erie, Ontario L2A 5X3

* Terms and prices subject to change without notice. Prices do not include applicable taxes. Sales tax applicable in N.Y. Canadian residents will be charged applicable taxes. Offer not valid in Quebec. This offer is limited to one order per household. Not valid for current subscribers to Harlequin Heartwarming larger-print books. All orders subject to credit approval. Credit or debit balances in a customer's account(s) may be offset by any other outstanding balance owed by or to the customer. Please allow 4 to 6 weeks for delivery. Offer available while quantities last.

Your Privacy—The Harlequin® Reader Service is committed to protecting your privacy. Our Privacy Policy is available online at www.ReaderService.com or upon request from the Harlequin Reader Service.

We make a portion of our mailing list available to reputable third parties that offer products we believe may interest you. If you prefer that we not exchange your name with third parties, or if you wish to clarify or modify your communication preferences, please visit us at www.ReaderService.com/consumerschoice or write to us at Harlequin Reader Service Preference Service, P.O. Box 9062, Buffalo, NY 14269. Include your complete name and address.

HWDIR13R

LARGER-PRINT BOOKS!

**GET 2 FREE
LARGER-PRINT NOVELS
PLUS 2 FREE
MYSTERY GIFTS**

Love Inspired

Larger-print novels are now available...

LILPDIR13R